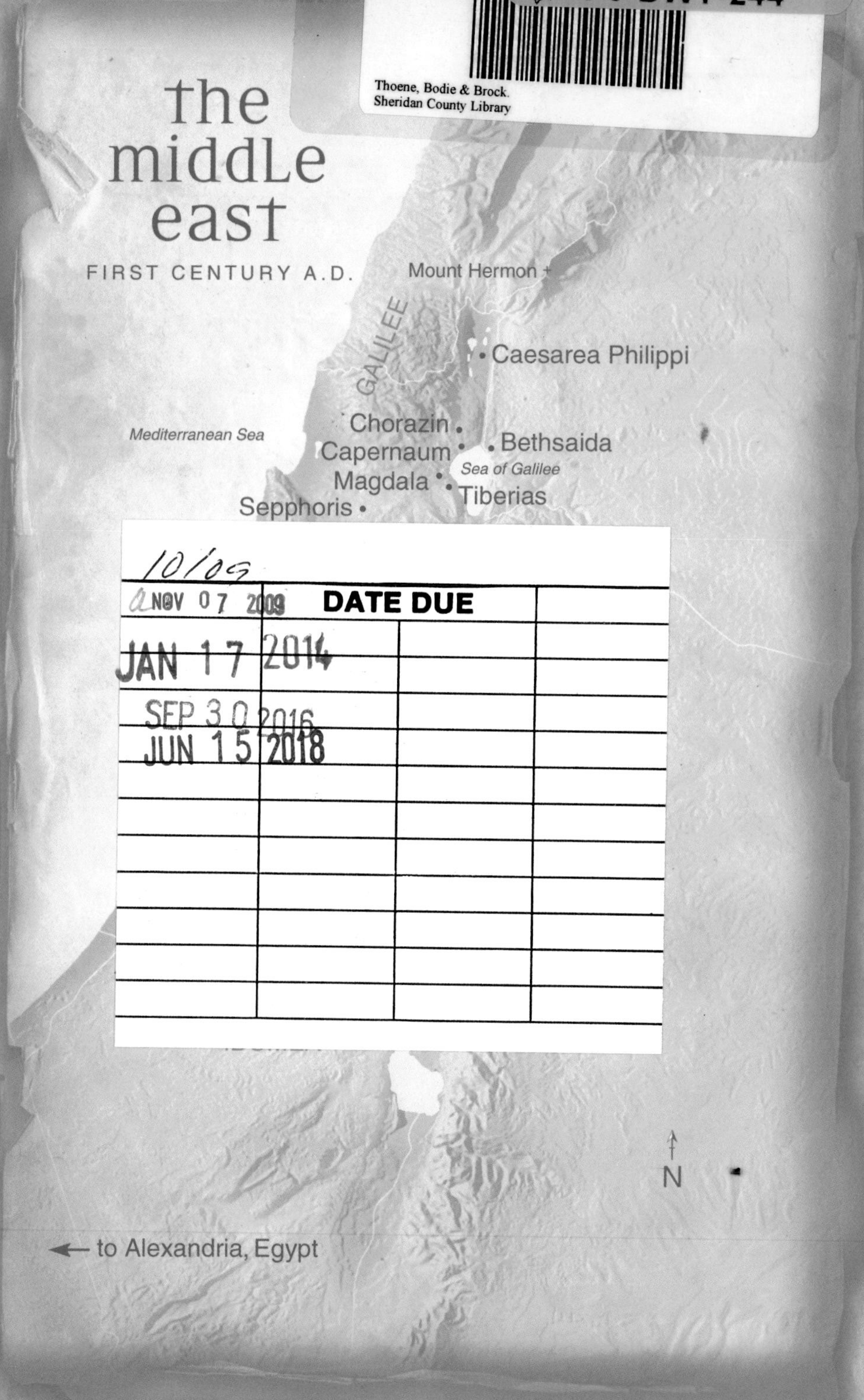

the
middle
east

FIRST CENTURY A.D.

Mount Hermon
GALILEE
Caesarea Philippi
Mediterranean Sea
Chorazin
Capernaum
Bethsaida
Sea of Galilee
Magdala
Tiberias
Sepphoris

N

← to Alexandria, Egypt

eLeventh quest

BOOK ELEVEN

A.D. CHRONICLES®

eLeventh quest

Tyndale House Publishers, Inc.
Carol Stream, Illinois

BODIE & BROCK
THOENE

Visit Tyndale's exciting Web site at www.tyndale.com

A.D. Chronicles series designed by Rule 29, www.rule29.com

Interior designed by Dean H. Renninger

Edited by Ramona Cramer Tucker

Library of Congress Cataloging-in-Publication Data

Thoene, Bodie, date.
Eleventh guest / Bodie & Brock Thoene.
p. cm. — (A.D. chronicles ; bk. 11)
ISBN 978-0-8423-7537-5
1. Bible. N.T.—History of Biblical events--Fiction. I. Thoene, Brock, date. II. Title.
PS3570.H46E43 2009
813'.54—dc22 2009016466

Printed in the United States of America

15 14 13 12 11 10 09
7 6 5 4 3 2 1

We dedicate Eleventh Guest *to Poppy Irwin,*
much-loved daughter of Jesse and Rebecca Irwin.

Nineteen weeks of Life on earth.
Forever alive in heaven with Jesus.
MATTHEW 6:28-30

I AM the vine; you are the branches.

JOHN 15:5

Prologue

LONDON, PRESENT DAY

A steady downpour drenched London and slowed noon traffic to a crawl. Shimon Sachar gazed out the bus window at a canopy of black umbrellas. The pedestrians packing the sidewalks of Oxford Street moved faster than the red Number 10 bus.

Alfie Halder stood and lumbered toward the exit as the bus slowed and stopped across from Selfridges Department Store.

The old man ducked his head and grinned over his shoulder at Shimon. Though Alfie was always pleasant, Shimon had rarely seen him excited. Today his eyes glistened with childlike anticipation. "Eben Golah! Eben Golah," he murmured again and again.

They inched forward amid the throng on the bus.

Outside, opposing black conveyor belts of umbrellas flowed east toward Oxford Circus and west toward Marble Arch. Except for the occasional moving punctuation point of a Burberry pattern or a floral print, the pedestrians might have been stationary.

"Too slow. Too slow," Alfie declared.

The interior of the bus smelled of wet wool overcoats and over-liberal applications of cologne. At least the rain reduced the choking cloud of diesel fumes Shimon always associated with London.

Would they be late to the meeting?

The headlines of a crumpled London newspaper screamed from the floor beneath Shimon's shoes: *DIVIDED JERUSALEM?*

It seemed Israel's right to exist had been betrayed. The American president, who openly negotiated with and supported Islamic regimes, wielded a political sledgehammer, dictating an Israeli policy of appeasement: *If you want our continued support,* America now declared to Israel, *you will abandon the Golan Heights and everything back to the pre-1967 boundaries.*

Back to indefensible borders.

Destruction of the Zion Covenant, sealed by the blood of six million Jewish martyrs, was imminent.

The words *Never Forget* were now to be forgotten. The new American policy assured that the Jewish battle to keep Jerusalem as the eternal, undivided capital of Israel was as good as over. Israel's right to survive was a bone tossed to Islamic terrorists in exchange for "peace."

How many generations had died for the sake of a Jewish homeland? What would be left of Eretz-Israel after politicians carved it up?

Shimon's wife and mother had both died in an Islamic homicide bombing in Jerusalem.

Shimon pictured his wife's face, pale and lifeless, as the mortuary attendant had lifted the sheet so Shimon could identify her body. A single bolt from the homemade slaughtering device had pierced Susan's right temple. Such a small wound for such an enormous soul to escape through. Susan's eyes, half open in death, had gazed at something beyond him. Her lips were parted in a gentle smile. Her death had seemed incomprehensible. "*Susan? Get up! This cannot be happening!*" His voice commanding her to get up and live was without effect. His words of acceptance seemed to belong to someone else. "*This is Susan Sachar . . . my wife. . . .*"

That had occurred only a few years earlier. Now talk of dividing Jerusalem and surrendering more Jewish territory to Islamic terrorists was reality . . . and incomprehensible to Shimon.

Who would lift the sheet and identify what was left of Israel?

Shimon kicked aside the newspaper and wondered if this strange encounter with his father's old friend might shed some light on the future.

"Eben Golah," Alfie chanted. "Eben . . ."

Doors slapped back, disgorging passengers. Umbrellas popped open. They stepped down and melted into the current of the damp, Oxford Street crowd.

Alfie's head towered over the surging mob. The old man lifted his umbrella and peered out from beneath the rim. Spotting Shimon again, he called out, "Come on, boy! Shimon! Hurry! Eben Golah! You'll see. He'll be there. Waiting."

Shimon fingered the slip of yellow legal paper with the address.

St. Mark's Church
N. Audley St.
London

The old church was only one block away from the American Embassy. Shimon had heard about the place, though he had never been there. Shimon's father, Moshe, had often mentioned a man named Eben Golah. Moshe said that miracles happened in St. Mark's, North Audley, but when pressed for details, he had shrugged and said perhaps one day he would explain.

Time ran out. The story of the St. Mark's miracle and clues to the true identity of Eben Golah were buried with Moshe Sachar.

Shimon had once previously met Golah, also in London. Much about the man remained a mystery—such as how a 1941 comrade of Shimon's father could be in his eighties and yet appear to be a youthful thirty.

The mystery was increased by the recent, urgent summons to return to London. A packet had arrived in Jerusalem, addressed:

To Shimon Sachar,
Son of Moshe and Rachel Sachar

In it were two tickets from Israel to London for Shimon and Alfie and a time and date to meet at St. Mark's Church. The message was signed *Eben Golah*.

Now Alfie shouted, "Shimon! Come on! Don't want to keep him waiting. Eben Golah. I been waiting a long time to meet him. Come on!"

They left Oxford Street and headed down North Audley toward the American Embassy. The crowds diminished and the fervor of the rain increased. A torrent hissed from the sky and sluiced off the roof tiles until the buildings gushed miniature waterfalls.

Every doorway Alfie and Shimon passed was packed with people seeking shelter. The entryway of an Italian restaurant was jammed with those who had a sudden urge to get inside. Refugees from the rain mingled with others who had changed their minds about leaving.

"Come on," Alfie urged again. The old man trudged forward, oblivious to the downpour. "Almost there."

Shimon hunched his shoulders deeper into his raincoat. When he unwisely tilted his umbrella to locate their destination, a jet of cold water poured down his collar. Alfie, as usual, was correct. The columns of the portico loomed just ahead, but so did an unexpected barrier.

"What's this?"

Shimon blinked to clear his eyes. His father had described the St. Mark's steps as once enclosed by wrought-iron railings. Then he had explained how the iron had been removed during a 1940 wartime scrap-metal drive.

How had they reappeared?

A few paces closer revealed the truth: The entryway was blocked by a three-sided, chain-link enclosure. Signs warning against trespassing competed for space with handbills offering the secrets of Tibetan meditation and invitations to a retrospective showing of the greatest vampire films of all time.

"This can't be right," Shimon muttered aloud. "All the way from Jerusalem . . . boarded up?"

Alfie seemed undeterred. "Eben Golah said. Meet him here, he said. So here he will be." Methodically Alfie grasped the chain-link and rattled each juncture where an eight-foot-high section of fence met another.

In the center of the barricade was a narrow gate, chained and padlocked. Alfie grasped the lock and pulled downward. It fell open in his hand. "Come on," he urged. "It's open. See?"

Shimon looked up and down the block for police cars and witnesses, but the elderly man had already disappeared into the gloom beneath the overhang.

Shimon climbed the steps as Alfie searched for the way into the building. Massively tall double gates, designed to accommodate the ebb and flow of an enormous Sunday congregation, offered access through the center of the portico.

They were locked. Impassable. To the left, however, was an entryway sized for everyday use. Alfie pushed the door inward and it squealed open at his touch. "Not bolted," he offered, slipping in.

Shimon hesitated outside. The interior of the narthex was unlit and visible only by the thin streak of light admitted by the partially open portal. The passage leading to the sanctuary proper looked like a cave entrance.

Alfie again scolded him for lagging behind. Shimon shrugged and stepped over the threshold. After all, he reasoned, a church—even a derelict one in the center of London—could scarcely be as intimidating as the tunnels beneath Jerusalem.

The foyer was empty . . . emphatically so. Alfie's shoes squished and creaked, but Shimon's heels clattered unnervingly loudly on the black-and-white marble tiles and echoed from the vaulted ceiling. Even the walls were unadorned, except where bare patches of paint brighter than the rest announced where bulletin boards and memorial plaques once hung.

"Alfie," Shimon said with a hiss, "wait for me." Then, struck by irony, he mused aloud, "What am I whispering for?"

"A holy place." Alfie grasped Shimon by the wrist and pulled him forward into the gloomy interior. Shimon allowed himself to be led down the center aisle, reasoning that Alfie must see much better in the darkness than he could himself.

If the narthex was spacious, then the sanctuary was monumental in scope. Even as Shimon's eyes adjusted to the murkiness, his view was carried farther and farther eastward toward the high altar. On the way there his inspection went up and up and up, past a gallery ringing the auditorium, to end in shadows too deep to penetrate.

Enough illumination entered from the storm-shrouded skies to display stained-glass windows—scenes of David and Moses and prophets whom Shimon couldn't instantly recognize.

Another stained-glass panel, too dark to make out, topped the altar. The torrent of rain continued to pound on the roof like the fists of some living thing wanting to get in.

Shimon shuddered and turned to look back toward the light glowing dully through a window above the choir loft at the rear of the auditorium. He backed toward the altar in order to get a better view of an enormous stained-glass window that illuminated the loft. The figure of

Jesus, many times life-size, was central to the composition. The exterior light was too dim to distinguish any additional details.

At that moment something stirred in the shadows at the base of the west window. A portion of the darkness in the loft moved and separated itself from the rest.

"Shalom, Shimon Sachar and Alfie Halder," a deeply resonant voice called. "Come up." The words echoed and multiplied until the command came from all directions.

"What?" Shimon gasped.

"Maybe angels, eh?" Alfie said with a smile. "But also could be Eben. Shalom, Eben! How do we get up there?"

"The foyer," the disembodied voice ordered. "Turn left. Stairs behind the pillar."

Alfie lurched ahead of Shimon into the foyer. Shimon followed more slowly. What did he really know about this man, Eben Golah? What lay behind the cryptic summons and the—Shimon groped for the right word—*unusual* choice of rendezvous?

What drew him onward was Golah's association with his father. Despite being privy to many of Moshe's secrets, there was still so much Shimon did not know but wanted to be able to encompass.

He felt his way around the circumference of a pillar, guided more by the tramp of Alfie's ascending steps over his head than by his own limited vision. Could Alfie somehow see in the dark?

A staircase led upwards into even thicker gloom. A glimmer of light revealed a landing. The faint gleam glinted in an oversize mirror on the wall. Antique, with its silvering faded and streaked, the mirror offered the appearance of an old photograph, even a tintype. Shimon's reflection rose into view and grew in size. He stopped short in front of it. It seemed to be his father's face he saw before him, yet not the elderly Moshe. Unconsciously Shimon's hand rose to his cheek and tugged. It was a gesture he had seen Moshe employ often.

The mirror . . .

A young Moshe Sachar peered back at Shimon—Moshe as he would have appeared if he had stood in this church sixty years earlier. A dark comma of hair fell across a worried forehead above narrowed dark eyes. A prominent nose surmounted a mouth twisted into a wry expression.

Shimon rocked back on his heels with that thought. Moshe *had* been in this church many decades before, perhaps had climbed these very stairs past that same mirror. Moshe had been in this church during the war against the Nazis. Moshe had been in this church when the first postwar discussions of the resurrection of Israel had taken place here.

Is that what this meeting was about?

Shimon shook his head, and Moshe in the mirror offered the same disagreement. *There is more to this than you can even imagine*, his father's image seemed to argue.

Shimon took the rest of the steps two at a time, ascending two more flights before emerging on the level of the choir loft.

Alfie was already beneath the huge stained-glass window, beside Eben Golah, whose name he kept repeating over and over with delight. Shimon advanced to meet his father's old friend, but the words of greeting died on his lips. He was struck again by the same doubts as at their first encounter.

The man smiling beside Alfie must be an imposter. He appeared to be in his thirties, younger than Shimon, in fact. His face was unlined, his shoulders erect, though below Alfie's in height. A globe of wiry, light-colored hair topped a high, broad forehead, giving his head a too-large appearance for his thin neck.

Could it be this was not his father's old colleague, but rather the son of that man? If so, why the deception?

"Shalom, Shimon Sachar . . . son of Moshe. I always recognize your father in you. What a friend he was! Thank you for coming on such short notice."

Alfie's head bobbed. "You see! Eben Golah. Told you he'd be here."

Lightning flashed in the south, illuminating a row of arched, clear glass windows in the upper gallery. The boom of thunder followed, rattling the building.

"Right above us," said Alfie, rolling his eyes heavenward.

The image of the sanctuary burned on Shimon's retinas. High marble pillars supported interior archways like bridges made of polychrome bricks.

Eben Golah blinked at the flare as if some memory was jarred loose by the crack of thunder. He said quietly, "I was here with your father the night the bombs fell and shattered those windows. The prophets were all there in a row. How Lucifer hates this church. But the stick of bombs missed, you see. The church survived the Blitz. But the prophets in their alcoves shattered into a million pieces. We swept them up and your father . . . ah, well. It was long ago." Eben smiled and sat down on the dark rose–colored pew in the choir loft. With a wave of his hand he invited Alfie and Shimon to join him.

Shimon felt his breath catch at the implication of Eben's words. He would not ask, but the question burned in his mind: How could this young man have known his father?

Alfie steadied Shimon with a massive hand on his shoulder. "Your Papa told you, Shimon . . . he said to you . . . miracles happened in St. Mark's, North Audley. Eh? Sit down. Sit down. By and by you'll know."

Without thinking, Shimon grasped Eben's hand firmly and then released it. It was solid flesh. Eben was human, not spirit. Not angelic either, unless angels named Eben wore Levis and Nike tennis shoes.

A renewed cloudburst rumbled on the roof.

Eben remarked, "You are very much like him, you know."

Shimon lowered his chin in acknowledgment. Thoughts of seeing his father's face reflected in the mirror's image of himself cascaded through his mind. He answered, "You were old friends. Old. I knew that much."

The corners of Eben's thin lips turned up in amusement. "Yes."

"Why here? Why not in Jerusalem?"

"Because the missing piece . . . what you look for is right here."

Outside the church the clouds must have parted before the westering sun. In an instant light streamed through the window like the music of angels caroling.

Alfie sat transfixed as the face of Jesus, luminous, seemed to smile down upon the trio in the choir loft. The old man lifted his fingers in greeting and said, "Hey . . . it's him."

Eben nodded once. "I was sure of it the first time I laid eyes on the face."

Shimon wondered when that moment had taken place. Last year? A century ago?

"Yes," Eben declared with certainty, sending a chill through Shimon. "Look upon him. It is Yeshua." Then Eben asked, "Shimon, son of Moshe, look around you. What do you see?"

Shimon obeyed, drinking in the shifting hues.

The face of Yeshua the King, returning to reign, glowed bright above the seven golden candlesticks of the seven churches. A serpent twined around the third lampstand from the left. The words in Revelation 2 sounded plainly in Shimon's memory: *"I know where you dwell, where Satan's throne is. Yet you hold fast to My name and you did not deny My faith. . . ."*[1]

On the base of this particular candlestick was a small golden pelican. Few beyond the artist would notice such an obscure detail. The pelican was said to pierce its own breast for blood to feed its young. The bird was an ancient symbol of Jesus offering His life so others might live.

The bejeweled breastplate worn by the image of Jesus cast variegated pools of color on the warm, red wood of the pews, and on the trio of men. *"He put on righteousness as a breastplate. . . ."*[2]

A golden grapevine adorned the robes of the coming King and reached out green and living tendrils onto the walls of Jerusalem. *"I AM the vine; you are the branches."*[3]

Puddles of blues and greens formed on the black-and-white checkered floor, and a single brilliant shaft of gleaming white beamed down on the open Bible on the altar.

The interior of the church brightened as if someone outside had thrown a switch and focused floodlights on the stained glass. The storm broke. Darkness fled. Wood and stone and glass became radiant. Sunlight passing through colored panes transformed intangible energy into visions of history and prophecy.

Details of windows that had been obscured by the clouds became vivid. Above the gold-paneled altar directly opposite the Revelation window, Christ suffered agony on the cross. On either side of the cross were angelic creatures described in the book of Revelation.

There was no corner of the church that did not proclaim God's love for man. How could language describe it all?

Shimon chose his words carefully. "This building . . . it is the story of what was and . . ." He faltered. A holiness, a spiritual presence was in this place, making it difficult for Shimon to speak. Awe silenced him.

Eben fixed his eyes on the face of Christ and whispered, "What was . . . and what is. And what will be. Look there—the vision of Ezekiel and Revelation. What will be . . ."

The whole story of the end of history was there, though it would take years to read each visual detail: End of Days. Second Coming. Seven seals. The angels. Prophecy was recorded in glass and stone—some obvious; some secrets concealed, obscured.

Eben gestured up to the full height of the hammerbeam ceiling.

Round windows were positioned high so light could flood down from above. Blacked out, painted over during the Blitz; no one had ever bothered to remove the paint and restore the interior clarity after the war.

Eben continued, "But look closely: The Star of David pattern in each circle remains visible beneath the blackout paint. In this place, 125 years before Israel was reborn, someone wove the prophecy of the last days and the rebirth of the nation of Israel into the fabric of this building. Your father was part of the fulfillment of that prophecy. The Star of David crowns St. Mark's."

Shimon remembered what scant facts his father had given him about St. Mark's, North Audley, "The American Church." It was the church where Eisenhower had worshipped during the planning of D-day. Where American soldiers, destined to die in battle, had written their last letters home. Where Eleanor Roosevelt prayed before she met with the first UN members in 1947 to develop the establishment of the State of Israel.

The crown on the head of the victorious Christ glinted as the sunlight passed through it. Colors shifted, revealing new details in the stone.

"A treasure." Eben hummed and traced Hebrew letters intertwined in the carving of a wood panel. "*Nune. Sheen. Gimel.* 'To reach; to lay hold of.' And by the reverse, 'Goshen—the fertile land where the Almighty sheltered his children in Egypt.' So let us lay hold of a great blessing, eh?"

Shimon shook his head in disbelief at the Hebrew anagram. Backwards and forwards the word was significant. Who had carved the message into the panel? "Will it . . . will this . . . be lost?"

"Lost? Not lost. The end is within reach. The goal is in sight. We will take hold of the Truth. It is finally attained. St. Mark's is the gate, the portal between the past and the present."

Shimon understood the significance. Two blocks north was the old Roman highway by which the first converts to Christianity had carried the gospel throughout Roman Britain. Linked to modern history and the establishment of the State of Israel in 1948, the American Embassy in London was two blocks south of the church.

Eben rested his hand on the carving. "America's spiritual fortress in the northern boundary of the ancient Roman Empire. It is no surprise that this week the church is closed as America yields to great evil. This is none other than the gate of heaven, the dwelling place of the Lord in this outpost. The men who built it understood. The land beneath this church was deeded and dedicated to stand as the house of God in perpetuity . . . 'til the end. The End. You understand, don't you?"

"And if it is destroyed?" Shimon paused and waited for the answer.

"The future is written in the Book, is it not? What was. What is. What will be. Even this—" Eben swept his hand around the chamber—"even this is a sign."

Eben stood and faced west, gazing up at the window portraying the Second Coming. By a slight inclination of his head, he commanded Shimon and Alfie to also rise. He bowed slightly, touching his forehead as he enacted greeting the Messiah. In an ancient Hebrew dialect, which startled Shimon by the ease with which it was uttered, Eben whispered the prophecy of Daniel: *"Behold, on the clouds of heaven came one like the Son of Man, and there was given to Him dominion and glory and a kingdom, that all peoples, nations, and languages should serve Him. And His dominion is everlasting and shall not pass away. . . ."*[4]

Then Eben said quietly, "Shimon, you are an archaeologist. A linguist specializing in ancient language. You recognize first-century Hebrew spoken, like your father did. And Greek . . . it is elementary to you, eh? Hebrew, the language of secrets revealed. Greek, the language of mathematics, of proportion, of beauty. Complex. So tell me what language you read in the picture of Christ before you."

Shimon scanned the patterns in the stained glass. "It is . . . not so simple. A lifetime of study. A theme is here, certainly in the repetition of the geometric patterns. A doctoral thesis, possibly more than one, on the symbolism and meaning in the portrait."

Eben concurred. "You see, yes." He then spoke in fluid, melodic Greek. *"I was in the Spirit on the Lord's Day, and I heard behind me a loud voice like a trumpet. . . . Then I turned to see the voice that was speaking to me, and on turning I saw seven lampstands and in the midst of the lampstands one like a son of man, clothed with a long robe and with a golden sash around His chest."*[5]

Shimon blinked up at the image in the window. "The passage . . . this . . ." He faltered as visions crowded out coherent thought.

Eben said, "Language integral to the picture in the glass itself. More than art. It's prophecy. One letter, especially—a Greek letter within the glass—defines this church. Just as every measurement recorded in the ancient Tabernacle and in the construction of Solomon's Temple had significance. Can you find it?"

Shimon's eyes narrowed as he pondered the challenge and the narrative in the artwork. "Yes. It tells a story . . . the story of the End of Days. But far too much to summarize."

"Then begin with the obvious." Eben's gaze locked on the face of Jesus and His crown. "Plain language."

Shimon followed Eben's eyes to the two golden Greek letters woven into the halo around the crowned head of Christ. He raised his brows in surprise. Suddenly he understood Eben's premise. He answered, "I see *alpha* and *omega* in gold. *Alpha*: first letter in the Greek alphabet. *Omega*: last letter. Eternity. Beginning and End. The first and among the last words of Christ in Revelation . . ." Shimon paused and spoke the phrase in Greek, which sounded awkward and childlike compared to Eben's mastery of the ancient tongue. "*I am the Alpha and the Omega.*"

The omega letter in the glass was small. With its footed arch, like a golden horseshoe standing upright, perhaps it would be noticed only by a trained eye.

Eben instructed again in fluid original Greek, "*Jesus said, 'I AM the Alpha and Omega.'*"[6] The enigmatic guide reverted into modern English without trace of an accent. "Common enough in religious art, but this is only the smallest *omega* in St. Mark's. *Omega*. Shaped like a gate. The letter proclaims a passage out of time. The end of time, as we know it. The beginning of something new: eternity." Eben opened his arms to embrace the scene all around them. "Now look out over the sanctuary. Tell me what you see. Or rather, what do you read in the walls of this building?"

Clouds now dispersing, the afternoon light illuminated a geometric masterpiece, a perfect example of the golden mean: the floor plan of the sanctuary. The ratio of the lofty ceiling to the length of the nave, the proportions of the windows . . . mathematicians back to Pythagoras would revel in its symmetry.

But there was much, much more. The span and height of the warm interior were supported by a multilayered pattern of brick archways—one archway built atop another. From top to bottom, walls and window frames looked very much like a series of Roman bridges stacked upon one another, or the model of an ancient aqueduct built to carry water to a desert place, or a series of gates opening into the walled city of Jerusalem.

And within the multiples of tiered archways were some that had been clearly embellished to portray the Greek letter *omega*.

In Hebrew, Eben quoted the first words of the Messiah in the Book of Revelation: "'*I am the Alpha and the Omega*,' *says the Lord God*, '*who is and who was and who is to come, the Almighty. . . . Write what you see in a book and send it to the seven churches*.'"[7]

Alfie gasped. "I see it all right," he cried. "Look! There's one . . . and there and there. Everywhere."

Shimon summarized: "A geometric masterpiece. An Escher woodcut. No beginning and no end. The *omega*. Embedded in the stone structure in plain sight, yet concealed to the inattentive eye. The entire building is a three-dimensional representation—a celebration of the letter *omega*—written by the architect in brick and stone. Was this representation of the *omega* the conscious intent of the architect? It exists. It is fact. The stones bear witness."

"Well spoken," Eben said in a clipped tone, like a schoolmaster congratulating a student who finally understood the most basic of lessons.

Next, Eben led the way back down the dark stairs to the center aisle of the sanctuary. In the exact middle of the hall he turned and raised his right hand to where light streamed through the vision of the Second Coming portrayed in the Revelation window. The sheen on the pews just beneath it in the choir loft transformed the wood into a series of steps leading down from the feet of Jesus.

Powerful beams of white sunlight focused through three small arched windows set high in the wall.

In front of the Revelation window a central brick archway seemed suspended in air, forming the perfect *omega*. The Second Coming window floated in the exact center of the arch. The King seemed poised to descend and enter though this gate.

It was Alfie who said what Shimon was thinking: "A prophecy."

Shimon shivered at the implication. Now he spotted the *omega* everywhere he looked! Geometrically proportionate, the construction of the building had no visual beginning place and no end. Eastward, above the high altar, three tall arches framed scenes of the Crucifixion and the Resurrection. These images in glass would glow brilliantly each day with the rising of the sun.

Moving clockwise, Shimon guessed that the clear windows on the south wall, stained glass blown out during the Blitz and never replaced, would have originally portrayed Hebrew prophets.

On the north wall, stories of the miracles of Christ and the apostles inhabited the transept.

West, above the entrance, the Revelation window floated high. One day the sun, which illuminated the image from behind, would set for the final time on earth's history. Then the One who is the Alpha and Omega would appear like lightning flashing from east to west.

The prophecy portrayed in the window would come true.

Alpha and Omega. Eternity. There would be no beginning and no end.

Eben concurred. "The *alpha* and the *omega* are the tangible reflection of a spiritual weight placed within the covenant on the deed of this property when the land and the building were dedicated. The church will remain a church until the end. In perpetuity. When and if the covenant is broken—a small sign, perhaps, in a world filled with so many prophecies unnoticed, yet think of it!—the covenant is broken. This house of God, the congregation evicted, a fence blocking entry, has represented the spiritual home of America in England for two hundred years."

Shimon touched the smooth wood of the pew and imagined American soldiers sitting there. General Eisenhower. Over two hundred years of American presence in this neighborhood. From the days of John Adams' service as minister to the Court of St. James in 1785 and the adoption of the American Constitution in 1787, to the present American Embassy, just a short walk from here.

Eerily, Eben seemed to read his thoughts. "Yes, Shimon. Everything means something. The history of this church parallels American history. The closing of St. Mark's at this moment. The last pastor, evicted by a broken covenant, an American."

Directly opposite, at the far end of the hall, the carved marble pulpit beneath the scene of the Crucifixion directly faced the stained-glass vision of the Second Coming. Reached by ascending twelve steps, the pulpit enclosure also contained twelve arches—a facsimile of Revelation's description of the twelve gates of the New Jerusalem.

From this position, as the pastor preached, he alone could see the depiction of the Returning Messiah.

Christ, as the Alpha and Omega, was at the backs of the congregation. Thus only the Word, proclaimed by the shepherd, could warn the flock of His imminent return.

Window by window, Eben took them on a picture tour of the stories of healing recorded in the Gospels. Nearly every miracle was portrayed.

There was, Shimon thought, something unique about the faces shining in the stained glass.

They seemed familiar, real. The windows were alive in the shifting light, like photographs of the living, rather than portrayals of the ancient dead. It was as if the artist had known Peniel, the man born blind, and the paralytic, and the cripples who had met Jesus face-to-face. The thought came to Shimon that the artist himself had somehow been touched by Jesus of Nazareth and changed forever. At each window Eben pointed out some object or symbol that was worked into the pattern. Pomegranates, grapes, figs, citron, bunches of lavender, and the pink buds of almond trees all spoke to Shimon of prophecies contained in Torah.

Was the artist Jewish? Shimon wondered.

Strangely, the windows along the south wall were clear glass. "Also blown out during the Blitz," Eben explained. "Shattered too completely to be reassembled. Oh, the stories they could have told! But there was one . . . we saved the pieces, your father and I."

Eben glanced over his shoulder as the sun blasted through the face of the risen Christ in the resurrection window. He bowed slightly, as if he had received a spoken order.

"It is time." Eben turned on his heel and led Shimon and Alfie to the altar. He smiled and slid his fingers beneath the edge of the top, producing an old iron key. Inserting it into an obscure keyhole, he turned it. There followed the distinct click of the tumblers in the lock. A look of victory filled his face as he lifted the top of the altar like the lid of a child's school desk. Inside a shallow compartment were shards of broken glass from the unrepaired windows shattered in the Nazi bombing raid. There was an old twelve-by-fourteen-inch photo of the window as it had been, depicting ten ragged lepers—eight men and two women. A solitary figure of an old man sat across from the ten with an open scroll on his lap, as if he were instructing them in Torah. They feasted at a table heaped with the bounty of Israel's fruit: almonds and citrons and figs. Along the border of the table were depicted a sandal, a hammer, a fish, a Torah scroll, a pomegranate, and a bunch of grapes.

Eben reached into the compartment and produced a fragment of glass with the identical image of the scroll on it.

"What does it mean?" Alfie asked.

"It means I fear the window may never be restored. The journey of the ten is almost forgotten. The eleventh? The old man? Ah, well. Who remembers him? Here is their testimony."

Lying on the bed of glass was an aged leather portfolio secured by leather shoelaces. Stamped into the border of the cover were the same symbols portrayed in the shards of glass.

Eben explained. "Four manuscripts. Four love stories. Not as this world perceives love, but rather stories about the love that is stronger than death." He frowned. "Shimon, it is written. If this house falls, then surely this city will fall. This church has been the repository of these manuscripts for two hundred years. A drop in the bucket. Before then? Ah, well. They have been kept safe in many other places over the last two thousand years. But now? There is a prophecy written in the covenant of this church that it would remain in use as the house of God until the end. It survived the Blitz, but it may not survive the selfishness of this generation. We believed this treasure . . . and others . . . would be safe here. We must pass this on to you for safekeeping now, in Jerusalem. Perhaps we guardians of the north have come to the end. We have been betrayed."

"And if Jerusalem is betrayed?"

"Pity the betrayer."

"You believe the time is near?"

"Take these documents back to Jerusalem with you. I cannot leave Britain. You know what to do, how and where to preserve the documents until the day they will be revealed."

THE SHOEMAKER'S SON

They shall sit every man under his vine . . . and no one shall make them afraid.

MICAH 4:4

THE JOURNEY BEGINS . . .

Nine lepers and Lily, the widow of Cantor, gathered in Rabbi Ahava's stone hut in the Valley of Mak'ob. They were meant to be a minyan of ten, chosen by lot to go out in search of Yeshua the Miracle Worker. The Galilean Rabbi was said to be able to heal every disease.

Cantor's sudden death had whittled their number down from ten and disheartened the nine who remained. All but the four strong youths from Ahava's Torah school were downcast. Carpenter, who had counted on Cantor to lead them, was frightened by Cantor's unexpected absence from their task. Surely the hand of the Almighty had prevented Cantor from leaving the valley of lepers.

Carpenter explained to the rabbi, "With Cantor flown away? It's like this, Rabbi. Those of us with a few years on us—mind you, not these four youths, but the rest of the party—we're thinking maybe it's a sign. Maybe we're meant to stay Inside."

Other voices broke in while the four teenaged lads scowled.

"Aye," agreed Crusher.

"That's it," concurred the two Cabbage Sisters in unison. "Thinking it's a sign we shouldn't . . ."

Fisherman, who had grown content with a life without the uncertain sea, added, "Never was too keen on the idea of leaving the Valley."

Carpenter added, "So, if Your Honor agrees with what we're saying? Well, Rabbi, we'd rather just . . . you know."

Rabbi Ahava's wooly head bobbed as he considered their reasoning. The old man frowned. "What do you say, Lily?"

The young woman, her gaze filled with sorrow as she glanced up at the path that led Outside, responded slowly.

"I didn't want Cantor to leave the Valley. But it seems to me he wouldn't have wanted the rest of you to give up the quest just because he's not here to lead you."

Carpenter squirmed. "I'm not as young as I used to be."

The four young Torah scholars sat forward eagerly. Their leader, son of the Shoemaker who lay close to death, proclaimed, "But we're still young. Still strong! Ah, Rabbi! We've never been Outside since we were small. Since we entered. Let us go! We'll go." He included the other scholars with his sweeping gestures. "Let us go Outside on our own. If there's a Messiah, we'll find him."

Rabbi raised his hand for silence. "Fine lads, all of you. Cantor would be proud of your eagerness. You're sons of his brave heart, that's certain. But without a leader. Without Cantor or Carpenter . . ."

The widow clasped Carpenter's hand. He tried to withdraw it, but Lily clung tight and drove her words home like hammer blows. "Carpenter! Oh, Cantor loved you so. Made you second in command, just in case . . . in case something happened to him. He knew you could lead the others. Would you have turned back if he had died Outside, on the road?"

Carpenter considered her question and answered honestly. He had never considered himself a brave man. His disease had simply made him more reclusive. "I may well have done so," he admitted.

She demanded, "And what if Messiah was just over the next hill? if hope was within reach? Just a mile away? Would you have turned back?"

Crusher studied the patch of sky as if he saw the future there. "Well now, that's altogether another story."

Lily held up her clawlike left hand. "And if you knew a touch or a word could restore this? And the One we've all been waiting for was close enough for you to shout to him? to grasp his knees and not let him go until . . . until . . . ?"

Carpenter, ashamed of his willingness to stay in a familiar place and die, relented. "If you put it that way, Lily, of course we'd go on."

"Yes. Yes, Carpenter," the young widow encouraged. "Cantor would expect it of you. Expect you all to be brave."

Shoemaker's Son cheered her on. "My father! What if this Messiah could make him well again? I'd go to the ends of the earth."

Carpenter scanned the half faces of his fellow sufferers. "Sure. That's right. Just what Cantor would say, I suppose, if he could speak. Well spoken, Lily."

Lily leaned back against the wall.

Carpenter exclaimed, "I know. Lily can go with us! Lily can be tenth in our minyan."

Carpenter saw Lily's face cloud. "The baby. I can't. Deborah is my sister. My mother. As she grows weaker, she's becoming my child. I have no one left now but Deborah and the little ones. I can't leave them."

She closed her eyes, and her lips moved as though laying her case out before God. Carpenter did not interrupt. He scanned the eight who looked to him for leadership. Except for young Shoemaker's Son, no one in the group had a loved one they must leave behind. The Cabbage Sisters had one another. Their lots had been drawn one after another, and both had been pleased they had been selected.

Rabbi Ahava agreed. "I believe you must go. Go search for him and bring him back if you find him. The Almighty always leads us out to lead us in. Those of us who remain behind will pray for you."

Young Shoemaker's Son put a hand to his brow. "I'm leaving my father when he would not leave me. Will you care for him, Lily?"

Cantor's widow agreed that she would feed Shoemaker and look in on him every day.

Rabbi Ahava turned to Shoemaker's Son. "And I, as well. You must not look back . . . only to the road . . . set your heart on finding the One we seek. I'll take care of your father. He's stronger that Cantor was. Perhaps this . . . sickness . . . which fills his lungs will pass and you'll see him again, well and healthy."

And so it was settled. These nine would go Outside in search of the Messiah.

A meadowlark sang in the brush, a strange counterpoint to their good-bye. "We're leaving, Father." Mikki, the shoemaker's son, clasped his sick father's hand as he lay wheezing on the bed of straw beneath the chalky cliff.

"Not without me." Shoemaker tried to sit and then to stand.

Mikki pushed him back and he collapsed, as weak as a kitten. "Look here. An amphora of water. Bread and vegetables to last a week. We'll be back by then. We'll bring him back with us."

The bird sang a cheerful melody. If they failed, it would mean the end of the world for the 612 in the Valley. Their lives would be forgotten. Hope would be buried in the sandy soil of the dead riverbed.

"You can't go . . . alone."

"Not alone, Father. There are nine of us. Almost ten—almost a minyan, if Cantor hadn't died last night."

"I won't let you go . . . without me." Shoemaker struggled to rise again.

"We nine, we're the strongest. We'll bring him back, Father, I promise. If we have to sneak into his camp and bind him and carry him here, we'll make him come."

Strange how the meadowlark sang from the bush while father and son parted for perhaps the last time.

"I promised her . . . you can't go without me."

Mikki was kind, always. He placed his half hand on his father's fevered brow. "Father, you have the sickness—what Cantor died from. The cough. Water in your lungs. I hear it gurgle when you breathe."

"Why?" Shoemaker's face contorted in frustration. "I'm the one who can walk without limping. I can whistle, snap my fingers. Why me? Why now?"

Mikki rubbed his eyes and gazed down on his grieving father. "Listen to me. I was chosen by the casting of sacred lots to go Outside. Me and the others. Cantor was not meant to come with us, so his soul has flown away. Father, if you came with us, sick as you are—no matter that your feet are sound—your breathing would slow us down."

"I could keep up. I'm the only one . . . who should be leaving this place . . . for the Outside."

Mikki didn't let him finish. He reasoned with his father as if Shoemaker were the child. "Listen: You would slow us down, and then you would die."

"I wouldn't."

"Like Cantor died. You would. I am sure of it. The Lord has chosen only nine of us to go Outside. It is only the Lord . . . by lots. And your lot was not chosen."

"I wouldn't die," Shoemaker moaned, moving his head from side to side on the ragged blanket that was his pillow. "We must not . . . be separated. That's the way we beat this demon. We stay . . . together."

"And then we would have to stop long enough to bury you. Nine lepers on the road—that's bad enough. The people Outside, they'll stone us if they can. But if we have to stop and bury you?"

Shoemaker began to cough. He convulsed with hacking. His eyes brimmed with tears as he covered his mouth with a whole hand. Ten fingers. Ten toes. Why was his lot not chosen among the lepers of Mak'ob?

Mikki shook his head. "Listen, Father. Just stay and rest. Rabbi Ahava will tend to you. He promised. Lily said she will come and make certain you eat."

"Poor thing," Shoemaker croaked.

"Yes. She's just buried her husband from this same thing that now burns up your lungs. And now I tell you, Father, we are close to something—reaching out for something wonderful, like nothing Israel has ever seen. Do you hear me, Father? If we can only find him!"

Shoemaker nodded. He blinked at the high rim of the Valley of Sorrows where 612 lepers dwelt perpetually. The sun was a red ball snagged in the limbs of a storm-blasted oak. "I will try to . . . keep breathing," he surrendered, too tired to speak.

"Father." Mikki's voice trembled as he suddenly feared leaving his father behind. "You must not die of this thing filling your lungs. Not when the rest of your body is complete. Till now you are the strongest of us all. But clearly it must be the will of the Almighty that you stay behind. I must go and you must stay here until we bring him back. And then? Then he will heal us all."

Shoemaker nodded and closed his eyes. The fever burned in his brain. He shivered with cold. "All right," he gave in. "But don't be . . . gone long. Promise me."

The meadowlark burst from the bush and flew into the craggy rock.

"Father, please be here when I come back. We'll bring him. We will. The nine of us. And you can be our tenth—the minyan—only you are the one who stays behind to pray."

The eight lepers who followed Carpenter up the switchback trail were called "Faithful Minyan of Mak'ob." Though they lacked one person to form a true minyan, these were the strongest members of the community. There were scarcely any in the Valley of Sorrows who were not missing toes or feet or legs.

Carpenter was the strongest and the only one who knew Yeshua of Nazareth. At least Carpenter had known the family long ago.

Mikki was the leader of the four boys of bar mitzvah age.

Carpenter announced, "We will invite the prophet Elijah to travel with us, eh? The prophet Elijah will be the tenth member of our minyan."

"Carpenter, you met this Yeshua, eh? Tell us again," chimed the Cabbage Sisters as they made their way out of the Valley to the Outside.

"Yes, Carpenter," urged Fisherman. "Tell us what you know."

The four Torah scholars chimed in with Crusher, the vinegrower. "Tell us. What was he like? It will help as we set our faces to this task. Finding the Messiah. A daunting task."

Carpenter agreed. "Stories will help pass the time. This is what I know. All I can remember." He drew a deep breath of satisfaction as he recounted what he had seen and heard. "I knew the lad's father. The guild, you see. Carpenters. Yoses or Yosef—some such name. But he was the center of gossip for everyone in the guild. Something about his betrothed . . . pregnant before they married. Unusual circumstances about the child's birth. A miracle, Yosef said, but no one believed in angels. Demons were the big reality back then when Herod the Butcher King ruled." Carpenter spread his strong hands. "Well, he said an angel came to him. Said she was carrying the Messiah. 'Marry her,' the angel told him. No one believed it. But he married her anyway."

"Do you believe it?" asked Shoemaker's Son.

"Here's the thing. I met the lad later. Passover, it was. A few of us in the Carpenters' Guild traveled to Yerushalayim together. The lad was twelve years old or so." Carpenter sized up the four boys walking in a pack to his right. "Their size and age—bar mitzvah age. And this lad spent all his time in the Temple courts at Solomon's Portico, listening to the learned men. Not listening only, but discussing intelligently with them. They were amazed, these rabbis were. And the lad stayed on in Yerushalayim while we all left. Three days later his mother says, 'Where's Yeshua?' They turned back and found him where they left him: speaking with the learned doctors of the Law. Sleeping down in the quarry with the orphan boys, the link boys of Yerushalayim. One link boy became his brother in the end. Went home with the family to Nazareth, I hear. Nothing ever like this . . . wisdom . . . from the mouth of a boy. Kindness too. Everyone said so. And then he puts the Law into practice. Brings a child to his mother and father, and they adopt him."

"And then what?" asked Shoemaker's Son.

"Then I got leprosy and my nose fell off. From sticking it in other people's business, I'd guess." Carpenter laughed.

"There has to be more," Fisherman said. "What's all this about healing and miracles and such?"

Carpenter shrugged. "I know as much as you know."

Shoemaker's Son cleared his throat. "I think I saw him. I mean, I sold him sandal straps. Lots of them. If it's the same fellow."

Carpenter rubbed his forehead where eyebrows used to be. A thought struck him. "This is good. You can tell us. We'll all tell some story."

"Does it have to be true?" Fisherman was dubious.

"True? True? Of course not." Carpenter came to the fork in the road. "I've lived too long in Mak'ob to tell a good true story with a happy ending. No. I've forgotten all such stories. Just tell a good story, nu? Each of us as we go. All right. Which way would you head if you were the Messiah? Yerushalayim? Or Jericho?"

Shoemaker's Son smiled wistfully. "I'd go to Yerushalayim. The Temple Mount. Where else would the Messiah go?"

"Well spoken," agreed Carpenter. "So. We'll go to Yerushalayim and find Messiah. No doubt. No doubt. He'll be where his mother found him. If it's the same lad I remember, he'll be there, in the Temple. If he's the Messiah, we'll find him there setting things straight. Teaching Torah to the doctors of the Law, eh?"

Back in the Valley, Shoemaker opened his eyes as morning sunlight beamed through a hole in the tarp covering his shelter. He drew a deep breath and exhaled slowly without coughing. For the first time in—how many days?—the fever had broken.

He did not know for certain how long he had been ill. How many times had the kind face of the old rabbi hovered over him, praying, urging him to live?

Shoemaker sat up. He reached for the water jug and drained it dry.

Wiping his lips with the back of his hand, he shook the fog of fever-induced confusion from his mind. Where was his son? Somewhere amid the haze, Shoemaker remembered a dream. . . . The boy had come to him and declared that he was leaving Mak'ob, going Outside in search of a healer.

Shoemaker doubted the reality of this madness but still wondered where Mikki was.

The scraping and crunch of gravel announced a visitor. The quaking voice of Rabbi Ahava called, "Shoemaker? Are you still with us in the land of the living?"

Shoemaker's voice was rusty, like an unoiled hinge. "I am alive."

"Good!" The flap of the shelter was drawn back. The old rabbi's face beamed in. "You are sitting up! Good! Very good."

"I am feeling better." Shoemaker invited him in. His stomach rumbled at the smell of a warm loaf of bread. "Smells good."

"I brought you bread. Fresh."

"I'm hungry today. First time."

"Ah. If only I could smell it. I miss the smell of bread. I admit it. I do." The rabbi smiled and sat cross-legged on the woven mat. He broke the bread and blessed it as Shoemaker's mouth watered. Then he gave half to Shoemaker and began to tear off small chunks of the feast for himself.

Through a full mouth Shoemaker asked, "My son. Have you seen him?"

The bewildered expression on the rabbi's face alarmed Shoemaker. "But . . . he came to bid you farewell. Don't you remember?"

"Farewell?" Shoemaker tried to rise but found his legs still shaky. "What is it?"

"The minyan—surely you remember? You were displeased with the Lord that you were not—"

"But . . . you mean it happened? It was not a dream? They left? After Cantor died? Still they went Outside?" It all came back to Shoemaker in a rush.

"This is our choice: We either look for Messiah and bring him back, or we must be content to die without trying."

"But without Cantor . . ."

"Carpenter is the leader."

"I was willing for my boy to go Outside as long as Cantor was leading, but this . . ."

"Your son has his bar mitzvah, Shoemaker. In the eyes of Israel he is a man." The old rabbi raised his chin. "He was chosen. You were not."

"Carpenter leading? He's set in his ways. Told me he didn't care anymore if he ever left here. What kind of leader will he make?"

Rabbi Ahava contemplated his bread. "He will let the boys be men, I think. Cantor trusted him to keep their hopes up . . . keep them going."

Shoemaker reached for his sandals. "I'm going."

Ahava put a half hand on Shoemaker's arm. "You were not chosen."

"I promised . . . promised her . . . I wouldn't leave him."

"*He* left *you* . . ."

". . . told his mother I'd take care of him."

". . . for your sake, for the sake of all of us. He's gone to bring Yeshua of Nazareth back."

"That one. Trouble. I told my boy in Yerushalayim: Stay away from all that. There's trouble there."

"Yeshua of Nazareth. Our only hope, Shoemaker." Rabbi Ahava spoke to him kindly, like one trying to calm a frightened animal.

"The Romans. Herod Antipas. The high priest. This Yeshua is trouble for them. And trouble splashes all who get near him."

"They fear what they cannot control."

"Fear? Hate," Shoemaker corrected.

"The two grow from the same seed."

"Hate is the stronger branch. And they hate Yeshua and anyone who follows him. Maybe you've been Inside so long . . . maybe you don't know."

"Perhaps your son and the others won't be able to find him. But they must seek him. They must travel beyond their suffering, or they will not have any hope at all of living."

"Do you know what is done to lepers on the Outside?"

"So your son should stay Inside and die without trying?"

"I have to go." Shoemaker felt a surge of energy born of fear. He reached for the daylight, clawing past the rabbi. "I promised her . . ."

Rabbi Ahava followed him slowly, emerging from the shelter and grasping his stick to stand. "You're one of us now. You can't leave. Your lot was not chosen. To leave this Valley without the blessing of the Almighty is dangerous. Presumptuous."

Shoemaker waved the old man away. He scanned the steep switchback trail and mentally made note of what he would need to make a journey. Food. Water enough to travel back to civilization. "My son," he stressed. "My boy."

The nine lepers from Mak'ob traveled up the steep road on their way to Jerusalem in search of the Messiah.

Each evening they made camp, far from the highway. The four Torah boys gathered sticks and shrubs, and Carpenter, who carried the flint, built a fire. The sun set as they prayed for deliverance and shared their small ration of bread.

Each evening they fully intended to implement the telling of tales, but before they could begin, all nine fell into the deep, dreamless sleep of exhaustion.

It was Shabbat, and they were still two days' travel from their destination. The white marble of the great Temple gleamed in the distance like snow capping a mountain peak. The sun set and the Shoemaker's Son perched on a boulder to watch the final rays brush the stones of the city with a gold and then a pink before the light faded.

The Cabbage Sisters, who were surprisingly proficient in reciting the Shabbat prayers and Torah portions, prayed over the scant meal. Their cauliflower faces beamed as they welcomed Shabbat and invoked the coming of the Shekinah to their camp.

"Dwell among your people, O Lord!"

Carpenter sighed with contentment, as if the meal had been extravagant and the prayers spoken by a sage or a prophet.

Tonight no one seemed especially weary. Fisherman turned to the Torah boys and asked, "We're here until Shabbat ends. You, Son of the Shoemaker. It seems to me I remember that you once met Yeshua. You sold him . . . laces or something?"

Mikki nodded. "Not him directly. One of his followers."

"You're the only one who would recognize him," Crusher said with envy. "I'd like to hear your story."

"What is the story you will tell us, then?" Carpenter asked. "You owe us a story."

Mikki nodded and inhaled deeply. "I wish my father were here. He's a better storyteller than I am."

"But he's not," Crusher instructed. "So you'll have to tell it."

"Is it a true story?" asked the Sisters in unison.

"Stories are hardly ever 100 percent true," the Fisherman intoned, "because we tell only what we know. Only what we see. Let the boy speak. True or not. Let him tell us the story he wants to tell."

"Where is it set?" asked the Sisters.

Mikki answered, "Yerushalayim."

The Sisters clapped their hands. "Oh, lovely. Lovely! And what is it about?"

"A family. A son. A father . . . and a friend."

Crusher leaned back against a stone. "Sounds very . . . real. Can you tell it all before the fire dies?"

The Shoemaker's Son nodded. His gaze went to the final gleam of light high on the Temple Mount and far away. "If you listen closely, you will hear the sound of the shofar."

CHAPTER 1

Mikki, son of Tycho, walked back from bar mitzvah class with his best friend, Eli. The twelve-year-old boys rehearsed the day's lessons. The bond between them was strong. They had grown up together in Jerusalem on the Street of the Shoemakers. Their families attended the same synagogue and shared the same concerns. Their fathers had known one another since they were apprenticed into the Shoemakers' Guild.

Mikki, tall and dark, towered over Eli, who was thin and pale and suffered from a lifetime battle with asthma. Mikki knew Eli was smarter in studies, but the smaller lad often remained silent because he could not breathe and recite the answers.

Today was a particularly difficult day for Eli. His breath came in short gasps. "I . . . don't know . . . if . . . if I can . . ."

Mikki finished his thought. "Don't worry. You'll just go up there and open the scroll. You know you can read Torah better than any of us."

Eli patted his chest three times and shook his head in disagreement.

"At least you understand what you're reading, eh? Not like me. Just words to me."

Eli glanced at Mikki with disapproval. He paused beside a pillar to inhale slowly, though the shoemakers' stalls were within sight. "Drowning . . . ," he gasped. With a wave of his hand he indicated Mikki should go ahead to his father's booth.

Mikki waited, pretending to study the patch of sky and the plume of smoke rising up from the daily sacrifices. "No one but you is in a hurry," Mikki said lightly.

Eli doubled over in a spasm of coughing just as Mikki heard an unexpected clamor sweep over Jerusalem's Temple Mount. The summit crowned by the gleaming white and gold sanctuary was riotous at the best of times: the discordant bleating of hundreds of sheep and goats, the blare of trumpets, the enticing cries of the sellers, the babble of pilgrims.

All these combined in a most unholy cacophony of merchandising and worship, but this sound was different. Surpassing all the rest of the tumult was the rising bellow of angry voices.

Mikki linked his arm with Eli's, helping him the rest of the way to the market stall.

Mikki's father, Tycho, owned a Temple Mount concession where Mikki's older brother, Linus, sold sandals to pilgrims. Solomon's Portico, the columned arcade defining the eastern edge of the plaza, was packed with merchants and money changers.

Besides the irate murmur, there was a distinct change in the movements of the worshippers. No longer thronging *into* the courts of worship, now the multitude flowed *out*, away from the sanctuary. Thousands of footsteps approached the Roman garrison building called the Antonia, that grim, square block planted on the northern boundary of the sacred mount. It provided an ever-present reminder to all Jews that their magnificent Temple and even their worship itself existed at the sufferance of Rome.

Eli's complexion was ashen as the boys reached the stall.

Mikki's father, an older version of his son, gave the duo only a cursory glance. Tycho stood erect from his work at the shoe last.

"What? What's going on?" Tycho asked as Mikki found Eli a bench to sit on and fetched him a cup of water.

"Eli, you know . . . trouble breathing."

"No." Tycho lowered his chin to listen as another wave of sound moved toward them. "That."

Linus, Mikki's nineteen-year-old brother, snorted. "You know what it is, Father. Legionaries. The Court of the Gentiles is crawling with them. Maybe a fight . . . always something."

The consensus was that the Romans—*Foul pagans that they are*, Mikki thought—had again done something to defile the Temple Mount. *Like being there at all.*

Mikki was jealous for the honor of the One God of Israel . . . and curious. He told himself that duty required he look into the disturbance.

Mikki leaned close to Eli's ear and whispered, "I'll go see."

Eli, panting, grasped Mikki's sleeve and violently shook his head in disagreement. Mikki laughed and danced away. With a grin and a broad wave he slipped into a gathering current of pilgrims.

"Stay here," his father called. Tycho's command came too late to address anything but his younger son's departing shoulders.

Mikki ignored the command.

A rush of excitement surged through the boy. Tall and husky for his age, Mikki had no experience with treacherous, large crowds. He lived a sheltered and uneventful life. Rome had ruled Judea since before his birth, but Mikki had no firsthand knowledge of Rome's brutal suppression of rebellion. Roman swords and Roman javelins seldom discriminated about whether the blood they spilled was guilty or innocent.

Mikki pressed forward. The atmosphere was charged, but Mikki did not define it as danger. He emerged from the portico into the expansive north court. The view was startling. The throng of worshippers pressed against the extremity of the Temple platform. They shook their fists in the air and shouted. It was like the sea, stirred up by a violent wind.

He was sorry Eli was unable to witness this! These were not the excited, happy gestures of pilgrims, like at the Feast of Tabernacles. For that festival, Jewish visitors to Jerusalem waved palm branches and myrtle boughs and sang joyful psalms.

Today the air of the Temple Mount crackled with anger. The object of the hostility was clear. The previously unadorned wall of the Antonia now bore bright bronze standards depicting the features of Emperor Tiberius.

Blasphemy had bloomed overnight like obscene, poisonous weeds.

"Sacrilege!" a man in a brown-and-red striped robe shouted, spraying spittle over his neighbors. "No graven images! The Romans seek to defile our holy place!"

Mikki was drawn into the current like an undertow pulling him out to sea. He tried to slip sideways toward the edge of the swelling crowd but was hemmed in.

"Sacrilege!" was the chant and "Blasphemy" was the refrain.

All around him faces were red with rage. Mikki felt his own cheeks glow with righteous fervor. He shook his fist in the air, shouting against the Roman desecration. What a story he would have to tell Eli when this day was finished!

The furious horde threatened to overflow the plaza. The gates beside the Antonia opened. A squadron of Roman legionaries marched onto the Temple Mount, spear points glittering in the morning sun.

The mixture of mob and soldiers was a heap of dry tinder. Any moment the tiniest spark would ignite the pyre.

Mikki was jostled forward and back. Those nearest the advancing Romans shrank from the threat. Latecomers shoved in behind. There was a very real danger of being crushed. Young children, the elderly, and cripples struggled to remain upright.

Cries of fear now chorused with angry shouts.

Quickly, pallor replaced fury. The reek of human fear overpowered the aromas of incense and roasting meat coming from the Temple sacrifices. If the emperor-god of Rome was angry, what would *his* soldiers sacrifice to appease *him*? A man beside Mikki clawed his way backward, trying to escape.

Mikki suddenly regretted his own stupidity. Would he fall victim to foolish curiosity? be trampled without striking a single blow for the Almighty?

Mikki was above average height, already taller than many grown men. He saw the Romans advance. So far they cleared a path using only the butts of their javelins. The absence of screams of agony meant no blood had been shed . . . yet. The centurion in command of the legionaries traversed the plaza with steely eye and forceful stride. He stopped short of the low Soreg wall that warned non-Jews to advance no farther.

Mikki heard only fragments of what ensued as the centurion addressed the crowd: ". . . not disturb your worship . . . rioting must cease . . ."

Someone in the mob blurted, "Images . . . against our law!"

Now it will happen, Mikki thought in direct contradiction to his former bravado. *The fool has given the Romans the excuse to slaughter us all.*

Confirmation appeared certain as columns of tramping soldiers burst onto the Mount from the remaining three sides of the square. Panic replaced anger as the dominant timbre of the throng's voice.

In their efforts to flee, the crowd ran into and over each other. An old woman, bent at the waist and hobbling with a cane, caught the hem of her gown beneath others' feet. She pitched forward. Mikki caught her arms and held her amid the press. Using his elbows he kept a space clear for her to catch her breath.

From over the heads of the surging mob he thought he heard someone call his name. He strained to see. "Linus?" he shouted, but his cry was lost amid the clamor.

A new figure joined the drama. From his offices in the midst of the Temple buildings loped High Priest Caiaphas. His clothes were disheveled, and he ran awkwardly.

Mikki witnessed but could not overhear the solemn, earnest conversation between priest and centurion. All around Mikki the worshippers wore glazed and terrified expressions, like a flock of sheep surrounded by wolves.

A beefy, florid-faced man shoved Mikki down. The boy twisted to the side as he stumbled and cried out as he fell. His strangled call for help was lost as he struggled to protect his head. He could not breathe. Trying to scratch his way out of the melee, he began to take others down as well.

"Mikki!" someone above and behind called to him. "Mikki!"

"Here!" He raised his hand.

Suddenly Linus appeared, fighting to reach him, to rescue him, to pull him up from drowning in a sea of sweaty tunics and frantic bodies.

Mikki felt someone grasp his hair and drag him up, up and out to open air. He gasped as Linus' grim and determined face appeared. The older brother managed to look both angry and relieved at the same moment. "Stay close to me," Linus urged, setting him on his feet and breaking a path to safety beside a pillar.

Linus put himself in front of Mikki with the marble pillar at his back. "Get up there." He instructed Mikki to climb the base of the column where he had a clear view.

Mikki reported that a temporary resolution of the conflict was reached. As Lord Caiaphas looked on, the Roman centurion ordered his troops withdrawn to the gates of the Temple complex.

Commands were shouted by Temple officials: "Worship will continue, but worshippers are not permitted near the Antonia. Only groups numbering ten or less may congregate."

Crisis averted for the moment, the panic was quelled, and the crowds drifted apart. There was still a great amount of angry muttering, but no one had been killed; no massacre had occurred.

With a growl Linus rounded on Mikki, seizing him by the scruff of his neck and pulling him down from the pillar. "Are you trying to get killed?" Linus worried aloud. "Keep to business and leave politics alone! Isn't that what Father always says? You can be so much trouble, Mikki!" Then he walked Mikki back to their stall with his arm around Mikki's shoulders.

Tycho had also been searching for Mikki. He returned from the Temple Mount, grabbed his younger son and embraced him, but was unable to speak. Finding his voice, he stammered, "Linus, close . . . close the shop early. Things . . . are still too tense."

Eli gave a feeble wave of relief but remained seated. Mikki thumped his chest and inhaled deeply. For the first time he understood what it must be like for Eli to feel he was drowning on dry land.

Tycho closed his eyes, as if trying to erase the nightmare image of what could have happened to Mikki. He gulped. "Scared pilgrims don't buy shoes. But scared shoemakers can still make shoes . . . at home. Let's go there and open again tomorrow." He placed his forehead against Mikki's. "Mikki, please . . . never again! You boys are all that matters." And then to Eli, "Your parents will be worried. Come on, boys. Home."

Fearful words darted about like swallows in the Shoemaker's home.

"The Romans," Mikki's mother, Callisto, blurted. "That new governor, Pilate. Currying favor with the emperor. Doesn't care about our ways, our laws, our lives." Her eyes brimmed with what-ifs. "Mikki could have been killed!"

Tycho rubbed her hand in a calming gesture. "But he wasn't. We're all safe. No one got hurt."

"And little Eli. What if he . . . ? His mother was frantic."

Mikki frowned. "He was safe. I wouldn't—"

Linus confirmed, "Eli was safe, Mother."

Callisto fumed, "And what about tomorrow? What then?"

The Shoemaker shook his head. Mikki saw the lines on his father's forehead deepen.

"We can stay closed tomorrow, too." Tycho's words trailed away. He and his wife exchanged a look Mikki could not interpret.

"When word of this spreads, the pilgrims will turn back," Callisto said. "The crowds . . . a lot smaller?"

"It's evil," Mikki asserted, feeling again the wave of indignation he suffered when he saw the emperor's face staring down at the Temple. "Mocking our worship!"

His father turned and made a shushing motion with his hands. "You mustn't talk like that, do you hear? It's dangerous. This may not be over yet. Be glad your sisters and their families don't live here. There could be riots . . . crucifixions."

Callisto blanched and sat down abruptly.

"Listen," Tycho added, motioning for the others to sit. "So, it's a hard time to live in Yerushalayim—anywhere in Judea, in fact. The new governor has to prove himself. Can't allow rebellion. That motive beats all else. You know that prophet out in the desert, Yochanan the Baptizer? Openly challenging Herod Antipas and his queen. He'll be dead before a year is past. No doubt Antipas has spies watching him now. The high priest's men listen for sedition, too. Carry tales to the Romans. The way to get through this is to keep our heads down, stick to our last, eh? Stick to business and—"

"Stay out of politics," Mikki chorused. "But, Father, blasphemy?"

"Better a live dog than a dead lion, eh? If a thousand Jews attack the Antonia to make Pilate take down the images, there'll be a thousand fewer Jews living in the Holy City, and the images will still be up there. Now's the time to keep our opinions to ourselves. To ourselves," he emphasized.

Mikki nodded but despised his father's fear.

The image of Eli gasping for breath came to his mind. Every Jew living under the tyranny of Rome was drowning in fear, gasping to draw one breath of freedom.

CHAPTER 2

Much to Mikki's chagrin, his father forced him to stay at home and indoors for two days after the Temple Mount disturbance. Large numbers of Temple guards augmented the legionaries in keeping the peace. There seemed as many soldiers tramping through the streets as citizens.

So far nothing had been resolved.

The face of the Roman emperor maintained his staring contest with the One God of the Jews. Access to the courts of the Lord was strictly controlled. Jews were still not allowed to assemble in large numbers, and the tension remained unabated.

As Tycho said, resentment of Roman heavy-handedness was unavoidable. The trick was to not show it, not get caught between Romans and Zealots.

Roman troops garrisoned in Judea were mostly Idumean and Samaritan mercenaries. By both heredity and disposition they loved any excuse to break Jewish skulls.

"Don't let it be yours," Tycho lectured.

First rumors, and later eyewitness accounts, reached Jerusalem that the conflict had moved to the governor's courts in Caesarea Maritima.

Five hundred Jews—some reports said a thousand—occupied Governor Pilate's courtyard. They vowed to remain there until the offensive medallions were removed. When threatened with death, the Zealots refused to move. Citing their Maccabee forefathers, they preferred martyrdom to dishonor.

While not discussing his thoughts with his father, Mikki was elated. He understood how Governor Pilate was the one caught in a dilemma. What would displease the emperor more: having his image removed from Jerusalem, or having a thousand subjects slaughtered? It was Roman policy to not interfere with local religions, but here Pilate had done exactly that. What would Tiberius say if grumbling became bloody rebellion, and it was all Pilate's fault?

There were other issues to be considered. Passover week had arrived. Jewish pilgrims from all over the Empire and beyond were in the Holy City. Jerusalem was packed with many times its normal population. Those in charge of maintaining order had their hands full with pickpockets, petty quarrelers, and all manner of swindlers. If another riot occurred it could get much, much uglier than before. Word would quickly spread through all parts of the Roman world.

Tycho expressed his own personal concern about the timing. Many travelers walked a good bit of the journey and had worn out their footgear in the process. Next to the pilgrim festivals in the fall of the year, this was the busiest season for shoe sales.

The winter had been occupied with cutting and stitching until the shop was bursting with inventory. This was no time for unrest; it was time to do some business.

Weighing safety concerns versus commerce, Tycho finally relented. He allowed Mikki to accompany Linus back to the Temple Mount marketplace to assist with the stall.

So Mikki was present to see the epilogue to the graven image conflict. Pilate finally relented. The medallions of the emperor were being removed and placed inside the Antonia or in the governor's Jerusalem palace.

Pilate could claim the medallions still hung in Jerusalem, as promised.

The Jews would not care so long as the images were not visible.

Face would be saved.

And possibly many lives.

As Mikki looked on, Roman soldiers atop the Antonia's parapets hauled at the ropes suspending the roundels. One by one the copies of the emperor's visage were dragged upward and removed from view.

"Hoisted by the neck, as he should be," one Pharisee muttered.

Mikki grinned, then hid his smile before Linus noticed.

There was no cheering, but signs of joy and relief were visible on all the Jewish faces in the crowded terrace. It was the emperor who was retreating.

When Mikki pointed out this sight to his brother, Linus replied, "Good. Now get back to work sorting those sandal straps."

The Temple Mount quickly regained the hum of normal operations. A new drove of sheep entered the pens, with much bawling and squealing. A line of porters passed wicker baskets of doves from hand to hand.

Animals for sacrifice had to be approved by Levite inspectors. This meant a pilgrim either must pay a fee to have his offering examined or buy an already acceptable lamb at many times the usual price in Jerusalem.

It was all a great scheme to line the pockets of the merchants and the corrupt priests. The victims had little recourse if they expected to worship on the mountain. Many Temple officials, including High Priest Caiaphas, profited from the transactions. They were more than willing to turn a blind eye to the crooked practice.

Money changers called out the day's rate of exchange. Like the animal wares, the coin-changing practice also masked great wickedness. Only Temple shekels could be used for Temple purposes. Roman, Greek, and all other foreign coinage had to be exchanged. Mikki knew which money changers cheated, and which sold clipped, short-weight coins or charged exorbitant fees.

Mikki bit his lip as he labored at untangling the mass of straps. All the turmoil over the emperor's face on the wall, yet thousands of coins bearing the same profile flooded into the coffers of the Temple's businessmen. The emperor's face overlooking the plaza was blasphemy and a sacrilege, but using the identical image to cheat and steal was agreeable?

Mikki wondered if he should discuss these questions with his father. Tycho was an honest man who recognized dishonesty around him but preferred not to make waves.

At first Mikki did not respond when someone inquired about the price of the leather cords. Linus was so bossy he always took charge of every transaction as if Mikki were a witless servant.

When the customer repeated his question, Mikki saw Linus was engaged with three other purchasers haggling over expensive shoes. "Two for a penny," Mikki said, glancing up.

The man who stood before him was of medium build, with black hair and a curly beard that came almost to a point. It gave him a crafty appearance. He jingled a leather coin pouch.

"I want ten," the man said. "What deal can you make me?"

How cheap could this buyer be? Mikki wondered. He squinted in unconscious imitation of his father's "bargaining face." No one quibbled over sandal straps; two a penny was the going rate.

Still, no one bought ten at a time unless he was outfitting a Torah school.

"Come on! Haven't got all day," the shopper groused.

"The lot for three pennies," Mikki said.

The buyer grunted, counted out three pennies from the money sack, and accepted ten finger-width leather cords, each the length of Mikki's arm.

Curious now, Mikki watched the man retreat to join a group of about a dozen companions. They were clearly not from Jerusalem. Mikki studied them: rugged, sun-bronzed faces, paired with rough, homespun clothing, coupled to booming voices and broad gestures. When Mikki overheard the loudest of them mixing his *hets* and *khets* his guess was confirmed: Galileans.

Like many pilgrims they stared and pointed.

In their midst stood their leader, identified by the way the purchaser delivered the straps to him. The central figure was tall, with brown hair and beard. He was likewise tan of face, but not weather-beaten, and looked about thirty years of age.

Perhaps he was a rabbi?

While his friends or followers or students gossiped and gawked, the rabbi—Mikki decided to think of him that way—piled the ends of the straps in his palm. They hung down at length, smooth and straight, one atop the next.

What's he up to, Mikki wondered. *Ten cords? Like the Ten Commandments? Is he going to teach a lesson?*

The followers continued to overlook the actions of their teacher, but Mikki observed him carefully. With great deliberation the rabbi knotted the ends together into a kind of handle. Then he methodically proceeded to braid the loose strands together. Another knot near the end completed the whip—for clearly that's what it was—and prevented it from unraveling.

A whip? To drive what? Sheep? Goats?

The rabbi set off with a determined stride in the direction of the money changers' tables. By the time his talmidim noticed his departure and ran after him, he was already nearing his objective.

Cords standing out in his neck, shoulder muscles bunched together, the rabbi grasped the edge of the counting table and flipped it over! Coins scattered in all directions, rolling and jingling across the pavement. The startled money changer jumped up, stumbled backwards, tripped over a fistful of shekels, and went sprawling.

Nor was the sudden attack directed at only one exchange.

Despite the cries of alarm and shouts for him to stop, the rabbi proceeded down the row of tables, overturning some, swiping the neatly stacked piles of drachmae off of others.

Next to the counters of coins was a row of stalls containing sheep and goats and oxen. The whip popped and snapped overhead as the rabbi flicked his wrist. Opening the gates of the pens, he drove the animals toward the ramps leading away from the Temple Mount. Their owners corralled a few beasts, but many stampeded past.

The scene was soon a wild melee of flustered herdsmen, confused animals, and baffled visitors.

The rabbi approached the stall of a dove salesman. When he slashed his improvised whip through the air, it sizzled. "Take these things away!" Mikki heard the rabbi order. "Make not my Father's house a house of merchandise!"[8]

A crate of doves burst as it was overturned. A feathered explosion followed as the birds mounted up and up into the sky above the mountain.

The rabbi's talmidim caught up with their furious leader at last. They hustled him away toward the Eastern Gate leading out of the city and across to the Mount of Olives.

Mikki gasped for air when he discovered he had been holding his breath as the scene unfolded. Who was that, and what was this all about?

It could only end badly for the poor madman, Mikki thought. Even hating each other, Jewish priests and Roman officials would both be pleased to seize that man . . . whoever he was.

Eli was confined to his bed. The Jerusalem air had become poison for Mikki's friend over the last weeks. A walk across the Temple Mount was enough to send him to his knees in spasms of coughing. He was indeed drowning on dry land. Bar mitzvah classes were to be held at Eli's house in the evening, so Mikki had been given permission to join him in his studies. This made it possible for Mikki to work full-time during the day.

Mikki helped Linus close up the stall before they walked home together. His brother handed him the basket of shoes needing repairs and sent him on ahead.

"Three pair to resole and one for new laces. Pathetic." Linus shook his head. Business was very slow. "See you at home," he added. "Friend's coming by. No reason for you to wait. Tell Mother I won't be there for supper."

Mikki arrived at the Street of the Shoemakers. The lanes were empty of shoppers, as if it were a Sabbath or a Holy Day. He pushed open the rear door to the shop. There was no one to meet him. Setting the basket down by the other repair projects, Mikki went upstairs to change.

His parents' voices came from behind their door. The sounds were muffled, as if the words were being spoken underwater.

Callisto fretted, "But we ordered all that extra leather, expecting to sell a lot more sandals this year. The way pilgrims are staying away from Yerushalayim, we'll be lucky to sell enough to pay for the hides, let alone make any profit."

"Everyone's in the same boat," Tycho replied. "Lamp makers. Tinsmiths. Weavers. Since Passover, shoppers are staying home. Guilds are putting workers on half pay. After Eli's bar mitzvah Jabez says they are moving to Antioch."

Mikki heard his mother moan, "Antioch?"

Mikki blinked dumbly at the floor. Eli? Moving away? To Antioch?

If Eli left, who would he have to talk to? Who would listen to his blustering without hating him for it? Who would set him straight?

Drowning on dry land . . .

"Don't worry," Tycho said to his wife. "We'll manage. The tannery will give me more time to pay. They don't want the hides back. Who else is there to sell to? We're all in the same fix."

"How bad is it? Can we hang on?"

Drowning. Drowning . . . no one to pull Father to safety.

Mikki wanted to hear his father instantly say that everything would be all right. Instead there was a long, ominous pause.

"Let's not say anything about this to the boys," Tycho answered at last.

"Linus knows," Callisto responded. "He told me he waits all day for a single customer."

"Mikki, then," Tycho concluded. "It's his bar mitzvah year. I don't want him worrying we can't buy him that prayer shawl he wants . . . let alone fret about having to move to a cheaper house."

Move? From the house that had always been Mikki's home?

"You can't keep it from him forever," Callisto warned.

Mikki carried the box of new shoes across the great viaduct and onto Mount Zion. Instead of going directly toward the stall he turned aside, into the Temple courts. He was not being deliberately disobedient. The beauty of the pale, blue sky overhead framing the grandeur of the House of the Lord called to him.

The Levite choir began the psalm of the day:

> *"Sing for joy to God our strength; shout aloud to the God of Jacob!*
> *Begin the music, strike the tambourine, play the melodious harp*
> *and lyre."*[9]

Musicians performed exactly as the lyrics required.

Rhythm, melody, and words stirred Mikki's soul. He entered the Court of Women and approached Nicanor Gate's steps. Setting down the basket, he could both see and hear the worship.

"Sound the ram's horn at the New Moon,
and when the moon is full,
on the day of our Feast."[10]

At the end of the first passage the trumpeters raised the silver horns to their lips and blew three blasts. *Who would not be stirred by such a scene?* Mikki wondered. He wished Eli could be with him as the trumpet calls vibrated up his spine and down to his toes.

He swelled with pride. Soon, very soon now, he and Eli would not be limited to the Court of Women. They would pass through Nicanor Gate and take their places in the Court of Israel as men!

The priests faced the crowd. Their hands were raised in worship—worship offered to the Almighty, whose footstool was the Temple. As they sang, Mikki made their song a prayer for Eli's lungs and a prayer for his father's little shop.

"In your distress you called and I rescued you,
I answered you out of a thundercloud;
I tested you at the waters of Meribah."[11]

The threefold blare of trumpets echoed again across the courts and caromed off the storage chambers for wood and oil and spices. It reverberated amongst those making vows and those giving thanks for answered prayers.

The hair on the back of Mikki's neck stood up.

"Hear, O My people, and I will warn you—
if you would but listen to Me, O Israel!
You shall have no foreign god among you;
you shall not bow down to an alien god."[12]

An approving murmur swept through the throng and was instantly stifled. It was impossible to be before the House of the Lord and not remember how the Almighty had recently triumphed over the foreign god, Tiberius Caesar!

"If My people would but listen to Me,
if Israel would follow My ways,

how quickly would I subdue their enemies
and turn My hand against their foes!
You would be fed with the finest of wheat;
with honey from the rock I would satisfy you."[13]

The final trumpet flourish rang out, rolling around the Mountain of the Lord as if emerging from the thunderclouds in the hymn.

Mikki muttered his prayer. "Please, heal my friend Eli. His father's only son. And please wear out the shoes of the pilgrims before their time. Send customers to Father. Then I will serve you, Adonai. I will go to war. Defeat your enemies like King David did Goliath. Cut the Romans to pieces."

When the last echoes had died away, the normal hum of movement and conversation resumed.

Mikki stood transfixed, staring through the arch of Nicanor at the white and gold of the Temple itself.

"Beautiful, isn't it?" agreed a voice from near Mikki's feet.

A beggar, holding a clay bowl decorated with a rainbow, smiled up at him from a shady spot on the steps. The bowl contained a meager three pennies and one even smaller coin called a mite.

The beggar lifted his face. He was blind. The sockets were sunken depressions, mercifully shrouded with eyelids that sheltered no eyes.

"Ye . . . yess," Mikki faltered. "But how did you—?"

"No magic. Heard your breath speed up. Many stand where you are there and do the same. Peniel's my name. I'm here most every day."

Peniel was a thin teenage youth. He couldn't be much older than Mikki.

"It's beautiful," Mikki agreed.

Peniel nodded vigorously. "Tell me something about it. I always ask. Sometimes people have time to talk. I love a good story."

Mikki concentrated. "The smoke of the sacrifices is billowing up, thick and dark as night."

"Night. I know how thick night feels. Go on."

"It's climbing straight into the sky, like a giant pillar holding up the heavens. On either side I can see the pillars of the sanctuary itself, brilliant white, capped with shining gold and bright in the sun. The priests—" Mikki was suddenly embarrassed. "That's . . . that's all, I guess."

"Night and pillar holding the sky and shining sun. Thank you . . . you?"

"Sorry, sorry. I'm Mikki, Shoemaker's Son."

Peniel's head bobbed agreeably. "Can I repay your kindness? Do you know why the Levites sing that psalm on this day each week?"

Mikki racked his brain but could not answer. "Tell me."

"Because today is the fifth day of the week. It was on the fifth day of creation the Almighty created the fish and the birds and the creatures of the deep. The fifth was the first day anything had life and breath to praise the Lord! And since that day to this, all that has life and breath is ordained to praise the Lord."

"That's wonderful! My rabbi never told me that."

"I heard it from Reb Gamaliel."

"You're his student? The great Gamaliel?"

Peniel laughed. "Nothing so grand as that. I hear lots of things here at Nicanor. Funny. People must think a blind beggar can't hear, either."

Mikki's toe bumping against the basket of shoes reminded him he was late. He'd be in trouble with Linus if he didn't hurry. "I've got to go. Shalom, Peniel."

"Shalom, Mikki, Shoemaker's Son. Come again. I'm almost always here."

As Mikki turned to leave, he put his hand to where a fold of his tunic made a pocket beneath his belt. From it he withdrew a small silver coin given him by his mother to purchase his midday meal.

He dropped it into the begging bowl, and it rang as true as the note of a silver trumpet. "These alms are offered for the healing of my friend Eli. And for my father. Shalom," he repeated, darting away.

But there was no answer to his prayer.

CHAPTER 3

It was Elul. The month tradition said was the best month for a man to repent and for God to hear from heaven.

There was much to pray for, perhaps even much to repent of. Mikki had, in his thoughts, dishonored his father by believing he was a coward. Mikki prayed but did not feel or see evidence of divine pardon or benevolence. Worse than that, he still believed his father was a coward.

Business was bad. Father and Mother seldom spoke of anything other than Jerusalem's economic woes.

Eli's condition worsened day by day until he could not travel. At last his parents gave up plans to move to sunny Antioch. Eli's mother became grim and never smiled. The unthinkable rumor circulated among Eli's classmates that perhaps Mikki's best friend would not live to see his bar mitzvah. Most certainly he could not last through the winter.

As the High Holy Days neared, traffic dwindled on the Street of the Shoemakers. Pilgrims who had been regular yearly visitors to Jerusalem and the shop of the Shoemaker stayed home this year.

Eli's ability to breathe diminished as autumn chilled the air. The days for their bar mitzvah approached, yet Eli was unable to leave his house or attend classes with the other boys. His skin took on a transparent, ethereal glow. His mother called him her angel, which, Mikki knew, embarrassed Eli. And besides that, it was bad luck.

Mikki visited Eli each day and tried to keep his spirits up. He recounted tales of Zealot rebels holed up in the wilderness, but Eli had a faraway look in his eye.

"I will never forget the day that fellow overturned the money changers' tables, eh? Ah, Eli! If you had been there! A regular Judah Maccabee, this Nazarene seemed to me. The money changers ran from him, all right. They hate him plenty now. A troublemaker, my father says."

Eli drew a shallow breath and closed his eyes as if the effort was too much. His words came in a single exhaling of breath. "I would . . . have liked to see . . ."

The boy lapsed into silence as Mikki rambled on for long minutes about the gutless tradesmen of Jerusalem. Eli stared blankly at the ceiling.

"Come on." Mikki tried to cheer him up. "Are you thinking about living in Antioch?"

"Not thinking . . . of living anywhere." Eli punctuated nearly every word with a breath. "They . . . say . . . the sea . . . no smoke." He glanced out the window to the thick pall that hung over the city. "See the stars . . . at the shore."

"The desert has as many stars above it. After bar mitzah we could run away from here and . . . and join a rebel band." He lowered his voice, lest Eli's mother hear. "You and me . . . Zealots, eh?"

Eli smiled sadly and turned his face to the wall. "I . . . pray . . . I live . . . to see . . . the day . . . you . . . and . . . I . . ."

"Soon. A few weeks only. Bar mitzvah is the beginning of everything. After that no one can tell you what to do. Not to stay in bed. Or move to Antioch." Mikki's bluster faded as he noticed Eli was breathing easier. *Asleep?*

Eli's mother padded lightly outside the room. She poked her head into the chamber and with a finger to her lips let Mikki know it was time to leave.

The heaviness of despair settled in Mikki's bones as he hurried away from Eli's house. Sure, they had learned the prayers of praise and healing and thanksgiving together. Every time Mikki practiced the blessings for bar mitzvah, he had prayed, really prayed.

Where was the God who answered? Why was Eli sick? Why were shops of the tradesmen's lanes being shuttered and abandoned as business dried up?

Don't you care? We are drowning in Yerushalayim. Drowning in the sea of hopelessness.

Mikki raised his eyes, imagining Messiah, Son of David, breaking through the clouds to vanquish their oppressors and heal their land.

"*Oh, that You would rend the heavens and come down*," he whispered.[14]

But the clouds did not part.

A cadre of drunken, off-duty legionaries staggered past.

Orange and yellow gleams danced amid the Sukkot booths on all the rooftops of Jerusalem. Interwoven palm fronds and braided branches shattered escaping beams into a thousand pinpricks. Mikki saw spectral forms flitting about, like moths drawn to flames, as Jews gathered for the Feast of Tabernacles.

A just-past-full moon peeked over the mountains of Moab. Sunset had been an hour before—an ocher dusk that faded to pearlescent streaks.

Below the rising orb of the *Ruach HaKodesh* lay the pilgrim encampment on the Mount of Olives. This year only a handful of shelters tossed the moon's gleams back skyward. In the six months since the turmoil on the Temple Mount, tensions had gone from bad to desperate, and then grew still worse. Travelers, afraid both of bandits pretending to be patriots and of Romans eager to crush rebellious looks, stayed away from the Holy City. Mikki overheard his father say it was the worst year for business he could ever remember.

Mikki cared less and less about shoe sales. His concern was all for Eli.

The booth on the roof of Mikki's home was oversize, made to accommodate friends and relatives and pilgrims who came to visit. Constructed as much of hope as palm branches, tonight the tabernacle welcomed only Mikki's family and Eli's. Callisto and Eli's mother were in one corner of the booth. Shoulders touching, foreheads touching, like columns in need of mutual support, the two women whispered together.

Callisto asked, "Have you heard of the healer? The Nazarene? They say miracles are all through the Galil."

Chin tucked against her shoulder, Eli's mother offered a reply meant for Callisto's ear alone: "Too far! He's too sick to go. Coming here tonight is as far as he's been in weeks. I didn't want to bring him, but he insisted. Said it might be . . ." Her voice caught.

Mikki didn't want to hear more. For those same weeks he had gone to visit his friend every day, willing him to get well. Tonight was supposed to be a celebration.

Across the Sukkah from Mikki, Eli was propped against the wall. Though the night was mild, he was wrapped in a heavy blanket.

The light from the oil lamp darted about. In the interplay of shadows, all humans were dim reflections, as if seen through gauze or smoke.

But Mikki's view of Eli was like looking at a guttering candle. He was so pale that he, alone, seemed bright—another candle glowing in the darkness. His friend's features were sunken within the cowl of the blanket; his eyes were sunken pools in his waxen face.

He won't see another holiday, Mikki grieved. *Not another Tabernacles. He may not make it to Hanukkah.*

Eli's father and Tycho spoke politics. "The Baptizer's been arrested. Held in Machaerus, they say," Tycho reported.

"He'll rot there, then. No escaping that dungeon in the desert. Antipas will see to that."

"Aye. And the Nazarene's smart to keep clear of Antipas and the Romans both."

"The Nazarene's afraid," Eli's father pronounced.

On Tabernacles it was the custom to invite the patriarchs and heroes of ancient Israel to join the celebrations. Abraham, Isaac, Jacob, Joseph, Mosheh, Aaron, David—all the exalted wanderers, each of whom had spent time running from enemies or living as nomads—were bid to share the feast.

Mikki saw Eli summon his strength. "*Ulu* . . . ," he breathed. His gasp would not have extinguished a burning straw.

". . . *Ush-pi-zin*," Mikki continued forcefully, speaking on his friend's behalf. If Eli wanted to welcome imaginary guests to this, his Feast of Tabernacles, Mikki would make it so. "*Ulu Ush-pi-zin. I-la-in ka-di-shin.* Enter, exalted, sacred guests."

Someone pounded on the wall beside the outside stair leading from ground floor to roof, then called, "Shalom, the rooftop."

The voice was rasping, unfamiliar to Mikki. The four adults in the booth exchanged glances: father to father and husband to wife. No one recognized the voice, it seemed.

"Come up, and welcome," Tycho stammered.

The figure who appeared in the entry to the booth was lean and his features weathered. From the battered straw hat to the well-worn sandals and the plain, dust-colored robe, he looked exactly like Mikki conceived the patriarchs should look.

The guest arrived burdened. One under each arm, he carried sacking-swaddled parcels the size and shape of bread loaves. From each bundle a brown stick the length of Mikki's forearm protruded.

"Who are you?" Mikki challenged.

"Let . . . me guess," Eli offered. "Avraham?"

"Not David. Too old." Mikki added, "No offense."

When had Mikki's parents arranged this surprise? Hiring an actor to portray one of the Ushpizin was a wonderful treat. Tycho and Callisto were wonderful actors too, portraying surprise and astonishment.

"Wait!" Eli ordered. "*Tevu, Ush-pi-zin.* Be seated, faithful guest."

When the man was seated, Callisto poured him a cup of wine and passed him the platter of bread.

"What are those?" Mikki asked, pointing at the packages now lying beside the stranger. "Are they a clue?"

Leathery face split into a gap-toothed smile. The guest responded, "Let's change tradition tonight. I will ask you questions. What do you say?"

Taking consternation for consent, the old man said, "Each of you must think the responses. So. We begin: What is most important to you? On this holiday, when we remember the gift of manna that satisfied hunger in the wilderness, for what do you long? What will satisfy you?"

Mikki needed no pondering. He would be satisfied if Eli was well again. In the last six months, while Mikki had grown taller, broader, and stronger, Eli had shrunk. Instead of appearing the same age, now Eli seemed to have lost years in size and strength.

"What questions do you wish the Almighty to answer for you?"

Mikki knew his father was thinking of shrinking business and struggling finances. It was a fair question. Since Tycho was an honest man amid many who used dishonest measure, why should he be suffering now? Where was the relief promised to the righteous?

But Mikki's own thoughts were again all for his friend. Peering up through a gap in the leafy roof, he saw the wandering star called Tzadik, The Righteous King, leading the Moon. Beside the Moon floated the jeweled Pleiades, *Ki-Mah*, "Who made?"

The old man said, "Your forefathers lived like this, with nothing, not even permanent dwellings, yet the Almighty led them into blessing." Now the Ushpizin turned toward Tycho. "If you had nothing but this booth and your wife and two sons beneath the stars—" the wanderer waved toward Tzadik, shining overhead— "could you still praise the Lord?"

Mikki saw the struggle of Tycho's thoughts warring on his face.

"This year I would entreat the Almighty to send us work." He stared at his open hands. "I don't know. I've worked so hard. It's all for my family . . . my boys . . . ," Tycho replied.

The Ushpizin did not scold, did not correct, did not offer a solution. Instead he retrieved the parcels and handed one to each boy. "Grapevines," he explained. "Plant them in clay pots. Keep them sheltered from the cold. Next spring, when the last frost is past, bring them here to the rooftop. Give them cords to follow and they will embrace your homes with their tendrils. In three summers you will pick the fruit from your own vines."

Mikki shivered. Was it a promise? a prophecy? Would Eli live for three years to pluck the grapes?

"When Messiah comes," the Exalted Wanderer added. Then he quoted: "'*In that day,' declare the Lord the Hosts, 'every one of you will invite his neighbor to come under his vine and under his fig tree.*'"[15]

Without comment or explanation the old man grasped the bread and broke it. When he bowed his head, Mikki saw everyone follow suit. *"Blessed are You, O Lord God, King of the Universe, who gives us bread from the earth to eat. 'For He satisfies the longing soul, and the hungry soul He fills with good things.'"*[16]

There was a long pause before Mikki's father finally ventured: "Amen."

When they looked up, the Ushpizin was gone.

The bedchamber Mikki shared with his brother was at the front of the house, overlooking the street. His parents slept at the back, above the workshop. He heard his father's snores even now, a sort of gargling noise. The wind moaned around the eaves in a ghostly counterpoint. It was very late, beyond the middle of the night watch.

Unable to sleep, Mikki sat up. It was not the breeze keeping him awake. Nor was it his father's snoring. It was the absence of his brother. Linus had gone out after supper and had still not returned. At the moment Father stretched and Mother yawned and both headed upstairs, Linus had announced his intention to visit friends.

He was a man grown, after all. Tycho had warned him about the curfew and wished him good night.

That had been hours and hours ago. Had he been beaten and robbed? Had he been taken up by the watchmen for violating the Roman restrictions?

Mikki shivered and wrapped a cloak around his shoulders. The floor creaked when he stood, making him shudder. A square opening covered with an oiled leather curtain served him as a window. Mikki approached it and peered out.

He was looking east, toward Mount Zion. A waning half-moon floated above the Temple. One face of the sanctuary glowed with the moonlight. The shining white expanse seemed to pulse with Mikki's every breath, like the view of a sleeping giant.

The moon's glare washed out the other heavenly lights, except for a nearby wandering star. Mikki did not know its name, but it was pale yellow compared to the pewter shade of the moon.

Where could Linus be?

The city, though seemingly quiet on the surface, roiled with unease and the stories of plots real and imagined. Dagger-men, Zealot assassins, were abroad at night, kidnapping or killing collaborators.

The Roman authorities responded by setting up a system to reward Jews who informed on their neighbors. Many an old score having nothing to do with politics was settled by a timely accusation.

Syrian legionaries in disguise went abroad in the souks. These armed thugs had the authority to arrest troublemakers and any who spoke treason. Often their methods of arrest resulted in no need for a trial.

Where was Linus?

Away at the end of the street, where blackness shrouded the valley between Mikki's home and the Temple, a new orange star winked into existence. Its light wavered and flickered: a torch.

Four shadowy figures swam into Mikki's view like fish barely glimpsed beneath the surface of a murky pond. Two shared the firebrand: link boys.

Orphans, younger than Mikki, the Jerusalem Sparrows earned a penny for each pedestrian they escorted across Jerusalem's lightless lanes. They lived on the fringe of society, housed in an abandoned quarry and supported by Temple charity.

The other two forms were bigger. A pair of men walked with their heads almost touching. They spoke in low tones, but not low enough to prevent Mikki from recognizing his brother's voice.

Mikki's heart pounded in his chest. He stepped to the side of the window opening lest the torchlight somehow reach up and drag his presence into view.

The other man wore a hood over his head. Mikki saw nothing of his features, did not recognize his voice. All he heard was a last comment given to Linus as a command: "Say nothing of this to anyone. Not until all is settled."

Now Mikki's heart was in his throat and blood roared in his ears. Was Linus a Zealot? Had he been at a secret meeting of assassins?

The unknown man departed with the two link boys.

The latch clicked open and shut. A table's legs squealed briefly as Linus bumped into it in the dark.

Mikki dropped the curtain closed and jumped back into bed.

The stair treads groaned. Linus was moving as quietly as possible, intent on waking no one. He lit no lamp. By the moonlight coming through the oilcloth Mikki saw his brother feel his way into the room.

At the opposite end of the hallway Tycho snored loudly and snorted into his beard. Linus froze. A moment passed; then Tycho sighed and was still.

Linus tiptoed forward, spinning about when Mikki softly called his name.

"Shhh!" Linus said urgently.

"Who was that man? Are you a Zealot?"

Now Linus sounded angry even in a whisper. "You sneak! Don't say anything about this, you understand? Don't tell Father. Not a word. Agreed?"

Mikki nodded his agreement but did not close his eyes even after Linus was fast asleep.

His brother, a rebel!

Chapter 4

The two-day-old moon was a handbreadth high in the west when his mother called Mikki to supper. Bracketing it were a pair of wandering stars. The lower light Mikki recognized as *Nogah*, Splendor, the one the Romans called Venus. Opposite the other horn of the spiked crescent was another, but Mikki did not know its name.

Since Linus' clandestine late-night rendezvous, Mikki had prayed as never before. He was terrified his brother would be arrested and crucified, or more likely, clubbed to death and dumped in an alley. Every time Linus went off alone or returned after dark, Mikki fretted.

What if Linus carried out some mission of rebellion, then had to disappear? What if Mikki never got to say good-bye?

Almost as bad as the anxiety was the fact that Mikki had no one with whom to share it. Because Linus swore him to silence, Mikki could not even tell Eli. Eli was powerful in prayer; he would know how best to handle this situation.

But Mikki could not ask. Grieving thoughts occupied his days; horrific dreams tormented his nights.

Mikki's grapevine was planted in a tall, clay amphora in the shop corner nearest the street. He carefully watered it every other day at dinnertime. The stalk already showed signs of budding.

Every time Mikki visited Eli they talked about how soon the leaves would show. Eli was eager for warm weather to come again, to make the roof vineyard a reality. However tired Eli was from struggling to breathe, he always brightened when they spoke of eating grapes from their own vines. However inconsequential the vision of the vine, Eli once again had hope—a reason to see himself as part of next spring, next summer, three years from now.

Mikki was grateful to the Ushpizin . . . whoever he was. What an odd interlude that Feast of Tabernacles had been.

Family meals were torturous affairs whenever the talk turned to politics. Plenty of politics to discuss, too. Mikki waited for his brother to reveal his secret, silently urged him to, but Linus remained mute, shooting stern warning glances at Mikki every time.

Tonight's conversation had nothing to do with politics. After many false starts, Tycho announced he was closing the Temple Mount stall. "They raised the rent again. We're not selling enough. I'm sorry, Linus. You'll have to come back and work here."

Mikki set aside his spoon and stared at his bowl. Linus did not act morose; neither did he speak.

Silence reigned around the table. The change had been whispered long before, but Tycho had held on as long as he could. Having a stall where famous rabbis and holy men walked, selling sandals to chief priests and elders, was a source of enormous pride for Mikki's father. This was a painful loss. It seemed very clear there would be no answer to Tycho's Sukkot petition.

Someone pounded at the shop door, interrupting their communal gloom. This was not the knock of a late-arriving customer. There was something official, terrifying, in the force of the blows.

Mikki's eyes widened, expecting his brother to dash upstairs or out the rear exit, or grab a concealed sword. He nudged his brother and hissed, "Linus! Go!"

Instead Linus sucked up another spoonful of stew. A curious smile played across his lips.

"Shop's closed. Who could that be?" Tycho muttered, rising.

"I'll go," Linus offered.

"No! Don't!" Mikki countered.

Linus grinned with amusement and left the room.

Mikki gripped the table with both hands and waited.

His mother blinked at him in concern. "Mikki, you're white as a priest's new tunic. Whatever is—?"

Mikki's mouth opened, but there was no time to answer. His worst fears were confirmed as Linus returned with the visitor. Behind him strode the uniformed figure of a Roman army officer.

Mikki remained rooted in place, unable to move or speak.

"Father," Linus said, "this is Quartermaster Paulinus. He wants our shop to furnish two hundred pair of caligae boots for the Yerushalayim garrison. I made the bid long ago but just yesterday heard it had been accepted."

Tycho stabbed his awl savagely into the upper he was working, nearly knocking over the stitching pony. When he steadied it he pricked himself in the hand, drawing forth both blood and a curse.

Mikki kept his head down and his mouth closed. He was cutting out a heap of medium-sized boot soles, and he had a quota to fill before supper. Tycho made it clear failure meant working through supper instead of eating.

It had been like this around the shop ever since Tycho agreed to fill the Roman contract. Callisto and Mikki hated the idea; Linus enthusiastically supported it. Tycho wavered between the two extremes, but finally commercial success triumphed over scruples.

Now there was no time for anything but cutting hides, setting rivets, and lining soles with hobnails. Mikki saw Eli only on Sabbath days. He barely remembered to water the grapevine. Even his bar mitzvah studies had been put on hold.

If the venture proved satisfactory, who knew what additional government contracts would come their way, Tycho bragged. The House of Tycho and Sons would have to expand; add another location; hire more employees; could perhaps get some of the trade of the fancy, rich Roman ladies who previously did all their shopping in Caesarea.

Mikki was happy his father's financial woes had disappeared, but where had his father gone in the process? Tycho was harried and grumpy, despite the new contract.

Their rabbi from the synagogue in the Street of the Leather Workers warned Tycho he would alienate many of his friends and neighbors. It was one thing to sell a single pair of sandals to a Roman, but quite another to become an official supplier to the Roman legion occupying the Holy City. It was aiding the enemy. Who knew when troopers wearing those same hobnailed boots would use them to trample Jewish children? The next time Tycho saw legionaries leading a Jewish captive in chains, how could he face the man's family? What if the footprints leading to a crucifixion bore the nail pattern of Tycho's shop?

Mikki agreed completely. He was angry at his brother and distressed that Linus had got them into this mess, but he reserved most of his disappointment for his father. Linus wanted to prove himself, but his father should know better.

Tycho, red with embarrassment, and perhaps guilt-ridden, ordered the rabbi out of his shop, telling him to mind his own business.

When the other officers in the Leather Workers' Guild offered the same counsel, Tycho accused them of being hypocrites. "If this chance had come to any of you instead, none of you would have refused it either. Don't tell me you would!"

"Mark my words," retorted an angry former friend. "The Almighty will not let you profit from this . . . this treason. You'll be sorry you ever laced one strap of a legionary's sandal!"

"Get out!" Tycho bellowed. And when he noticed Mikki looking on, wide-eyed, he shouted, "Get back to work! What are you gawkng at?"

CHAPTER 5

The shop was a flurry of activity. Tycho, Linus, and Mikki worked from daylight until dark. Callisto tended any customers; there weren't many. After a round of visits from curious neighbors, most of them stopped coming.

Mikki hoped there would still be time for him to resume his bar mitzvah practice before his birthday arrived. On a Sabbath visit, Eli, in a strained but adamant voice, said to his friend, "Study! Stay up late! Go to the bema together. Us. Read . . . same day. That's the plan, remember?"

Mikki was so pleased Eli spoke about the future he didn't disagree. "Right. Just so you get the passage with the hard words. You're the scholar."

Inside, Mikki never believed he'd be ready. He fell into bed exhausted every night. He had neither time nor energy for study. He would never become a son of the commandments at this rate.

Mikki frowned at the thought. No bar mitzvah, but his father already treated him like an adult apprentice. This change was not turning out like Mikki expected.

This morning his father set him to stitching the hobnailed soles to the uppers. Mikki had never done it before. The amount of pressure required to jam the thick needle through two layers of dense leather was immense. Mikki stood over the stitching pony and leaned into each drive of the lance, as if spearing a wild animal. The resulting stitches had to be both tight and neat. His father was adamant the quality must not suffer.

His left hand underneath the boot, Mikki had to steady it to keep the force of his jab from flinging everything onto the floor.

Tycho approached to inspect the results. He picked up three complete pair from the basket and studied them critically. "Good," he said tersely. "But too slow, Mikki. Work faster. What's that?"

A folded cloth lay beside Mikki's work. It was stained with blood.

Tycho swiped his hand across the surface of the work counter beneath the boot. The wood was dark from years of oiled leather, but his palm came away glistening and wet. When Tycho raised it to the light it was bright red.

"What's this? Have you cut yourself?"

Mikki shrugged but allowed his father to grasp his left hand. The tip of every finger oozed blood. Each was swollen and pricked in many places.

"We have thimbles," Tycho said, uncertainty evident in his tone. "Doesn't that hurt?"

"I'm too clumsy with the thimbles, Father. Besides, it doesn't hurt. I'm keeping it cleaned up, really."

Wincing visibly as though he were the wounded one, Tycho squeezed the pads of each fingertip in turn. "Don't you feel that?" he demanded.

"I feel you mashing, but it doesn't hurt."

Tycho pressed the cloth into Mikki's hand and folded his fingers around it. "Stay there! Don't work anymore." He called out, "Callisto. Callisto! Come here and look at this."

On the shop door hung the sign *Closed until further notice.*

Inside the shop a row of sentinels lined one wall: Rabbi and priest were in the center, heads together, whispering. Mikki's mother and father clung to each other at one end. Linus, looking grim and surprisingly young, glowered from the opposite corner, nearest the potted grapevine.

Across from this rank of somber-faced witnesses was Mikki. He sat forlornly at the workbench, feeling like a condemned man must feel when his judges have just pronounced sentence.

Mikki overheard his rabbi pleading his case. "He's just a child—not even bar mitzvah yet. There must be some allowance, some room for doubt."

The priest, a long-faced, black-robed man, stroked his iron-gray beard. He shook his head and pursed his lips before replying, "No, the diagnosis is clear. It's *tsara*, plan and simple."

"The separating sickness," the rabbi murmured.

"What's that mean?" Linus demanded savagely. "He's only twelve."

"It means," replied the priest, "that after the period of observation he has to leave the city."

"And go where?" Linus persisted.

The priest sniffed. "Not for me to say. Perhaps one of the settlements. The Valley of Mak'ob, perhaps."

"After observation?" Mikki's mother said hopefully.

The priest narrowed his eyes. "May as well make ready now," he said firmly. "I've seen many of these cases. There's really no doubt."

Once Mikki had seen a drover kill a sick donkey with the same lack of emotion. "Never saw one this bad live," the drover said. "May as well get it over with."

Mikki shuddered at the memory. His hands, one with fingers bandaged till they resembled plump sausages, were tucked in his armpits, as if Mikki were trying to hide them.

If only he'd never shown his father the wounds! If only he'd used the thimbles. If only he'd been more careful with the needle. Mikki couldn't breathe. It had nothing to do with his hands. He felt like he was drowning. *Leave home? Go somewhere unknown? Live with strangers? Never come back?*

Mikki knew what *tsara* was. He'd seen lepers begging outside city gates. He'd heard the horror stories of how they lived around graveyards and in tombs while their flesh rotted. They were the living dead—always treated as unclean, the same as a dead body.

When Mikki was seven and Linus fourteen, there was a noseless leper who used his deformity to gain sympathy and alms. Linus had noticed Mikki's fear and teased him by popping out of dark corners while pushing his nose up with his thumb.

Mikki caught Linus looking at him. His older brother winced and dropped his gaze. Perhaps they had shared the same vision.

Lepers were nameless beggars. Mikki had never known anyone who became a leper, never met anyone personally who contracted the disease. He could not think of himself as a leper. *Tsara* happened to others.

"We have a place of confinement in the Valley of Gehenna," the priest noted. "I'll take him there now."

"No!" Linus and Callisto cried out as one.

Tycho said forcefully, "Don't be so eager, Priest. We'll keep him in his room. I alone will have contact with him during the waiting period. You," he said forcefully, "will keep your hands off him."

The priest shrugged, and he and the rabbi turned to leave the shop.

Callisto moaned as she asked, "Why? Why our boy? Why?"

The query was addressed to Tycho and to God, but the priest chose to answer anyway. Hand on the latch, he turned and said, "Perhaps this household harbors secret sin. Perhaps it's rebellion or uncleanness making its consequences known. Stubborn pride or even blasphemy. Remember the punishment for worshipping other gods: visiting the iniquity of the fathers on the children to the third and fourth generations."[17]

Mikki saw the blood drain from his father's face. He watched Tycho clutch his chest, but he could not run to him. He was forbidden to come near.

The dawn of Mikki's departure from Jerusalem—from his family, from his life—came with a rush. Though Mikki begged time to slow down, the week of waiting flashed past. There had been little change in his condition, except now he had lost the feeling in his thumb as well.

His mother wept inconsolably. Tycho and Linus restrained her from crushing Mikki in her embrace. She refused to be parted from him, saying over and over, "I don't want to live."

Mikki had once heard a grieving widow, clinging to the coffins of her drowned husband and only child, say the same thing.

Callisto threatened to kill anyone who took Mikki. She brandished a pair of hide shears. In the end, when the priest came, she could barely move. She stood rooted in the doorway of the shop, wavering like a tree about to topple in a high wind.

The priest said, "So he's going to Mak'ob? Good." He added, magnanimously, "You may send him supplies. You may write to him. But it's better if you don't. The sooner he adjusts to his new life, completely accepts that he'll never be back, the easier it'll be for him."

Callisto lunged at the priest, but Tycho caught her and wrenched the shears from her hands. Mikki's mother sank to the floor.

Physically Mikki felt no different from a week before. He was not sick then, was not sick now, but his father seemed to have aged ten years between Sabbaths. His face was thin, his eyes hollow and red-rimmed. Tycho's shoulders were stooped and he shuffled when he walked. He gasped for breath before beginning a sentence, as if emerging from a deep pool of water.

"Father," Mikki called across the room as if over a broad chasm, "please take my grapevine to Eli's. I want him to have it to remember me by."

All were weeping now. The little procession assembled outside the front door.

"Pay attention," the priest ordered, holding one hand over his nose as if Mikki already had the stink of death. "You must keep ten paces behind me at all times. You will call out 'Unclean! Leper! Unclean!' every ten steps. Is that clear?"

Mute, Mikki nodded.

The priest scowled. "Do it now."

Mikki's voice quavered and broke. "Unclean," he piped. "Leper."

Knots of people in the street magically parted at the cry of "*Tsara!*" as if they were the Red Sea and the call "Unclean" the rod in Mosheh's hand.

It had been planned for their last good-bye to be at the shop entry. But there had been no time to say all that must be said, no ability to speak the words of love and remembrance.

So Tycho, supporting and dragging Callisto, and Linus staggered along the opposite side of the lane, dodging people and calling to Mikki: "I love you. Don't give up hope! We'll see you again."

"Unclean," Mikki said hesitantly.

"You'll be well! You'll see!"

"Lep—" Mikki's voice caught as if an unseen hand seized him by the throat.

"Louder!" the priest demanded.

"My boy! My baby!" Callisto sobbed.

"Un . . . clean."

"I can't! I can't do this!" Mikki heard his father assert. "I can't let him go alone. I'm going with him."

Mikki saw Linus struck with the same idea. "Father! I'll go! Let me go!"

Faint hope rose in Mikki's heart, tantalizing.

"No, no. You're young. Your whole life is ahead of you. This is my fault. I must go! You understand, don't you, Callisto? Linus, you run the shop. Take care of your mother, yes?"

"If you go into the Valley," the priest observed sternly, "you may never come out to live again, except as a leper, outcast from city and society, unclean as death. Do you understand?"

"Yes," Mikki heard his father shout.

His father ran to embrace him, snatched Mikki up in his arms. A deep breath, and then his father cried, "Unclean! Leper! Unclean!"

THE JOURNEY CONTINUES . . .

The Shoemaker's Son paused in his telling of the story. He gazed around the circle of comrades as the Shabbat fire faded.

He faltered. "I-I wish my father was here. He could tell you the rest. How the Shoemaker went with his son. Gave up everything. Left Yerushalayim behind and . . ."

One of the Cabbage Sisters asked gently, "My dear, dear boy. Is it true, then?"

The boy bit his lip. "My bar mitzvah was in Mak'ob. Rabbi Ahava helped me with my studies." He nodded at his three silent friends. "We are brothers here."

"And your father . . ."

"For a year or more, the sickness did not touch him. But now a spot. A small sign. He says he will walk with me anywhere, and if I am to be declared unclean, then so will he be." The boy's lower lip trembled. "I pray I am not too late. That we can bring Messiah back to Mak'ob. They say he heals everyone who asks . . . who believes. I only wish my father was here."

Behind them the brush rustled and parted. A figure swathed in black stepped into the firelight.

"Mikki." The newcomer released the veil that covered his face, revealing the Shoemaker.

The boy leapt to his feet and ran to his father. "Father! We are going home, Papa! Yerushalayim! Together! Going to find Messiah and then—you and me, Mother and Linus. Oh, Father!"

The Shoemaker's eyes scanned every face around the ring. "I'd like to come with you."

"So," Carpenter said, "we are truly a minyan now. Now we are ten."

The last rays of the setting sun ignited the highest pinnacles of the Temple, sparking them into golden candles that shimmered above the Mount. The lower courses of honey-colored stone still radiated subdued warmth, like an oven cooling in the evening air.

Between the iridescent gilding of the day and the banked fires of a watchful night lay the gleaming white of the marble-covered sanctuary. It appeared to Mikki that the dwelling of the Most High did not just reflect light; it radiated light from within.

When the Minyan of Mak'ob located Yeshua, would He also have that quality? Would Yeshua's divine light be so apparent that Mikki would know the truth instantly, even before his body was healed?

The young man hoped so. If he immediately sensed that quality in the man from Nazareth, then all the other stories would be confirmed, even before Mikki's body was healed.

It could not happen too soon, he thought wearily. The glorious illumination of Zion did not reach as far as Golgotha, the Place of the Skull, where the lepers took refuge. The gap between Paradise and Gehenna seemed no greater than that chasm between the Jerusalem of the living and the suburb of the dead.

Outside the city walls on the west of the Holy City was an extensive burial ground. Tombs cut from solid rock, some whitewashed and others neglected, dotted the misshapen dome of barren limestone.

During daylight hours it was a place of mourning and respectful observances. After dark it became the exclusive realm of unclean corpses of both sorts: interred and still breathing.

The minyan discussed how to enter the city. The consensus was that the twilight hour was best to make the attempt. After full dark, torches drew too much attention to travelers;

going without them suggested evil designs and brought the scrutiny of the guards.

"We'll go," Shoemaker insisted. "Mikki and I. We know the city. We won't get lost. We'll learn what we can and return as fast as we can."

There was no argument from the others. The confines of Jerusalem were the most dangerous place for a leper to be found. One or two might be ordered out at spear point—pelted with garbage, hounded through the streets—but ten traveling together was a loathsome threat.

They would all be stoned to death before ever pleading their mission.

His hands concealed within the oversize sleeves of his mantle, Mikki's disfigurement could not be detected. In the gathering gloom the mark of *tsara*'s kiss on his father's face would not be noticed either.

Such was the confident way Shoemaker expressed himself. But he and Mikki knew if they encountered a party of Herodian watchmen or Jerusalem Sparrows bearing torches, their secret might be uncovered at once.

"Stay downwind of whoever you pass" was Carpenter's parting advice.

Mikki and his father were fortunate all the way to the Street of the Shoemakers. No one gave them so much as a second glance as they passed through a city winding up its business day and preparing for its evening meal.

As Mikki passed the home of his friend Eli, he spared a glance for the rooftop. There, dimly seen by a pair of oil lamp flames, was a trellis of grapevines. A pair of wrist-thick stalks rose from twin clay pots just over the doorway of the house. From there they split into layers of creeping tendrils that reached across the facade in both directions. The lush growth suggested a dark green wall, half the height of a man. Though the two gnarled trunks continued their separate existences, their foliage was so enmeshed and entwined that the life of one could not be distinguished from the other.

"Mazel tov, Eli," Mikki breathed. "Thank you for still caring. I hope you're praying tonight!"

There was a light in the window when Mikki and his father reached the shoe shop. The pent-up excitement raging in Mikki with each step nearer home drove him to pound on the door. He gave no thought to whether a stranger—or, even more dangerous, a neighbor—might be within.

The door opened at once. Linus—older, heavier, care-worn—said, "Can I help—?" Then he recognized his father at Mikki's side. Hugging and dragging, he seized Shoemaker around the middle and hoisted him before any warning could be given.

"Don't!" Shoemaker cautioned. "You mustn't—"

Linus ignored the threat. "Father! It's so good, so good!"

Mikki saw his older brother's eyes widen with surprise. Linus' gaze took in Mikki's familiar face located above a much taller and more mature body. "Mikki!" Linus exclaimed. His hug expanded to an arm wrapped about a father and a brother.

Mikki shrugged off the embrace long enough to kick the door shut. "Blow out the light," he said urgently, as much concerned for his brother as for himself. "Move back."

Before he completed the sentence, the entry to the dining area opened and his mother emerged. Unlike Linus, Callisto recognized Mikki at once. She was a thinner, grayer version of herself, and she swayed at the sudden revelation.

Mikki ran to support her, and the four withdrew from any prying eyes that might wonder at the reunion.

"You must not cling to us," Shoemaker ordered, while unable himself to relinquish his grip on Callisto's hands. His voice was hoarse and fragmented. "We . . . we can't stay. We want . . . we need . . . but can you . . . do you? Mikki, help!"

Taking a deep breath, Mikki began: "We, father and I and eight others, have come from the Valley in search of Yeshua, the Healer from Nazareth. We think . . . we want to ask . . ."

Why had they made this perilous journey? What was it that drove them to leave the confines of Mak'ob? "We think he may be the Messiah and can heal us . . . us lepers. If we can only find him."

"But no!" Callisto moaned softly. "You're back, Tycho! You can't leave again!"

At last Shoemaker was strong enough to pick up the thread. "The others. They're waiting. We've got to find Yeshua. Take him back to the Valley. More than six hundred waiting. We're just the strongest . . . the others, so hurting. He's our only hope."

"Do you know where he is?" Mikki asked. "What have you heard?"

Linus and his mother exchanged a glance compounded of hope and grief. "The stories are true!" Linus asserted. "You remember the blind beggar at Nicanor Gate? The Nazarean healed him."

"Peniel?"

Callisto nodded eagerly. "And a cripple by the Pool of Bethesda," she added, her words spilling all over each other. "And—"

"And Eli!" Linus said triumphantly.

A mighty wind roared in Mikki's ears, and his mother's face swam in front of his eyes. *Eli, healed?*

Then the stories were true! The journey was not pointless! There was hope for the lepers of Mak'ob!

"But he's gone. Yeshua's gone . . . left Yerushalayim," Linus added. "Antipas and the priests—they hate him. Want to kill him. He left a long time ago."

"Where?" Shoemaker asked. Though the word was expressed as calmly as a pilgrim's when asking directions, Mikki heard the terribly desperate longing behind that one syllable.

"No one knows for certain." Linus clenched his fists in frustration. "He's in hiding, or always on the move."

"But where . . . give us a direction at least!"

"We heard Joppa. Some say he's gone to the seacoast. Perhaps you can find him there."

The minyan of the *chedel*, the living dead, sagged under the weight of the news brought by Shoemaker.

"A true healer was in Yerushalayim . . ."

". . . and we missed him?" the Cabbage Sisters chorused mournfully. "How much longer . . ."

". . . can we keep going?"

Like an ocean swell piling up on a distant shore, dejected grimacing circled the group until despair broke at last on the rocks of Mikki and the other Torah boys.

"We keep going until we find him," Mikki asserted.

"Easier for you to say than others," Crusher wheezed. "Strong limbs."

"We all have strong legs," one of the students asserted. "It's how we qualified, remember?"

It was true that the young scholars appeared healthier than the rest. As outward signs of their terrible affliction, one merely had thickened and shiny ears; another possessed a curiously flower-shaped nose; and the last had distended, coarse lips.

"Joppa is on the seashore?" Mikki regarded Fisherman. "I've never been to the sea."

"Nor have we," asserted the boy with the swollen mouth. He spoke sharply to overcome the mangling his lips applied to his words, but his eyes betrayed excitement, not anger. His inquiring gaze swept over his companions. They nodded encouragement. "I was just a baby. I don't remember anything of Outside."

The one who had the ears of a wrestler added, "We all grew up in the Valley. We've never been anywhere else. Why would we turn back now?"

Around the council backs straightened and chins lifted at the words.

"Then it's settled," Mikki pronounced, as if a formal decision had been reached. "Tomorrow we press on toward Joppa."

FISHERMAN

You shall take on the first day the fruit of splendid trees. . . . And you shall rejoice before the LORD your God seven days.

LEVITICUS 23:40

THE JOURNEY CONTINUES . . .

The breeze from the sea swept past an olive-tree-crowned knoll. The bracing updraft carried with it the tang of salt and the sweetness of citrus, even to mostly unresponsive nostrils.

"You must have . . ."

". . . loved it here," the Cabbage Sisters observed.

Fisherman ducked his cheeks into his broad palms and rested his forehead on what remained of his fingertips. When he parted his hands, he was surrounded by caring, sympathetic expressions, but he focused on none of them. He saw only his old home across the lane at the bottom of the hill.

Fisherman tried to review the scene with the detachment of a stranger . . . and failed miserably.

The stone wall at the back of the garden had been repaired. It was straight and level and sound, maintained by someone who loved it.

One of his sons? Fisherman wondered. Jason, his eldest? Or had the property been sold long since? Was he staring into the fulfillment of someone else's life, someone else's dreams?

A row of five citron trees punctuated the garden. Blossoming and bearing continuously, it was their misshapen fruit that perfumed the night air. Fisherman stretched out his right hand toward the orchard.

"My trees, my boys," he said. "So tall. All grown."

A figure rounded the corner of the house to drink in the evening sky. A tall, broad-shouldered man lifted his arms heavenward in a worshipful, respectful gesture of praise.

A sharp intake of Fisherman's breath. He held it, considering, wondering, fearing the answer. Was it one of his sons?

Was it anyone who knew his name or had ever known

his face while it was still whole? Fisherman touched the place where an ear had been.

Gently, Carpenter drew him by the elbow to a sheltered spot. "It's your turn," he urged. "Sabbath eve. Tell us your story."

CHAPTER 6

The fire basket hanging from the prow of the boat roared with renewed vigor as the wind backed into the northwest and increased in force. Judah the Fisherman lifted his head and sniffed. "Smelling rain. But not yet, leastwise."

"Swells are up," commented Lech. He sniffed loudly, imitating his boss. He jerked the hand missing the thumb toward where the new hire, Breen, hung over the side, puking yet again. "Want to haul in and run for shore?"

Judah shook his head. It had not been a profitable night. The sardines were skittish. Each time the net went in, the shoal moved off before the circle could be closed around them. Only a single basket of the silver-sided darting creatures awaited transport to the sale dock.

They had just now reached the midst of a large school of fish. Judah bellowed, "Breen! Stop feeding the fish and get back to work unkinking that line!"

The young man, pale even in the reflected firelight, nodded weakly and wiped his mouth on his sleeve.

A few moments later Judah ordered, "Now start rowing!"

Breen on the forward thwart and Judah on the rear grasped their oars, struggling to set the boat in motion as Lech paid out the net. The row of lead weights caused the bottom of the mesh to disappear into the depths. Cork floats kept the top of the purse seine bobbing on the waves.

"Pull hard! Pull to windward! We need to get upwind, then drift down around the fish!"

Judah glanced behind him. Breen had no breath for replying, but the skinny eighteen-year-old bent his back, giving his best effort. Rowing into the rising wind against the additional drag of the net was hard work even for Judah's brawny shoulders. He caught Lech's attention and jerked his chin at Breen's effort. The boy had no experience and little muscle, but Judah would see to the one. Hard work would take care of the other.

"That's it," Judah said with approval as the boat completed its upwind leg. "Now it'll come easier; runnin' downwind. A bit more oar to starboard. No! Your other starboard. That's it. Give the school plenty of space. Don't let 'em know they're caught just yet."

At the end of the circuit Lech, at the stern, peered northward. "See that, Judah?" he asked, indicating the stretch of black horizon. Less than an hour ago a full swathe of heavenly lights twinkled overhead. Now the lower half of the bowl of night was obscured. The star called the Tentpole of the Sky was already shrouded. The overcast raced to swallow up the outline of the Chained Woman, Andromeda.

The fire baskets of Judah's two other fishing boats winked orange and gold against the inky blackness as their crews also labored in the night. Without warning the more distant light disappeared.

Moments later, so did the second.

"Squall coming!" Judah warned, the shriek of a gust tearing the words from his mouth and flinging them toward Joppa. "Heave on that purse line. Heave! Once it's secure we can ride this out."

The purse line was a drawstring that closed the bottom of the net so the catch could not escape downward. Breen jumped forward to obey. He hauled with one hand, then held the gain with the other as he reached overhand for a new hold. Breen stowed the slack at his feet.

Another blast of wind accompanying a torrential downpour of rain tossed the stern of the boat upward. Breen shouted as he was flung across a thwart and into the bilge. The purse line flew out of his hands and began to unwind over the side. The cord sizzled against the rail from the combined drag of lead weights, fish, and surge.

The rain hissed as it sliced into the waves.

Breen sought to stop the cord's flight. As he leapt toward it, he planted his feet in the unspooling coil, which grasped his knees as suddenly as a snake.

Before Judah could complete his shouted warning, wave and wind and plunging cable sucked Breen over the side and into the depths.

Ripping his knife from the sheath at his belt, Judah bit down on the blade and threw himself headfirst into the sea after the boy.

Hand over hand Judah found the line and followed it, pressure building in his ears and lungs. There had been no time to shed his tunic. Now the clothing threatened to drag him to the bottom.

God of my fathers, Judah prayed, *help me now!*

Breen had to be close by. Once the bottom of the net had fully reopened, the force on the cord would relax. Surely the boy must be near.

Judah's hands found Breen's hair and seized it. He struggled to yank the young man upward but gained nothing. Judah dove deeper. Finding the rope around Breen's legs, he sliced it free. But still the boy did not rise.

The net! Breen's arm was caught in the fabric of the net.

Hacking downward, lungs on fire, movement hampered by tossing surge and sodden clothing, Judah begged, again, *Almighty, help me!* Judah thought of his own boys, safe at home, and wondered if he'd see them again.

The knife slipped out of Judah's grip and went spinning away.

Judah clawed at the mesh with his bare hands and finally Breen was free. One arm about the young man's neck, Judah kicked powerfully toward the surface. Air! He desperately needed air!

The boat had already drifted away. Did he have enough strength remaining to reach it?

When his head broke the surface, Judah was grateful to see Lech extending an oar to him. There was just enough light from the flickering fire basket to see. Lech pulled Judah, towing Breen, closer to the boat.

Judah was barely able to help heave Breen into the boat. When it was his turn to clamber aboard, he clung to the rail, resting, before rolling himself over it.

The squall passed as quickly as it arrived. Stars reappeared in its wake.

"Breen?" Judah inquired of Lech, who was pounding the boy's back.

A gush of seawater surged from Breen's mouth. He coughed and sputtered, waving his arms wildly about his head, then gasped, choked, and coughed again.

"Saved his life, you did," Lech said.

Judah nodded but said nothing. At last he dragged himself upright. "Let's get the net hauled aboard. Still an hour's row back to harbor."

A flaming beacon gleamed atop Andromeda's Rock, assisting mariners to enter Joppa Harbor. Judah was grateful for the comforting reminder. On a night like this it was easy to imagine the sea monster, Cetus, emerging from the depths to devour the princess chained there.

Tonight no hero on a winged steed had appeared to assist the rescue effort. Judah leaned on the oars for a moment and ran both hands through his graying hair. Breen, wrapped in a blanket, shivered where he lay propped in the bow, like a quivering, waxen figurehead.

It had been a near thing, this rescue. Judah had jumped in without thinking of his own safety, and it was a good thing too. In another moment Breen would have been impossible to locate until they hauled in his drowned body still knotted in the net.

Judah snorted. The sea was a challenging and dangerous adversary at all times. No mythical sea serpent was needed to make it more so.

He reviewed what the night had cost him. The catch of fish had escaped, the net would have to be mended, the purse line was so chopped up it would need to be replaced, and a whole night's fishing had been wasted, but praise the Eternal, a life had been spared.

Among the houses of the fisherfolk of Joppa town there were many empty places at tables where the sea had not been so forbearing. Judah was grateful to God he did not have to report such a fate to Breen's father and mother.

After the weary row back to Joppa Harbor, Judah wanted only to sleep. Instead he dispatched Lech to help Breen get home.

"I'm sorry . . . my fault . . . stupid," Breen kept repeating.

"Go home." Judah pushed the young man away good-naturedly. "To be a fisherman you learn many lessons. Look at Lech there." Judah gestured toward Lech, who waved his truncated hand aloft.

"Anchor line caught around it," Lech said proudly. "Popped that thumb off like spitting out a grape seed. See that? Popped it clean off."

Since Breen had already heard this tale, he only nodded wearily.

Judah resumed, "Just thank the Almighty that tonight's lesson didn't cost you your life and . . . don't ever step in a coil of rope again! Better to lose catch, net and all, than go overboard in the dark. Now get home! But out of your next pay packet, save enough to buy a thank-offering for HaShem your next trip to Yerushalayim."

"You mean I still have a job?"

"After I saved your life? You'll be years working that off."

Breen looked worried.

Judah offered his crooked smile to relieve the tension. "'Course you have a job. Be back here midday. Nets to mend. Now go!"

Judah himself did not go home. He waited on the docks for the other two boats to return. If they had made good catches, it would ease the pain of his losses.

One of the remaining fishing vessels appeared within the hour, but not bearing good news.

"First blast of the squall she heeled over, right flat to the mast," Zebulon, the skipper reported. "Had her belly full of fish, too. Lost about half 'fore she come back up. All that whipsawing sprung some of her timbers. Spent the next two hours bailing and trying to fish at the same time, but it was no good. Leaks kept getting ahead of us, so we come in."

Judah bit his lip, chewing his wiry beard in frustration. "Be back at noon. Get her caulked and dry, even if you miss tomorrow night's fishing. Get it done right."

Zebulon agreed and turned to leave, but Judah stopped him with a question about the remaining fishing boat: "Did you see Targ?"

"Not since the big blow," Zebulon reported, clearly concerned. "Saw his light go out just before . . . *whoosh*, it hit us. Been hoping he come in ahead of us."

Judah shook his head and sent Zebulon and the crew off while he sat down again on the end of the breakwater, watching all the other returning vessels.

Dawn broke as Judah pried open gummy, salt-crusted eyelids. He stared at one last black speck dancing on the water: Targ's boat, minus its mast, missing all but one oar, but with everyone safe and a half hold's weight of fish.

"Praise be to the Eternal!" Judah boomed aloud.

Now only one more treacherous circumstance still lay ahead.

The sun hung in the wind-scoured sky above the gnarled olive trees topping the knolls east of Joppa. Judah lifted the latch of his back door and pushed it open, wincing when it creaked. He stopped, listened, then shoved it another few inches and squeezed through.

Could he get out of his soggy clothing and into a dry tunic without having to explain? A bit of warm breakfast wouldn't be amiss either.

A little uninterrupted sleep was too much to hope for. Anyway, Judah was eager to hug his boys, even if they would not understand his need.

He made it as far as the pantry without being discovered. The storeroom floor was planted thick with cats. All broke into simultaneous purring. Shelves rattled and jars of dried beans buzzed in resonance.

Judah tried vainly to shush them but gave up when the orange tabby rubbed against his legs and the gray-striped twins both begged to be picked up. Judah bent to oblige, then looked up to see his wife framed in the portal. She eyed him suspiciously.

Self-consciously he put one hand over his bald spot, then unbent rapidly. "Good morning, Emma," he said as brightly as he could manage. "Sorry if I woke you. I thought if I came in—"

"You only come in the back way if you have something to hide." Emma's curly, sand-colored hair was pulled back from her face, emphasizing her prominent cheekbones. "What happened?"

Her intuition was as accurate as ever.

Judah abandoned stealth as a strategy. It had never been his style anyway. "Storm last night. Nearly lost Breen, but we fished him out, none the worse for it."

"When you say 'we fished him out,' you mean you had to jump in to save him?"

Could the village gossip mill have churned this far this fast? Judah imagined it could, indeed. Lech and Breen left the harbor hours ago. Lech was such a talker, he'd probably regaled Breen's mother with stories of how near her son had come to death.

By now the whole town knew.

"Yes," he concluded.

"And you could have been killed," Emma protested. "Then where would I be? And your four boys and this, from my lips to God's ears, this girl I'm carrying? Answer me that: where?"

Judah tried to step forward to embrace her, but she backed away. "You're soaked and you stink, and you could have been killed. You never think of me at all, do you?"

"Emma, what if it had been one of the boys? You'd want someone to—"

"Never! Our boys will never risk their lives out on the ocean in those foolish, dangerous, little boats. They will own a fishing business, not be smelly fishermen."

Judah rubbed his twice-broken nose. It was an old habit he used to keep himself from firing an angry retort.

And this was an old argument. Judah had tried many times to explain that before there was a successful fishing business, there had to be a smelly fisherman. No one, not even one of Judah's sons, could hope to run a fishing business without knowing the trade from the waterline both up and down.

Now was not the time to reengage in a never-ending, no-win struggle, but Emma wasn't ready to stop yet. "And why are you out on the water anyway? Don't you own the business? Don't you have three boats and all those men who work for you? Why can't you be home at night and go to an office like the Carpet Importer or the Dried Fruit Merchant?"

The wives of those two shopkeepers were two of Emma's best friends. They often came up when comparisons were required.

Judah was too tired and too trapped in the pantry. Raising his voice, he snapped, "How many times must I tell you? I am the trainer. No one else. I train all the men so they do it my way . . . so they're safe."

"Ha! Safe!" Emma retorted. "Like last night?"

"Yes!" Judah shot back. "We all came home alive; nobody got seriously hurt, praise the Eternal."

"And how much profit did you make last night?" Emma demanded.

So she had heard about the other boats too. Judah made a mental note that he might have to strangle Zebulon and Targ, as well as Lech.

"Did you forget that the workers are coming to measure for the new sideboard today? Mahogany inlaid with ivory, remember?"

The only reason Emma would bring up the new furniture is because she anticipated his response. There was no help for it.

"Emma, we can't afford it right now. Last night set us back at least a week in repairs and lost income."

"And you call yourself a good provider," Emma sneered. "You break more promises than you keep. You never think about me or the boys."

"Woman!" Judah bellowed. "Not now! Not this morning!"

"Papa's home!" shouted six-year-old Rin, leading the parade of his two-year-old and eight-year-old brothers. The oldest of the trio looked just like their mother. The rest, including twelve-year-old Jason, were dark and squarely built of frame and hands, like Judah. "Papa! Time for breakfast. Come on."

Jason hung back from the others, frowning. When Judah tried to put a hand on his arm, the boy flinched away and moved to put his mother between them.

When did she change? Judah pondered wearily, recalling the loving, laughing beauty of his bride.

Sweeping the toddler up in scarred and calloused hands, Judah flung Tor onto his shoulders. The child squealed with delight.

CHAPTER 7

It was a magnificent fall day. The Feast of Tabernacles was just a short time away. Judah and all the cats napped in the pleasant afternoon warmth.

The Fisherman was roused by the screech of an ungreased axel traveling the main road near his home. He squinted at the sun: still plenty of time before heading out for the night's fishing. The twin gray cats dozed in a pile. The black-and-white female sat atop the rock wall, her tail swishing.

With a practiced eye Judah tallied his children: all present or accounted for. The toddler was by Judah's side. Rin and Tamuz played a game with stones under the dilapidated grape arbor. A single scrawny grapevine languished on the trellis, its handful of red and orange leaves surrendering to the season. Jason was away at bar mitzvah lessons.

The complaining axel drew nearer, accompanied by the clopping of small hooves and the rolling grind of cart wheels. All noises stopped.

A shadow fell across Judah's head from behind the wall. "Ho, friend," called a gravelly voice with a pleasant ring.

Judah roused himself. "Shalom to you," he returned, rising above the shadow's reach.

The shade was the product of a broad-brimmed straw hat crowning the head of a peddler. The face of the man himself looked like the Judean desert: wind-dried, sun-baked, and deeply creviced.

"I see you have a garden."

Judah looked around with embarrassment. A handful of rows sported dead plants, onions gone to seed, and weeds. The only thing bearing fruit was a mass of untrimmed creeper devouring the sunny side of the fence. *Prophet's cucumber*, the spiky globes were called. They were not edible.

"No time," Judah said. "My wife . . . children . . . all boys."

"I was referring to your boys." The peddler smiled. "But I may have something that will interest you." He gestured toward the cart, then cupped his gnarled hand to summon Judah.

A diminutive red donkey stood, head bowed, in the harness. In the bed of the two-wheeled wagon was a mobile orchard. The peddler indicated a cluster of small trees, roots bound in sacking. Their leaves waved at Judah in the thin breeze and they sported pale green, egg-shaped fruit.

"Etrogs," the peddler said. "Citron, some call them. Bear fruit all year. This Tabernacles you'll have your own supply."

The bitter-tasting green etrog was the "choice fruit from the tree" that Mosaic law required as part of the celebration of the upcoming feast. Citrons and palm fronds, together with myrtle and poplar boughs, were to be waved before the Lord.[18]

"Good for seasickness and intestinal woes."

Judah spread his hands. "I have no skill for gardening. I'm a fisherman."

"Friend," said the tradesman, "plant them in a row along there. Water them three times between Sabbaths. They will do the rest. Can't you just see them? Shading that half of the yard on a sweltering summer day? And when the breeze picks its way through the leaves and blossoms, the aroma is heaven-sent."

Judah warmed up to the notion. "I thought citrons didn't grow tall."

The peddler's scrawny chest puffed out in pride. "Mine are the best. These will be tall as you in two seasons . . . three times your height in five. And the fruit is the purest—no black specks at all. Sound as your boys, there. How many children do you have?"

"Four and one coming." An idea struck Judah. "I could get one for each of us . . . a way to mark the years. One each for the boys and baby and Emma and me. Seven, eh?"

"No man should be without a tree of his own planting—to say to the earth that he was here. Trees for shade. Trees for your boys to climb. Trees for you to rest beneath to dandle your grandchildren on your knee."

Emma came from the house in time to hear Judah asking the price. "Don't even think about spending money on something as useless as citron trees," she warned. "Buy citrons once a year. Nasty, bitter things."

"Ah, but the leaves will perfume clothing chests," the peddler entreated, tugging at his braided, grizzled earlock. "Never have moths where citron leaves are found."

"Don't you dare waste money on trees for us," Emma repeated scornfully.

"Did I mention that citron juice is a sovereign remedy for poison?" the peddler added.

Judah made up his mind. "Woman," he said firmly, "I will have five of these trees. One for each boy and one for the new baby. We'll watch them grow together . . . the boys and the trees."

Judah enlisted the aid of all four of his sons in planting the trees. He did not fully share his thoughts just yet, merely said he needed their help.

Playing in the dirt, digging with spades and fingers, was fun. The quintet of citron saplings, braced against the wall of the house, awaited the completion of the task.

Judah delved deep into the rocky soil, cutting a trench twice as wide and three times as deep as the size of the root balls. He and Jason sweated over the task together, though the breeze off the Great Sea was cool.

The middle brothers hauled buckets of dirt aside, sorting out the larger rocks. Tor toddled around, wooden spoon in hand, generally pouring more earth back into the hole than he removed.

They all chuckled when he tumbled in. His lower lip protruded for an instant; then he too broke into gales of laughter.

Judah harvested loamy topsoil from the derelict garden to mix with the soil from the trench. Throughout the labor he kept up a running commentary on the uses of etrogs and memories of past Sukkot festivals.

"First noticed your mother on Tabernacles," Judah said, staring into a lone white cloud that hung above Joppa. "You know how neighbors go visiting? That's when it happened. Most beautiful girl I ever saw . . . still think so, too. Asked my father to make the match then and there."

The trees were carefully moved into a line beside the ditch. Judah, using the peddler's knowledge, prepared the bed for drainage, support, and nourishing soil.

The boys assisted in patting the dirt firmly in place around each sapling.

Not a single baby citron was lost. Judah explained that etrogs never fall from the tree. "Hang there growing and growing," he said. "Get so big they break the limbs if they don't get picked in time. Grow big as your head," he said, poking Rin's nose.

"Ah, Papa," Rin and Tamuz groaned.

"No," Judah insisted, holding up a dirty hand with a row of black fingernails. "Peddler swears it's true."

Buckets of water hauled painstakingly from the well completed the assignment. Jason toted his alone, Rin and Tamuz together.

Judah hefted a bucket and Tor at the same time, sloshing pail on one side and giggling baby on the other.

But they were not finished just yet.

"Now line up," Judah instructed. "Jason, you here, at the far right. Next Tamuz. Then you, Rin. That's it." Judah sat on the ground, holding Tor in front of him. The toddler yanked a citron leaf from the sapling and rubbed it on his nose. "Perfect. Just like reading your names."

"What is, Papa?"

"The trees. The one you're standing in front of right now is your tree. It'll be yours forever. Next year, five years, ten years, when each of you comes here with your own babies you'll say, 'I remember when my papa and me planted this . . . 'course he was a lot stronger then.'"

There was a chorus of "Really?" and "Mine, Papa?"

Judah nodded and pointed to the last tree on the left. "And that one'll be for your baby sister when she gets here."

Judah felt Emma's eyes boring into the back of his head. He had invited her to come to the "ceremony," but she had refused. "Dirt and smelly trees?" she griped. "Are you trying to make me sick? You know how dirt and smelly things make me sick."

Even now she came no farther than the doorway of the house. She leaned her back against the doorframe, the bulge of her pregnancy prominently displayed.

"Thank you, Papa," Tamuz said, hugging Judah around the neck. Not to be outdone, Rin hugged even harder from the other side. Two-year-old Tor stared and said, "My tree," as he patted a branch.

Judah wiped his cheek. "Got dirt in my eye," he said. Then, "Wash up good, boys. Hands, faces, and necks. And don't track anything into the house."

Emma was no longer watching.

Jason grabbed his father around the neck just as the younger boys had. "Thank you, Papa. Best Tabernacles ever."

One day Emma left to visit friends and coconspirators. The confabulation of females was a plot to ensnare the nineteen-year-old son of a wealthy olive grower in the bonds of matrimony. The wife of the Rug Merchant had a daughter of marriageable age.

If the daughter was anything like the mother, Judah thought, those bonds might be very weighty chains indeed. When Emma departed, he wisely said nothing of his thoughts and continued casting up his accounts.

Thanks to Judah's hard work and some cost-cutting measures, the fishing business had fully recovered from the night of the terrible squall. By driving his crews to be the first out of the harbor at night and the last to return near dawn, the holds were full almost every night.

The Almighty had also blessed him in the timing: The weeks since the storm had been the period of month from the waning moon to the early crescent of a young New Moon. Everyone who knew anything about fishing realized that fish feed best in the dark of the moon, so are easier to catch.

Not only had all three boats, now fully repaired, taken full hauls of sardines, on three occasions they had run across schools of the even more valuable mackerel. It was as if the squall had blown good fortune in the form of shoals of fish into Judah's grasp. The fact that he was working longer hours and away from home more was a temporary necessity.

When he did come home, Judah reflected with a grimace, Emma chastised him for being gone too much. He was also in trouble for being too tired to work on her projects around the house.

It was easier to just stay away.

There had been a time when Emma was proud of him—proud of his ambition and his drive. She had been happy to be a fisherman's wife and excited to help him succeed. Where had that partnership gone?

In any case, at this rate of business success Judah would soon have important decisions to make: Should he purchase another boat and expand his fleet, or should he use the savings to buy a share of the fish market?

At present Judah sold his catch to the fish merchants. They resold some as fresh, salted or smoked the rest to preserve it, and made five times the amount of money Judah made. One of them was getting on in years and might be agreeable to taking a partner if the terms were satisfactory.

Moreover, the one Judah had in mind had no children. With four boys to raise up, Judah had to give serious attention to their futures. It might be possible for two of the brothers to join him in the fishing business, but Judah doubted the wisdom of trying to make it support five families. Tamuz, the eight-year-old, already showed a gift for negotiating trades in which he came out ahead: "I'll give you this handful of raisins for just one of your figs, but you have to give me your toy soldier too." He might grow up to be the perfect fishmonger.

Judah had a head for business, but not the hardness of heart. If a cripple begged a copper, Judah would often provide a whole meal instead. Jason, the oldest boy, was just like him.

Judah was so proud of his sons.

The last income recorded and the last expense tallied, Judah shook the leather pouch of coins with satisfaction. Prying the loose board free of its spot next to the fireplace, Judah tucked his savings into its hiding place and sealed up the cover again.

Today was also the day for the washerwoman, Mara. Emma had let Judah know none of the women of quality in Joppa did their own laundry.

Jason sat at the dining table reading. A sudden thought struck Judah and he acted on it. "Jason," he said, "come with me to the chandlery, and then to the yard."

Jason looked excited for a moment; then his face fell. "Mama told me to watch the brothers while she's away. I can't go."

"It'll be all right," Judah assured him. "I'll get Mara to do it." For the extra pay Judah promised, the laundress was happy to babysit "until the Mistress of the House got home."

How grand the title sounded! Too grand for the wife of a fisherman?

"Do you like fishing?" Judah asked his son on the tramp down the hill to buy supplies.

"Yes," Jason replied with a question in his tone.

"But?"

The boy glanced at his father's face, then away with embarrassment. "The sea . . . scares me," he admitted.

Judah put his arm on Jason's shoulder. "A captain must never let his crew see him be afraid," he instructed, "but—" he leaned close to the boy's ear—"but only a fool is not afraid of the sea. You have to know its moods and understand its signs. You can work on it and make a living from it, but it's not to be trusted. Understand?"

Jason bobbed his head, then with a sideways glance inquired, "Are you afraid, Papa?"

There was a long pause while Judah looked into his soul for a truthful answer. "I respect it, and I never turn my back on it. Truth to tell, there's other things I fear more."

Alarmed, Jason asked, "What, Papa?"

"Like ever not having you boys. You are my life. Someday you'll have children, and you'll know what I mean."

CHAPTER 8

It was as Judah and Jason passed an alleyway just beyond the Spice Merchant's shop that they heard a cry for help. At the far end of the narrow passage a lone man was being set upon by two others, who had beaten him to the ground. One arm raised above his head, the figure on defense was trying to fend off the fists of one attacker while being kicked in the stomach by the other.

It was then Judah saw the victim had only one arm.

"Stay here!" Judah warned his son, pushing him into the spice shop. He barreled into the fray, bellowing at the top of his lungs. The force of his charge carried him into the tumult, knocking one attacker into the dirt.

The second assailant leapt back, seized a stick, and swung it at Judah's face.

He managed to duck, partially deflecting the strike with his back, but the glancing blow to the side of his head made him see stars. As the assailant raised his cudgel for another swipe, Judah drove his right fist into the man's throat, then followed through by landing his elbow on the aggressor's nose.

"Papa! Look out!" Judah heard Jason shout. Without even seeing the danger, Judah jerked his body sideways just as a knife thrust by the other foe missed his ribs by inches.

Now he was berserk with fury. Dodging another sweep of the blade, Judah jumped for the hand wielding the weapon and seized it with both fists. With a cry of rage he brought the attacker's arm down across his upraised knee, like snapping a twig. The knife flew off into a heap of rubble.

Satisfied with the scream of pain that resulted, Judah discarded the disabled attacker and turned to find the other already in flight, out the other end of the alley.

His damaged arm tucked close to his chest, the remaining enemy also stumbled away from the scene.

Judah started after him, but the victim gasped, "Don't try to . . . chase him. Not worth it. Another alley . . . more of them . . . jump you. That . . . happened to me."

Thinking of Jason, Judah stopped himself from pursuing. Extending his now-bloodied right hand to the one-armed man, Judah pulled him upright and asked, "What was that about?"

"Robbed me" was the reply after a pause for breath. "Caught the tall one . . . cutting my money pouch from my belt. Chased him. He popped in here and . . . the two of them started in on me." The victim's eyes were nearly swollen shut from the beating, and gore matted his hair and beard.

By now Jason was at his father's side, staring wide-eyed at the carnage of the man's face.

"How much did they take?" Judah asked.

"Everything," the man said ruefully.

"Can I help you to your home? Or to some friends?"

The man shook his head gently, as if something inside rattled. "Just arrived here from Caesarea. Shomer, I'm called. Shomer the Weaver."

"A one-armed weaver?" Jason blurted.

Shomer grinned with split lips and bloodstained teeth. "Means I'm really fast. Came here to get work." Then he grimaced. "Not sure what to do now, though."

Judah thoughtfully extended his hand toward Jason, who understood the gesture. The boy passed him the handful of coins brought along to purchase fishing supplies. Judah jingled them thoughtfully, then presented them to Shomer.

"I can't take this," Shomer protested. "You already saved me from a beating . . . or worse. Can't take your charity, too."

"Can you weave nets? Fishing nets?" Judah inquired.

"S'pose so. I can weave anything if I have a frame and a pattern to follow. Why?"

"Then it's not charity. Call it an advance on your pay. I'm hiring you to work on my nets for me. Now take this, get a room and a meal, and come to harbor tomorrow at midday. Ask for Judah the Fisherman. Anyone can tell you where to find me."

Nearly everyone in Judah's household sought safer locations at the first screech. Peering around corners and out of doorways, five cats and three small boys were onlookers only.

Center stage of the living room was occupied by Emma and Judah, with Jason standing aside, head down. Only moments before, Jason had proudly announced that his father was a hero.

"You could have gotten him killed!" Emma shouted, putting her arms protectively around the twelve-year-old. "Getting mixed up in a fight that was none of your business?"

"A stranger here. Unable to fight back," Judah said stoically. "Who else would help him?"

"So that makes it your business? Are you now looking for fights? Look at you! Bloody from head to toe!"

This was an exaggeration, but Judah merely said, "Most of it's not mine."

The contradiction drove Emma into a frenzy. "So what are you teaching your boys? How did you know who started it? See a fight, get in it? Is that the message?"

"Two against one. A man with only—"

Emma went roughshod over Judah's reasoning, making him muse that he was getting beaten up worse at home than in the alley. She turned sideways to display the bulge of her pregnant belly. "Are you trying to kill me? What do you think news like this does to me? What if you were lying in the alley back there? And what if Jason had been hurt? I'd never forgive you! Never!"

There was some comfort for Judah in that. If he had been killed, he might have been forgiven, so long as Jason was safe. Involuntarily Judah's crooked grin appeared at the corner of his mouth.

"Don't you mock me!" Emma wailed. "You see," she said to the boys, "see how he abuses me?"

"Emma," Judah tried. "I didn't mean to—"

Tears were flowing down her face now and she gulped back sobs. "And you . . . took Jason with you . . . to your brawling."

"Business, not brawling. He went with me to learn—"

"The man's going to work for Papa," Jason reported, trying to intervene. "Weaving nets."

Emma's next words were cold as ice. "You . . . hired this . . . this . . . stranger? Already gave him money, too, didn't you? Didn't you?"

Judah nodded.

"You really hate me, don't you?" Emma accused. "No money for even little things I want, but throw it away on someone you'll never see again."

Judah could not take any more. He snarled, "That's enough! I can use the man! Less time rigging means more time fishing . . . more precious money for you!"

The cats disappeared completely at Judah's bellow. Instantly he regretted allowing her to provoke him, but it was too late.

"Ooooh!" Emma wailed. "You . . . you're nothing but a bully! Defend a stranger, then come home and attack your pregnant wife! Is that what you want your boys to learn? Is it?"

Jason said, "Papa, don't yell at Mama."

Judah raised his fist toward the boy, and Emma stepped between them. "Go ahead! Hit me! Hit your pregnant wife!"

"I'm not . . . I won't . . ."

Judah exited then, shutting the door with a thunderous slam. His departure rattled all the dishes on the shelves and made all the boys cry.

The time came for Judah's fifth child to be delivered. He recognized the fact instantly when he arrived home from a night's fishing. There was a clutch of women in his front room, though the sun had not yet risen.

He also knew Emma was in labor by the low muttering pervading the group. Hostile looks came his direction every time a cry of distress emanated from behind the closed door of their bedroom.

"Emma . . . is she . . . ?"

"She's doing as well as can be expected, no thanks to you," the Carpet Seller's wife replied sharply. "Not even here when she went into labor. Had to send your boy to fetch the midwife."

"Jason? Where is he? Where are the boys?"

"At my house. Why don't you go join them? Men are so worthless, aren't they?"

The last observation was not addressed to Judah, but just that quickly he was dismissed. He was only the father, after all.

He did not leave. Instead, he paced up and down outside their cottage. With increasing frequency Emma made cries of pain and shouts of effort. For each of these exclamations she was rewarded with a wave of sympathetic murmurs from the onlookers.

Judah felt more miserable all the time.

At last there was a cry louder than all the others and the commentary changed to shouts of "Mazel tov" and "Well done, Emma."

A plump, round-faced midwife, not from their neighborhood, parted the cohort of women with authority and demanded they locate the father. Judah advanced, wondering how much abuse he was about to receive for his absence and the clearly difficult experience Emma had undergone.

"My wife . . . how is she?"

The midwife snorted. "Fine! Soaking up the sympathy if you ask me. My head hurts! So much unnecessary shouting and moaning. For a woman on her fifth delivery, I ask you, was that really needed?"

Judah realized this query called for no response from him. Instead he inquired, "And the baby?"

The midwife brightened. "A fine, healthy son. Mazel tov, Judah of Joppa."

"A . . . son? Not a daughter? Emma had her heart set on a girl."

The sounds of weeping came from within the bedchamber.

The midwife continued as if she had not heard this blasphemy. "A brace of sons, you have! Like the psalmist says: like arrows in the hand of a warrior, eh? Blessed is the man whose quiver is filled with them."[19]

Judah shook his shaggy locks. "Not a girl?" Then, confronting the disapproving frown on the midwife's face, he added, "Can I see her? Them, I mean?"

"Of course, if we can make a path through these harpies. Follow me. Make way there." At the door she turned and said, "All but one of you, go home. The new mother needs rest and quiet. Take turns helping, but no more than one at a time. Now go."

Judah rapped softly, called lovingly, and entered. "Emma? Love? Well done. You are the best wife and mother ever."

"Another boy. Five boys!" Emma groaned into her pillow. "Boys! Not even one little girl to dress and teach to cook and sew and shop." Her eyes went from tear-filled to hard as nails in an instant. "You!" she said sharply. "You better get that new room built that you've always talked about, unless you fancy sleeping in the pantry with the cats."

"Why? What?"

"You know what!" Emma said with finality. "This is now my room. There's the door. Close it quietly on the way out."

The third night after the baby was born was a Sabbath. The fishing crews did not go out on the day of rest. Judah was not asleep, though he was physically and mentally exhausted.

Boys were heaped together next to Judah's bed on the floor, like a pounce of kittens. Unwinding himself carefully from his blanket so as not to wake them, he removed Rin's arm from around Jason's neck.

Tor had migrated to the outside of the pack. Judah hefted the toddler, tucked him into the warm spot in the center, and carefully covered him. Tor never once abandoned his stinkbug position while this maneuver took place. He only smacked his lips and burrowed his nose into his hands.

Emma had not bolted her door tonight. Judah listened carefully when she retired, and he was certain it was not bolted.

Holding his breath and lifting the panel so the hinge would not squeak, Judah entered the room. As he approached the bed, his heart stuck in his throat, pounding. Her hair, spread across the pillow, gleamed silver in the moonlight. Her lips were parted. Wispy sighs escaped with each breath.

Her face was drawn up in an unhappy frown.

Judah wished her good dreams.

Then he moved to the far side of the bed and carefully removed the newborn from beneath the quilt. Enfolding the baby next to his chest, under his heavy cloak, Judah slipped from the chamber.

Once outside he spoke to the sleeping infant with the rosebud mouth. "I cannot call you by name yet, little one, because you've not yet had your *Bris*. But there's something I want you to see."

The trip into the garden was a matter of seconds. Overhead the full moon was the flagship of an armada of clouds attacking Joppa from the sea.

The citron trees were a row of dark, silent, fragrant sentinels. Judah counted each one by name, "Jason, Tamuz, Rin, Tor . . . ," and stopped beside the last.

"And this one," he whispered, turning the baby to face the sapling. It carried a single, fist-sized etrog and a forest of blooms. "This one is yours. Forever. Next year we'll come here on Tabernacles and I'll tell you all about it."

CHAPTER 9

Judah sat beside the new sideboard, pondering his crew assignments. Targ and one of his crewmen were both sick with some lung ailment and would not work tonight. Judah could beach Targ's boat and stay home himself, but the fishing continued to be superior. Who could say how much longer that would last?

Judah idly rubbed his bald spot and tugged reflectively at an earlobe. What was the best way to keep all the vessels at work?

Lech could captain one craft, with Breen and a day-hire for crew. Zebulon's crew stayed intact, the way he preferred it. If Judah took the last boat himself he'd have one experienced hand from Targ's crew and one day-hire.

It would work.

Judah felt satisfaction about all aspects of his business. Hiring Shomer had turned out to be an unqualified success. Not only were all the nets in top repair, they were stronger than ever. True to his claim, the one-armed weaver was so speedy that he produced more mesh than Judah could use—nets that could be sold to other captains for a handsome profit.

The Joppa fisherman smiled at his son Tor, who was playing at his feet. If only things at home were sailing so smoothly.

Despite what Judah's friends told him about the moods women go through after childbirth—especially the birth of a fifth male, it seemed—there had been no change in Emma's resolve. She and the newborn were bolted into the bedroom at night. Judah slept by the fire in the living room.

The younger boys thought it was fun to join Papa in sleeping on the floor.

Only Jason looked at him strangely.

Tor, the toddler, was playing with a broken netting shuttle Shomer had given him. The boy sailed the scrap of wood around the chair and table legs as if piloting a boat through treacherous surf.

When this amusement had gone on for an hour or so, the boy looked up abruptly and said, "Seepy, Papa." With no further preparation he laid his head down on his arms and was asleep.

Judah was overwhelmed with tenderness toward this child and all his children. He suddenly realized he had transferred all his love, all his affection, from Emma to his sons.

Moreover, he did not feel sorrow. He felt sorry for her, but not sorrow. Judah was immensely proud of having five sons.

Judah bent and pried the shuttle from Tor's grasp. If he woke from his nap with a crease on his cheek, Judah would somehow be responsible.

There was a scrap of line still attached to the device.

By dangling it a foot off the ground, Judah enticed the orange tabby to jump for it. The male cat was the most agreeable, friendliest soul imaginable. He never asserted himself and got along with all the others—except with one black-and-white female who delighted in tormenting him.

A familiar scene played out now.

As soon as the tabby grasped the toy, the female rushed in, growling, to demand he relinquish it. The orange male did so and the female seized it, only to drop it in a corner and saunter away as if no longer interested.

As soon as the tabby retrieved the toy, the female charged back at him, batting and slashing. The tabby retreated under the table in confusion.

"You should quit trying," Judah advised. "I don't think you can win."

On the third encounter the tabby tried to stand his ground. His tail fluffed out to three times normal size, and his back arched in time to a deep-throated growl of warning.

Resistance infuriated the female. She slashed at the tabby's face, then sunk her teeth into his forepaw. When the orange cat attempted to retreat, the female pounced. She scored the tabby's ear and chased him, with every appearance of being ready to kill.

This was not play.

The tabby sought refuge in the highest, most inaccessible spot he could reach quickly: Judah.

Swarming upward with all claws digging for height, the male climbed Judah's bare leg, then his back, then the side of his neck and ear, to arrive at the top of Judah's head.

With a roar of pain that woke Tor, Judah swept the cat aside.

The screeching of the cats, the wail of the startled toddler, and Judah's bellow brought Emma at a run.

"What have you done now?" she demanded, snatching up the toddler to cradle him.

Judah, bleeding from a dozen wounds, controlled his tone. "I haven't done anything. The cats! Tabby tried to climb me like a bit of drapery. Look at me!"

"Yes, you're bleeding all over the floor and your new tunic." Emma sniffed. "Go clean up. Especially your ear."

"Hurts like the devil," Judah muttered. "Bet I can count every claw mark by the pains. Two on my leg. Two on my back. Two on my neck . . ."

"And don't forget your ear," Emma added. "Big baby. You're dripping all over everything. Get out of here! Get cleaned up."

Outside, plunging his head into a bucket of water, Judah marveled at the amount of blood still gushing from his ear. "Leg and back and neck all hurt worse," he mumbled to himself. "In fact, ear doesn't hurt at all." He fingered the gaping gash in the lobe. "That's strange. Feels almost tore off."

Down at the dock that night Judah was the object of some good-natured ribbing by Lech and Zebulon. Both tried to imply an amorous cause for Judah's scratches.

"Cats," Lech muttered, snickering.

"She-cat, eh?"

Fingering the pad of blood-soaked gauze bound to the side of his head, Judah growled the comedians into silence. Every scrape hurt, especially when he bent or stretched. Judah tried not to think about how painful rowing was going to be with the lacerations on his back and thigh.

It was a good thing the ear wound didn't hurt. There was even a flap of loose skin where a claw had torn the lobe. The cuts on his neck burned like fire, and it felt like needles had been poked into his scalp, but the ear was mercifully subdued.

"Shalom, Judah," Shomer greeted his employer. Gesturing toward the bandage he queried, "Been rescuing more unfortunates? Might want to invest in armor."

Judah explained, with a rueful grin, how the damage had come about, then added, "Like being stuck all over with fishhooks. Almost tore my ear off, too, but praise the Eternal, it doesn't hurt anything like the rest."

"Oh?" Shomer said quizzically. Reaching up he stopped his one hand inches from Judah's ear. "Forgive me." With that smallest of warnings he flicked his middle finger against the wound.

Judah did not flinch. He only narrowed his eyes and awaited an explanation of this strange behavior.

Then Shomer slapped Judah on the back, directly over the double row of scrapes.

Judah jerked aside, batted Shomer's hand away sharply, and roared, "What're you playing at there?"

The weaver made calming motions with his hand. "Judah," he inquired, "was there ever a spot on that ear? A pale bit, or perhaps even yellow?"

Judah tried to recall. "Don't look at myself much. I suppose it was whitish, but my earlock covered it most always."

"Do you mind if I see?"

"It's nothing, I tell you! Every other scrape hurts worse, and I'm not such a baby as to complain about those."

"Judah." Shomer drew his employer away from the others, who had been watching this strange business play out. "Judah," he repeated softly, "have you ever wondered how I came to lose this arm?"

"No business of mine."

Shomer frowned. "It might be . . . more than you think. Just listen for a minute." The net mender pulled his benefactor still farther aside. He touched his empty arm socket. "I did not lose this arm in an accident, and I was not born this way. I had a good trade, good prospects . . . even a girl I thought loved me."

Judah tried to imagine where this conversation could possibly be leading. What did Shomer's arm have to do with a catfight?

"One day I was working at top speed, plying a threading hook. It was brand new, sharp as a razor. Anyway, I jammed it into my arm. Deep. Deep." Shomer shuddered at the memory. "But it didn't hurt. Not a bit."

Judah started to speak but Shomer raised his hand for continued silence. "I went to a doctor I knew—a Greek, luckily for me as it turned out. Judah, it was leprosy—*tsara*—the separating sickness."

Involuntarily Judah stepped back with a horrified expression. "And it cost you your arm?" he whispered hoarsely.

To his surprise Shomer shook his head. "Judah, I let the Greek cut it off. It was the only way! I don't want to be a beggar. I don't want to be forced to live in the Valley of Anguish. The Greek told me it would save me, and no one would know, and . . . here I am."

Refusal plastered on his face, Judah argued, "But that . . . that's not me! My ear, it's nothing! I've just got tough hide. Why are you trying to scare me like this? Is this a joke?"

As soon as the words left his mouth Judah regretted them. Shomer would not joke about losing his arm.

The Weaver pressed ahead with his tale. "Saved my life but not my girl. Wouldn't marry a one-armed man, so I left Caesarea and came here. But I have a life, and it's not dying by inches in Mak'ob. Be careful who you tell about this—that's all I wanted to say. Better to lose an ear than your freedom, your family."

Judah was stunned. It could not be true. All night he was distracted, making stupid mistakes as he pondered the awful possibility. Heading the list of his distresses was worry for his boys. Judah had to learn the truth at once before he endangered them.

Cradling baby Joel in her arms, Emma stood as far from Judah as the length of the room would permit. Two sons had already been hastily sent away to a friend's home. Judah would not see them again, even to tell them good-bye. This parting was hard enough as it was.

Jason, restraining the toddler, Tor, stood by his mother's side. The twelve-year-old was openly weeping. The distress communicated itself to the small child, who wailed and struggled in Jason's grasp.

The morning after hearing Shomer's terrifying suggestion about the wound on his ear, Judah went directly to a public bath. In the privacy of a dressing cubicle he stripped and examined every inch of his skin.

Underneath his upraised arm, on his rib cage, he found the additional evidence he both sought and feared. A broad patch of flesh, the size of his palm, displayed a yellowish discoloration. Worse, it had no sensation of touch, even when he gouged it with the edge of a *strigil*, a carved bone sweat-scraper. There was feeling above and below the area, but the pallid stretch of skin was like that of a corpse.

A Tyrian doctor in Joppa's Street of Physicians confirmed the diagnosis. The practitioner offered to concoct an expensive cure of oils, unguents, and potions but, when pressed, admitted it came with no guarantee of cure.

Unlike Shomer, whose concern had been all for himself, Judah's apprehension immediately attached to his family. There was no thought of keeping the illness secret or dealing with it by either medication or surgery. There was no solution, no matter how radical, that could keep his boys safe.

Judah had to leave. Now. At once.

Nor had Emma protested his decision.

Once the tragic news was reported, Judah's wife had only two concerns: how she would live and whether she was at risk herself.

Judah wrote out detailed instructions concerning the value of the business, the worth of the fleet, and prices for all the equipment. He suggested the name of a scribe who would oversee the liquidation of the operation, whether in whole or in pieces.

As a request, Judah suggested to Emma that she keep one boat and let Zebulon run it. It would give her additional income and provide a future for at least one of the boys.

Then he added that she must do what she thought best.

Emma sniffed, refused to touch the parchment, and managed to hint that fishing was somehow connected with leprosy. Her features set with marble-like sternness, Emma spent the entire time Judah was saying good-bye bemoaning her fate. She worried aloud about her future finances and nervously touched her face, ears, and throat while peering into a hand mirror.

When the moment of departure came, Jason wrenched himself away from his mother. Over her screeching protests, he clung to his father's waist and begged him not to leave.

Throat husky and unable to speak, Judah thrust his son from him. Holding Jason at arm's length, he managed to say, "You'll be . . . good man. Make me proud. Know you will."

Outside, facing a road with no clear route and no destination but the grave, Judah stared at the row of citron saplings.

He knew they would grow, just as his boys would grow, but he would not be there to see it.

The stone wall between Judah and his son was nothing compared to the one in his heart. "See to the trees. I won't . . . I can't. You show your brothers . . . tell them . . . remember me."

Then he was gone.

THE JOURNEY CONTINUES...

"You don't have to do this," Carpenter said kindly. "One of us will go."

"We . . ."

". . . will."

"I'll go," Crusher announced, standing.

Fisherman shook his head ponderously, as if balancing a great weight atop it. "I want to . . . I mean, I don't . . . but it's mine . . . do you see?"

The young man glimpsed beside Fisherman's old home still stood in the garden between a pair of citron trees. The light of a fat crescent moon showed his hair to be dark and his forehead high. Fisherman felt his pulse quicken. It was his Jason! It had to be! That form, those features, were once Fisherman's own—those recalled from many a painful dream in the Valley of Anguish.

Jason . . . a man, grown!

Stopping much farther away than he wanted, Fisherman halted before his own features, or deformities, could be distinguished below the hood of his cloak.

"Shalom," he called. "Shabbat shalom. May a traveler ask a question?"

"Of course" was the reply.

The voice! So like his own at that age, full of youthful confidence.

Then his son continued, "But come and share Shabbat supper with us."

"No, no," Fisherman refused hastily. "I am expected . . . elsewhere. But my friends and I . . . can you tell us if the man named Yeshua of Nazareth is here?"

"Here?"

"In Joppa."

Beneath the plainspoken question Fisherman longed to reveal a deeper, stronger query: *Don't you know me, Jason?* his heart cried. *Don't you recognize your father? These trees, so tall! I missed watching you become a man. I missed so much. Did you look for me in the faces of travelers? Can't you show you still think of me sometimes?*

"The healer from Nazareth? Why do you seek him?"

Fisherman said nothing.

The figure shrugged in the moonlight. "Not in Joppa, but my brother just arrived tonight from Yerushalayim. Said something about many healings over Jordan. Beyond Jericho, think he said. Wait. I'll call him."

Fisherman's breath came and went in quick, brief sips. His eyes darted toward the house. Another of his boys here, tonight? Was it too wonderful or too terrible?

"Jason," the man in the garden called.

The name replaced Fisherman's excitement with confusion. If this wasn't Jason, then . . .

"What is it, Rin?" a deeper, older voice replied. A heavier, more squarely built form rounded the corner. "Supper's . . . sorry. Didn't know you were with someone."

Rin? Rin? Last seen as a six-year-old.

Had Fisherman forgotten how to distinguish his own boys, one from another? He steadied himself with a hand on the cold stone of the wall, then snatched it back before the moon's glow gave away his secret.

"This man asked about the rabbi from Nazareth, Jason. You know the one. Has he been in Joppa?"

"Not that I've heard. Perea, I think. Other side of the country, anyway."

Fisherman barely trusted himself to speak. What if they recognized him now? He didn't think he could bear it. "Good . . . fine . . . thank you," he said. "Sorry to disturb." He shuffled away into the closest shadow he could find.

"Shabbat shalom," both sons called after him.

Fisherman heard Rin ask Jason, "Did you notice anything *familiar* about that fellow?"

"Can't say I did. Why?"

"I don't . . . but for just a minute . . . but that's silly. Let's go in to supper."

Only after an entire day's journey toward Jericho did Fisherman come out of a daze. He felt as if he'd awakened from a dream to find the Cabbage Sisters taking turns leading him.

They also took turns speaking reassuring words: "Good news, Jericho."

"We know it well."

"Our home."

"Now we'll find Yeshua."

"You'll see."

"You'll soon be back in Joppa, healthy and whole."

"It won't be . . ."

". . . long now."

THE CABBAGE SISTERS

Is the seed yet in the barn? Indeed, the vine, the fig tree, the pomegranate, and the olive tree have yielded nothing. But from this day on I will bless you.

HAGGAI 2:19

THE JOURNEY CONTINUES . . .

As the lepers of Mak'ob neared Jericho, they left the main highway to travel by back roads and grassy tracks. There had already been talk about how the priests wanted to kill Yeshua. It could only make matters worse for Him if ten lepers openly sought Him. The Pharisees despised Yeshua for welcoming beggars and cripples and being merciful toward sinners. Imagine, the minyan reasoned, how the authorities would hate Yeshua if He was known to attract the living dead.

"Like we're the plague," Crusher muttered, "instead of the victims."

A valley nestled between two hills was filled with well-tended sukomore-fig trees. From a distance the minyan noted signs posted near where a cart track gave access to the grove. As they got nearer, they saw the placards were written in Hebrew, Greek, and Aramaic:

DEFILED BY LEPROSY!
ENTER NOT THIS GROVE!

"What does that mean?" Shoemaker grumbled. "How can an orchard be defiled? Did some greedy person put that up to keep beggars away?"

As the minyan neared the turn, they spotted a beautiful young woman approaching them. At the sight of her Carpenter rasped, "Unclean!"

Instead of recoiling in horror as expected, the woman did the unexpected: She peered toward each leprous countenance as if renewing old acquaintances. There was no trace of fear or loathing on her features—only joy and recognition.

With a glad cry she ran toward them, causing the minyan to shrink back in dismay. "Carpenter," the apparently crazy woman called. "Crusher. Look, all of you! It's me—Shimona!" She embraced the two Cabbage Sisters, who tried to fend her off.

"Please," one Cabbage Sister protested.

"We're *tsara*!"

"Unclean."

"Defiled."

"Woman," Carpenter uttered sternly, "don't touch us!"

Laughing and crying at the same time, Shimona showed them her unmarred hands. "But I was one of you, in the Valley! Yeshua came! He came to us one evening after the minyan had left to seek him and . . ."

Carpenter, voice muffled by the strip of cloth over the hole where a nose had been, said, "It is Shimona! I know the voice. But why are you here? And you're restored, but . . . what is that sign posted back there?"

Shimona explained. "The people are afraid their eyes are bewitched. They can't accept that I've been healed. So I'm here. Until, well, I don't know how long. But they want to be certain."

Fisherman muttered, "We've been looking for the Healer. But every time we hear he's one place and go there, he's gone to another. Now you tell us we could've stayed in Mak'ob and let *him* find *us*?"

There was a moment of silent anguish before Fisherman continued, "Missed him in Yerushalayim. Never was in Joppa, perhaps. Then Bethany. Raised a dead man to life, they say. But the high priest got wind of it and put a price on his head. They want to kill Yeshua and the man he raised as well!"

Shimona's words spilled out in a rush. "Kill him? Kill? Oh, Carpenter! You must find Yeshua! He is life to us!"

Crusher shook his head slowly. "We're afraid they will kill him before we find him. What then?"

The Cabbage Sisters cried, "Our only hope!"

Shimona sighed. "Friends! Yeshua healed everyone in the Valley. *Everyone*. It's not a fable. Everyone who came near, he healed them all. He laid hands on us and healed us and sent us out of the Valley and to our homes. But my family was afraid. My mother wouldn't touch me. The rabbi and the priest and my father—they don't believe what they see, even though their eyes tell them I have no spot or sign of sickness. They are afraid it is witchcraft. So I have been here in isolation according to the law of Mosheh."

"Alone?" asked the Cabbage Sisters in unison.

"It's not so bad. My father rents the grove from Zachai the Publican for a share of the harvest. I have a cottage. I tend the sukomore trees. I wound the figs and harvest them and dry them. Once a month my father's servant comes. He takes the figs and leaves me food and such." She gestured toward a basket beside a tree trunk. "But I missed him today. Didn't hear any news from the world. Didn't hear what happened in Bethany. Raising the dead. Oh, such news! Every day I pray, 'When is Yeshua going to set up his kingdom?'"

Crusher raised fingerless hands to the heavens. "Omaine to that. Omaine!"

Fisherman agreed. "The people are desperate. Hopeless, but hoping Messiah will restore the throne of David. So many believe Yeshua will overthrow the Romans. Call down fire, you know. Like Elijah."

Shimona said, "Please. Come stay with me. Stay here. You'll be safe here."

Carpenter answered, "We must go on. We have heard Yeshua is hiding from the authorities over the Jordan. We're going there to find him. Shimona, come with us!"

"I can't. I made a promise to my father. To the rabbi and the priest. I made a vow that I would stay here and work, that I would not cross the boundary and leave the grove. I'm happy. Really." Shimona opened the basket that contained heaping loaves of bread. "I don't have money, but take what I have. Here. There's plenty to get me through the month. Take it, my dear friends, and go quickly. Cross the Jordan. Find the Lord, and you will find life!"

In place of near exhausted despair the minyan received a new level of energy from Shimona's words. Yeshua was not only a healer, He had healed lepers! He had raised the dead. Nothing was too hard for Him, it seemed. Surely He would not reject the appeals of those who had come so far, staked so much of what little remained of their lives on His compassion.

One of the Torah scholars scooped up the basket and bobbed his head with gratitude.

"We know the way from here," one Cabbage Sister announced.

"Our home was near Jericho. All the news from over Jordan comes through it," the other continued.

"When we've found him, we'll come again and bring you word," Carpenter promised.

"Yes, dear friends," Shimona said. "Better still: Bring him back with you, if you can. We'll leave the warning sign where it is; then Yeshua'll be safe with us!"

From the clearing where the road topped a rise all ten of the minyan looked back toward the sukomore grove. There, waving from one of the tallest trees, was the earnest money—the promise—of their healing: Shimona, once a leper of Mak'ob, now healed and whole and strong.

The conversation among the minyan was not only about her healing, however.

"Why is she confined? And alone, when she is so plainly well?" Shoemaker wondered aloud. "How can her family permit such a thing?"

"*Do* such a thing," Carpenter corrected. "Fear. Fear of what they do not understand."

"More afraid of healing than of *tsara*?" Fisherman said incredulously.

"When she was Inside, Shimona was one of us," Mikki explained to his father. "She had family—us. Now, when she's Outside and healed, she has nobody. How can that be right?"

"Isn't right," Shoemaker replied grimly. "But it's the way the world is sometimes. Those who are afraid to admit they have anything wrong with their own lives hate and despise those who have admitted their problems and asked for help."

The main highway leading to Jericho was broad and busy with the coming and going of caravans. The minyan of lepers followed the route but remained far off the main road and out of sight, lest the stink of their rotting flesh draw comments from those on the main highway.

Carpenter warned that they must not speak as they made their way to the fortress city. In spite of this, the Cabbage Sisters giggled and babbled in hushed tones as they limped forward. Their heads together, they shared some secret with one another in sentences as broken as their bodies.

Nearby was an orchard of date palms, heavy clusters hanging ready for harvest. Bags of dates already picked were propped against the trunks of the trees. One sister looked at the other and said, "It's within our right."

"Oh yes, perfectly! Yes!" agreed the other.

"But you know they'd kill us if we did."

"Oh yes! Certainly they would kill us." She stopped and placed her hands on her hips. "Even so . . ."

"Well, yes. I suppose." The one Cabbage Sister summoned Mikki, the Son of the Shoemaker. She peered at him through red, glassy eyes. "That bag of dates belongs to me. A quarter part of it is rightfully mine. Now, if you consider all the bags and all the dates, then more than one full bag is mine. So come with me and we'll take that one away with us. Dates are so healthy."

Mikki blinked down at the wizened, rotten creature. "Healthy for who? Stealing dates. A capital crime. Prison. Torture. Maybe death."

"Not stealing. It's mine, I tell you," she argued petulantly. "You're strong lads," she said to the four Torah schoolboys. "One of you pick it up and carry it away. You have my permission."

The boys looked to Carpenter for assistance. None of them had ever seen the Cabbage Sisters insistent or demanding. It seemed that every mile they traveled nearer to Jericho, some memory of life Outside awakened in the Cabbage Sisters. Assertive and certain of their claims, they would not be denied.

Carpenter took the men aside as the two women shuffled off to talk of womany things. "I don't know who the Sisters were, exactly . . . I mean, when they lived Outside. But for a long time the gifts that came to them were many. You've seen their little stone cottage. The garden. I think, maybe, if they say they own a sack of dates? Perhaps it's true."

Shoemaker asked, "But how could we prove it? Say we take it away. And someone sees us take it. If someone thought we had stolen it, what then?"

Carpenter put a hand to his empty belly. "Who's going to take anything from a leper, I ask you? Who?"

"That's right," Fisherman concluded. "And if the penalty is death? Well, we're already starving, aren't we? Already dying. What else could they do to hurt us?"

So Shoemaker and Fisherman went together to the date palms and took a sack of dates. From time to time along the road to Jericho the Cabbage Sisters paused, pointed with the stubs of their hands, and laid claim to raisins on the vine or nuts still on a tree.

The minyan ate well, off the fat of the land, as they searched for Yeshua.

On a major trade route, Jericho was the first city inside the boundaries of Judea just above the Dead Sea. All overland trade coming from the incense-producing desert regions of Nabatea and Arabia entered the Roman world through Jericho.

The Jews themselves, at the conclusion of their exodus from slavery and wilderness wandering, had also entered the Promised Land nearby. Their encounter with the Canaanite inhabitants was the reason Jericho existed in three parts: New City, Old City, and even older, uninhabited ruins.

A day's travel from Jerusalem, Jericho was the gateway to the land of the Jews. It was the spigot of customs revenue from which the Romans never released their hand.

Between the rundown Old City, which welcomed smelly,

flea-bitten camel drovers, and the New City, domain of the rich and powerful like Zachai the Chief Tax Collector, was the Customs House.

From their hilltop hideaway the Minyan of Mak'ob saw all of this but approached none of it.

"We'll be safe here," Carpenter noted.

Crusher nudged a rock with the toe of his sandal and crushed a scorpion that bristled defensively beneath. "Safe . . . if we watch where we sit."

The hill was barren—all tumbled boulders from the size of a man's head up to the dimensions of his cottage. Besides rocks, all that grew well were clumps of flexible creepers. They looked invitingly like dark green vines until too-close inspection revealed finger-length, needle-sharp thorns.

It was a cursed place. After this version of Jericho capitulated to the arriving Hebrews, it should never have been rebuilt. Those who attempted to do so regretted it.[20]

"The smell of death is on this place," Fisherman said, shuddering.

No one took him to task for the irony of his observation.

"That's why we're safe here," Carpenter concluded.

The Cabbage Sisters, clinging to one another, stood on a mound and gazed longingly toward the city.

"Look there. . . ."

"Yes, look."

"The fig tree."

"The roof of the synagogue."

". . . the synagogue."

"The pomegranates will be ripe."

"Pomegranates. I dream of the juice from our trees. . . ."

"Juice. Yes."

The men set about gathering scraps of wood and dried brush for a fire. The sun began to set as lights of the great trading center winked on.

The Cabbage Sisters leaned upon each other as they sat beside the campfire. "They'll be closing the gates."

"The gates . . ."

"Evening prayers."

"Oh yes."

"I wonder if . . ."

". . . he's still there?"

The minyan shared a meal of fruits and nuts gleaned from fields and orchards the Cabbage Sisters had claimed were their own.

Carpenter wiped his mouth on the sleeve of his tunic and said to the women, "Your night to tell a story."

The women exchanged a glance. "All right, then. A love story."

"Yes. Love story."

"Two women. One man."

"Sisters."

"Like Leah . . ."

". . . and Rachel."

"Only . . . beautiful."

"Yes. Beautiful."

"Not us."

"No."

"This story is not about us."

"Although we are sisters."

"No. It's about two other sisters."

"Beautiful girls."

"Lived in Jericho."

"Yes. Jericho."

"A very long time ago."

CHAPTER 10

"We could share him." Tabitha looked into the eyes of her identical sister, letting Terabinth know she was as serious as death.

"Two women cannot marry one man." Tera sat down on the bed beside her twin.

Looking at their faces was seeing one visage with two sets of eyes. Twin daughters were a reason for much pride in the rabbi's house—God's double blessing on the womb, like Jacob and Esau, only more so.

People commented on how much the daughters of the Jericho rabbi looked alike. It was uncanny. They played tricks on guests. Made their mother and father guess who was who. Each pretended to be the other.

And now a suitor had come to ask for the hand of Tabitha, who was born a mere ten minutes before Terabinth.

Tabitha, not wanting to be wed without her lifelong companion, replied, "It is in Torah. They used to do it all the time. One man may marry two women. Two sisters, even."

Tera snorted. "Jacob. Rachel and Leah. Trouble."

"Not for us."

"Jacob always loved Rachel best. This caused the sisters grief."

"Never between you and me. No man could come between us."

Tera instructed, "Father would not allow it. Polygamy is not in fashion these days. Only among the Moabites and the Arabs. A new woman every day."

Tabitha's eyes misted. She was the more emotional of the two. "It isn't fair. I am first born only by minutes. Why should I have to marry this fellow, and you get to stay home in the garden?"

Tera patted her sister on the shoulder. She embraced her and wiped her tears. "It is just the way it's done. The first born is always the first to go."

Tabitha began to cry in earnest. Tera seemed so heartless in this matter. Why could she not comprehend that this husband would not know the difference between them in daylight or dark? They could continue to share the same bed and eat at the same table. If they lived all together in the big house in Jerusalem, they could still play tricks on the servants and . . . "If I am forced to marry and leave home without you, where will be the fun?" Tabitha brooded.

Tera chirped, "Children! Marriage means children. You won't be lonely for long."

Tabitha proposed a solution, a magnification of entertainment. "Suppose we each had twins—twins by the same husband. Oh, Tera, I tell you, it could happen. Think of it!"

Tera frowned. "Tabitha, you know I love you as I love myself. But I got a glimpse of the fellow downstairs when he went in to speak with Father."

Tabitha drew herself erect. "What? What! What?!"

"He is not young," Tera confided. She was pleased that her sister was first born.

"Not . . . ?"

". . . young."

"You mean he is . . ."

" . . . advanced."

Tabitha stammered, "Well then, he would not be demanding. We would have more time to spend together." Tabitha clasped Tera's hand in desperation. "Don't make me marry him alone."

Tera had always been the more independent of the two. "Dear sister, it would be like marrying our own father. Or grandfather."

"Grandfather is dead."

"Yes. My point. Exactly."

"Then our husband would not trouble us at all. Everything could go on just as it has always been. We will not be separated. He is a very rich fellow, Mother says. And he will die eventually. Maybe soon. Then we will inherit, and everything will be just the same."

There was no hope of Tabitha convincing Tera of the joys of polygamy. And Tera was only the first in a long line of participants who would have to be convinced for the plan to work.

Tabitha, first born, turned her face away from the mirror image of herself, hung her head, and sobbed. Not small sobs, but great gulping sobs that the disaster about to come upon them was inevitable.

For the first time, Tera did not attempt to comfort her wombmate. With a sigh, she rose and went to the lattice window that looked down on the students gathered in the courtyard of her father's Yeshiva school.

Tera peeked under a limb of the pomegranate tree that flanked the window. It and its twin had been planted on the very day of the sisters' birth, a decade and a half before. There was some family story about a strange man, perhaps a prophet, who had appeared with the saplings, but Tera had never bothered to pay attention to the legend.

There was no magic about it. It was the wealth from Grandfather's successful cloth-dyeing business that had built the school and Father's reputation as a scholar that attracted the pupils.

At the flash of her pomegranate-hued dress, the eyes of the tall, handsome rabbinical student turned upwards. *A Greek god! Adonis!* Tera waved, holding up her little finger in the secret signal she had given to him as proof it was she.

His eyebrows arched with pleasure. A furtive smile played on his full and beautiful lips before he looked back at his fellow students. He was her father's favorite scholar of the thirty-six young men who lived and studied in the wing beside the synagogue.

Tabitha's racking sobs stopped suddenly. There was the rustle of fabric as she joined Tera at the window. "What are you looking at?"

"Nothing. Poor students taking in the morning sun."

Tabitha's eyes narrowed as she followed Tera's field of vision to the most prominent creature in the garden. "He loves us both." Tabitha sighed. "What will he do when I am gone?"

Tera did not reply. She reached out and snapped the shutters closed, blocking Tabitha's view of their beloved.

"What difference does it make? He is poor and has nothing. He could never marry you . . . or . . . or . . . anyone."

Tabitha frowned as some thought flew through the blank sky of her mind. "What were you looking at, Tera? Do you think I am entirely stupid?"

Tera strode away from the window, then whirled to face her sister. "I don't know what you are talking about."

Tabitha raised her oval face in challenge—a gesture Tera despised so much that she fought very hard not to imitate it. Tabitha said, "I see it clearly. Marry off the first born daughter to . . . to a relic! And then . . . *ha!* Then when I am out of the way, you . . . *you*, my own sister . . . you marry this Yeshiva Adonis!"

Tera could not deny that this had crossed her mind. "But you! You would have me, your own sister, marry with you . . . to this old fellow . . . and share your misery. You would marry us both to this decrepit inhabitant of an ossuary just so you would not be lonely!"

Poised like cats with claws unsheathed, the sisters glared at their own reflections in their faces.

Fury! Betrayal! Jealousy! Resentment roiled the depths of their evenly matched souls. So, Tera would have love and youth and the challenges of poverty, which knit one's soul to its mate, while Tabitha would have wealth and impotence and a life without passion or joy!

Tabitha glowed red with anger. "So, Tera, I am not blind! I may be your twin, but I am not stupid either. You and he . . . you have plotted this very thing to get me out of the way. Did your lover plant this idea of matrimony in the stagnant pool of my suitor's ancient brain?"

Tera could not deny that the love of her life was also nephew of the rich merchant who now hammered out the matter of Tabitha's dowry with their father downstairs. "What of it?"

Tabitha raised her arms and thundered, striking Tera hard across the face. With a small shriek of surprise Tera tumbled backwards, slamming her ear hard against the bedpost.

Tabitha instantly regretted her act of violence. Little white hands rose to her flushed cheeks in horror. "Oh! Oh! Oh!" She fluttered to Tera's side and leaned over her.

Tera, shaken, blinked up at Tabitha. "Oh!" Tera groaned and made no attempt to sit up. She touched her ear. Blood. "Oh!" She stared at the dark red stain on her fingers. "You've tried to kill me."

"No! No, never!"

There was little pain, but Tera felt woozy. She closed her eyes and the room spun.

Tabitha begged, "Please! Oh, please, forgive me. Oh, Tera, they're coming!"

The sound of footsteps outside in the corridor roused Tera. She sat bolt upright and snatched a towel from the washstand. She held it to the wounded ear and scrambled to her feet.

A soft rapping on the door drove the sisters into each other's arms. They both said at once, "Mama! Papa!"

Their mother's doting voice emanated from the door panel. "Tabitha, honeycomb! Tabitha, darling. Your papa and I have come to speak to you. Open the door, girls!"

The duo exchanged horrified looks. Their world was coming to an end. As much as Tera loved the Yeshiva Adonis, she did not want her other self to be banished to the barren desert of an old man's affection.

Tera opened the door. There was blood on her shoulder.

Her mother's grin vanished. A cascade of hysteria flooded the bedchamber. "Oh, darling! What has happened? What?"

Their father was likewise shaken by the sight of blood. "Which one is it? Which? Who is injured?"

Tera identified herself with a wave of the bloody cloth. "I stumbled." She protected Tabitha, who trembled against the wall at the self-revelation of her own violent nature.

Tera pulled away from her mother's cloying embrace. "I am not hurt. Not so much. What is it you have come to tell us?"

The mood swung back to something like honeycomb stuck to the bottom of a shoe.

The rabbi turned his crinkled face toward the daughter who was not bleeding. "Tabitha!" He hesitated. "Which one are you? You are Tabitha? Yes. Yes, my angel! At last we have such news for you!"

Tabitha dabbed her eyes. "Oh, Papa."

"Yes! A wedding for my first born daughter."

Tabitha moaned, "Only by ten minutes. Only . . ."

Their mother embraced Tabitha. "A bride. A bride! To think of it: our first baby girl."

Tabitha sank to the edge of the bed as Tera looked on grimly.

Tabitha replied flatly, "Tell me, then."

The rabbi whispered the name of the old merchant as if it were holy. "Nachman the Elder."

Tera questioned her father's announcement. "What, Papa? Nachman is elder?"

The rabbi corrected, "*The*. *The* elder. Very wealthy and honored. Sits among the council."

Tera muttered behind her hand, "*Because he can't stand.*"

Tabitha began to weep loudly again. "Oh, it is too much!"

Mama giggled. "You see how overjoyed she is? I told you she would be pleased. Cannot hold back the tears of joy."

Tabitha sniffled. "Too much . . ."

Tera, ever the smug observer, considered how much was too much.

Tabitha the elder marries Nachman the Elder.

Tera the younger is then free to marry Adonis the scholar and live a long and passionate life.

Perhaps Tabitha would learn to be happy with a man who nodded off at dinner.

Tera dabbed the blood and examined it, making sure that Tabitha noticed her pained expression. Guilt was a lovely weapon. It was worth a bump on the noggin to now have something on Tabitha. *Dab . . . dab . . . dab . . .*

Tabitha groaned and put a hand to her head. "I am . . . oh, dear Tera! Are you all right?"

Tera examined the blood more closely. She batted her lashes and replied weakly, "It was an accident. I am sure of it." All the while she was trying to remember the technical Roman name for attempted murder of a sibling. Latin. There were many family murders among the Romans. *Patricide or matricide or sister-cide or some such cide.*

Papa turned to Tera with concern. "And as for you, Terabinth, soon enough we'll find a proper husband for you as well."

"Oh, not too soon, Papa." Tera did not want him to get ahead of the lead horse. "I am the younger, after all."

The flash of a dagger leapt from Tabitha's eye with the intent of piercing Tera's heart. So thoughts of homicide still lingered.

Tabitha simpered. "Oh, Papa, promise me that whoever Tera is to wed will be as rich and esteemed as Nachman the Elder."

"There, there." Papa patted Tabitha comfortingly. "There's my thoughtful girl. Tabitha, always thinking of your younger sister. Of course. Of course."

Tera paled but not from loss of blood.

Tabitha grinned evilly at the flash of hatred in Tera's glare. Tabitha said, "Oh, Mama, Papa, Tera—do you mind? I need a little time alone . . . to give thanks to . . . yes. Give thanks."

What was Tabitha plotting?

The correct Latin word leapt to Tera's mind: *Sororicide.*

CHAPTER 11

The day of reckoning approached and still Nachman the Elder had only one bride. Neither life nor death nor principalities nor powers could convince Tera to join Tabitha at the altar.

Tera avoided her sister, sleeping in the second bedroom.

Tabitha grew surly and short-tempered with her mother and father and the household servants. She wept copiously when congratulated by the young female members of Jericho's Congregation Beth Isra'el. It was all very normal behavior for a woman about to wed an old man whom she barely knew and by whom she wished never to be known.

Tera sometimes returned the winks of her beloved Yeshiva Adonis. Her hopes for a match with him were fixed. Identifying her by the raised pinkie signal he passed her a message: *After the wedding I will approach your father.*

Tera's heart soared at the news. She stood at the latticed window and with upraised finger signaled her love that all would be well.

She had, since the attack, severed her welded heart from Tabitha's. Well, perhaps the separation had come before that, but now Tera had a swollen ear to point to as the cause. The breach, though unrevealed to Mama and Papa, was open between the sisters.

Tera did not care if she ever visited Tabitha when she was installed as princess in Nachman the Elder's estate. Tera was content with her little garden and dreams of passion with the Yeshiva scholar.

This was the stable condition of all things between the twins until the day a wail rose up from the bedchamber of the rabbi and his wife. The cry was one of such extreme anguish that the birds outside Tera's window fell silent and fluttered away.

Tera charged out the door shouting, "What is it? What's happened? Mama! Mama!" She dashed down the corridor and burst into her parents' room.

The physician was present. His face was grim and stern.

Mama was collapsed, weeping, on the sofa. Papa wrung his hands in despair. And in the shadowed corner sat Tabitha, devoid of any emotion.

Mama pleaded with the doctor, "But it's nothing. Nothing! A spot!"

Papa said, shaking his head, "She's to be wed . . . next month."

The doctor shook his ponderous head. "No. Not next month. Not ever."

Tera's heart pounded wildly. She stared at Tabitha, trying to read whatever had gone so terribly wrong. Tabitha gave no signal. Her eyes were blank. Tearless. Accepting some terrible fate without protest.

"This cannot be!" Mama's hands were clasped, begging.

The doctor said firmly, "I have seen enough to know. The quarantine will tell. But I am 90 percent certain." He looked to Papa for help. "Rabbi, you know the law."

"Yes." Papa choked out his agreement. "Isolation and—" he looked up at Tera—"ah. There is some hope to avoid shame. Tera, you will take your sister's place. Nachman the Elder will never know the difference. His eyes are bad. One sister is the same as the other to him."

Tera could hardly believe what she was hearing and seeing. "What? Papa!" Then to Tabitha, "Tabby—" She used the pet name from their days in the nursery. "Tabby! Sister! What has happened?"

Tabitha replied calmly, holding up her right hand. "Oh, Tera, I am . . . dead while I live—*tsara*, a leper."

Papa looked everywhere and focused on nothing. "By the time it is confirmed, the wedding will be over. Nachman will never know the difference."

Tera felt a fire of rage well up in her. The unfairness of life! Tabitha, beautiful and exactly a duplicate of Tera, doomed to perish of a disease beyond any imagined horrors! And Tera, doomed to marry a man who was half corpse.

Tera rushed to embrace Tabitha. Her parents and the doctor cried out that she must not—must *not*—touch Tabitha! Not now, not ever again. Tera's father and the doctor held her back as she struggled to reach her sister.

"Tabby! Tabby! Forgive me! Forgive me . . . for everything!"

Tabitha's lips moved almost soundlessly. "Sure. Sure. You know I love you, Tera . . . more than anything." She stretched out her hand, displaying the disease on her index finger. It had appeared so quickly. She spoke to Tera with such pity. "But don't come near me, dearest. I am sorry. They are right. You mustn't."

Tera denied that this horror could be possible. Why? In the family of such a righteous rabbi? Tera prayed to wake up from the nightmare. To no avail.

"You still have one . . . one beautiful daughter," Tabitha said in farewell to her parents. "Tera, now you will have to live for both of us."

With the promise that this catastrophe would not be revealed from his lips, the physician led Tabitha away to some place of isolation.

Laughter fled from the habitation of the rabbi of Jericho. All linens and clothing were taken away by night and burned. The walls were scrubbed with strong spirits and whitewashed under the pretext that all things must be made new for the festivities. Plans for the wedding were a mockery of joy.

Tera prayed—really prayed, for the first time in her life—prayed that when the proscribed period of isolation was complete, Tabitha would be examined and declared clean.

Tera would stand in her place at the wedding to Nachman the Elder. A bargain: Even if she was forced to be a wife to him for the sake of Tabitha, she would do so.

"But only, please HaShem, will you not give her back to us? For Mama. For Papa. She may have my life and I'll take hers. She may marry my young man . . . have children. And I will hold steady for everything. But only just . . . I want my sister's life back."

But it was not to be.

Tabitha was examined for the last time the day before the wedding. The doctor came alone to the house.

"Leprosy." He pronounced the sentence of death.

Mama held tightly to Tera, yet it was Tabitha whose name she cried again and again.

The doctor said, "Tabitha is resigned. Accepting that this is God's judgment for her sin."

"What?" the rabbi exclaimed. "She is seventeen! Sin? Judgment?" He grasped Tera by the hands. "Dear daughter, do you know what it is your sister is talking about?"

Tera knew. Tabitha thought their anger at each other had brought on the punishment. Tabitha felt the pain of their disagreement as well, but surely the Almighty was not so cruel in judging the vanity of girls. God had not joined in and taken sides in the argument between two siblings. The Almighty would not cause one to die of sickness and the other of a broken heart because of a silly argument.

Tera would not tell her father the details of what had passed between them. "It was nothing. She was afraid to marry Nachman the Elder; that's all."

"Afraid?" Papa sat down slowly. "Afraid is not a sin. I am afraid now." He spread his hands out on his lap and said slowly over the low weeping of Mama, "No . . . no judgment. This sickness, our beautiful daughter—just the way things are in this world. Oh, Messiah! That you would rend the heavens and come down!"[21] Papa cradled his head in his hands. *"The Lord gives and the Lord takes away. Blessed be the name of the Lord."*[22]

The doctor, who had seen many such cases before, explained it was best if they did not meet Tabitha again. There could be no last embrace. The finality of parting would be too painful for them all. Best to make a clean break now. He would see to it that she was accompanied safely to the Valley of Mak'ob. There were many formerly prominent people living in Mak'ob. She could live there . . . as long as she lived.

The family could send her provisions and write to her, of course. But not even the smallest scrap of paper touched by a leper could ever come out from that place.

They would never again hear directly from Tabitha.

CHAPTER 12

Vain and vapid, self-absorbed and selfish, Tera grew up in an instant.

The night before the wedding, Tera dreamed of Tabitha alone in the dark Valley of Mak'ob. She had become a stone—still pretty, still living, but a stone nonetheless. She was balanced precariously on the edge of a cliff, which dropped into a wide sea. Waves roared beneath, undermining the cliff as the weight of her sorrow pressed down heavily on the verge. The wind blew at her back, pushing her toward the edge.

Tera called to her, but Tabitha could not hear her. Instead, Tera heard Tabitha say to the sea, "I'm going under. My own weight dragging me beneath the waves. I know it. Who loves me enough that he will give his life for me? Who will die in my place so I will no longer be stone, but live, redeemed?"

Tera shouted, "I will!"

Tabitha answered her, gasping out each word. "Oh, Tera! It can't be. You dying for me. Or me dying for you. Our Love. It isn't enough. Our Love can't fix this. No matter who dies for who, we each still suffer for the other. Sorrow will drag us under in the end."

Tera cried out, "Then who? Who can save us?"

Tabitha did not reply. The wind pushed and the waves pulled until she vanished beneath the water.

Tera stood rooted on the shore. She could not save her. "Someone! Lord of heaven, help us. Save us!" she cried.

The waves thundered. The wind howled.

Lightning cracked, rending the heavens and striking the sea. And then? Then the gentle voice of a man sighed from somewhere far away, "I will go. I will die for her. And you."

"Who are you? Who? Where? How will you save us?"

Silence. The sea grew still.

Tera awoke, sweating and reaching up into the darkness, but Tabitha was not there. It was almost dawn before she slept again.

That morning, Tera awakened to the sound of music in the courtyard. She went to the latticed window and pushed aside the pomegranate leaves. Her Adonis was below, serenading the bride with the Torah schoolboys. He flashed a smile at her, not knowing which sister she was. He raised his little finger just in case, but Tera did not respond in kind. He looked away, disappointed.

What would her beloved say if the truth finally came out?

The wind pushed and the waves pulled. Truth was a heavy burden. Its weight would pull them under.

The game was over. Tera's dream of happiness was finished. She would become Tabitha today, a stone incapable of love. Tabitha's name was on the marriage *ketubah*. For the sake of fulfilling the marriage contract, Tera must stand in the place of her sister and marry an old man who did not know or care which of the rabbi's daughters he took home.

Tera's father had warned her sternly that a great fortune depended on the illusion. Tera must now become Tabitha in the eyes of the world.

Both sisters would suffer, each in a different way. Their great love for each other could not save them from life. Love demanded that no matter who suffered first, both would suffer.

Nachman the Elder was a kind old fellow.

Living with him in the enormous Jerusalem palace was just as Tera imagined it would be: like living with her grandfather. He called her Tabitha and often dozed off in the midst of conversation.

His children from former marriages were older than she was. By the age of eighteen, she was a grandmother to eleven grandchildren, two of whom were older than she by years.

She was good to their father, so they tolerated her, accepting that he had signed a document assuring that his child bride would have a lesser share of his vast fortune when he died.

They could live with that.

He made no demands on her. None whatsoever. She was given her own chambers.

She lay in her wide barren bed and tried not to think of the boy who had smiled up at her from her father's courtyard.

In the beginning of the marriage, the nephew, Tera's Yeshiva school Adonis, often came to visit. A rumor circulated that one of the twins had become ill with a dread disease. Exactly which sister was where remained a mystery. Perhaps the Adonis suspected the truth about his uncle's bride, but he did not voice his suspicion. He was courteous, respectful to the bride of his aged relative. Only once he greeted her with his hand raised and his little finger extended.

She pretended it meant nothing to her. From then on he seldom came to the house.

13 CHAPTER

It was Passover and all the family of Nachman the Elder gathered in the great house in Jerusalem to celebrate. Tera knew and recognized only a few. They were polite and respectful to her, while recognizing that she was only a token, a placeholder in the old man's life.

That night Nachman the Elder had a dream.

Bare feet exposed beneath his nightshirt, he wandered through the halls calling for his first wife, who had died in childbirth forty-one years before.

"Jerusha!" Desperate, he shuffled along the stone floor like a broom. "Where are you? Jerushaaaaaa!"

Tera sprang from her bed and wrapped her cloak around her. The servants, sons, daughters, and various sizes of grandchildren poked their heads out to see what the old man was up to.

"What's he doing now?" His eldest son peered at Tera as if she would know.

"Shouting for someone," Tera answered.

Nachman howled, "Jerusha! Come back to me. Come back here at once. Jerusha!"

The son said quizzically, "Jerusha was my mother's name. I never knew her, but Jerusha was her name, I'm told."

"Jeru-shaaaa!" Nachman called down the stairs.

The daughter-in-law snapped, "Don't wake him! It's bad luck to wake someone who is dreaming!"

The son said to Tera, "He's your husband. Do something, will you? He'll wake all of Yerushalayim."

Tera, understanding the confusion of nightmares, ran after the aged master, as was her duty. "Nachman! Husband! Beloved!"

The hallway was lined with familial spectators who parted to let her through.

Nachman turned slowly from the banister. The panic in his cataract-marbled eyes eased a bit. He reached out his thin, brittle arms as she approached and sighed, "Jerusha, there you are!" He embraced her, or rather, enfolded her in an embrace that supported his weight.

"Yes, Nachman, I am here," she soothed. She felt it was no burden to pretend she was someone else.

He began to weep with joy. "Jerusha, such a dream I had. I dreamed . . . dreamed that you had flown away. Left me as you gave birth to our son."

"No, Nachman. I am here. Wake up. Wake up. Just a bad dream."

"And I thought I had lived a long and lonely life . . . other wives. A dozen children I loved but never knew. They never loved me . . . oh! Such a long, lonely dream. Jerusha! I am so glad—so glad you did not leave me to live such a life alone . . . without you."

"Just a dream, Nachman." Tera stroked the old man's white hair as he wept.

"And I dreamed I was very old . . . ancient." He raised his gnarled hand and stared at the back of it. Blue veins, a road map to reality. "Jerusha?"

"Just a dream. I am here, my husband."

Lifting his eyes to the audience in the corridor, he gasped. "But . . . who are they? Who? Jerusha?"

Silence. Tera turned to take in wide eyes and gaping mouths illuminated by flickering oil lamps.

She did not dare tell the old man these were all his: the offspring of the forty-one long and loveless years he had lived since his one true love had flown away.

"These are our guests, my dearest Nachman." Then, with authority, she told them all, "Go back to bed. Haven't you ever had a nightmare? It is rude to gawk!"

They stirred a bit but did not retreat.

Nachman blinked at them. He looked down to study her face through the haze of his vision. "Jerusha. My beauty. Still as you always were. Kind. Kind to me. Such a fool I have been. Would you . . . forgive . . ."

"Yes. Yes. Now come to bed, Nachman my dear." She took his hand, attempting to lead him back through the mob of relatives, but Nachman's feet refused to budge. He stood rooted like a stone on a cliff—the wind pushing from behind. The sea raging before his eyes.

"What? Jerusha? My love? What's that you say?" he whispered. "Ah yes. Jerusha! Waiting . . . for me . . ."

His knees buckled slowly. He did not fall, but rather crumpled and collapsed as his youthful soul stepped out from his body and into the arms of Jerusha, who had surely been waiting for him these forty-one long years.

Trunks and bags were packed. The estate had been divided. Though the rest of Nachman's relatives bickered and haggled over the inheritance, Tera, according to the terms of the marriage contract, had received a miniscule portion free and clear. She bought two orchards and ten vineyards and set tenant farmers to work them. The income was enough to live comfortably all the rest of her life.

Still young enough to have a life, Tera returned home to Jericho to live with Mama and Papa in the very room she had shared with Tabitha. The young Adonis of the Yeshiva had married and was the assistant rabbi of the Jericho congregation.

Tera did not notice him much. He was a stranger to her now.

It was, rather, Nachman's last dream that awakened her.

His life had ended forty-one years before he died. He never stopped loving the one he had lost. Though he kept breathing and searching and living, the separation from Jerusha was a wound from which he had never recovered.

On the night before Tera left Jericho again—this time forever—she had a dream.

She and Tabitha were little girls again, sitting beneath the giant fig tree in their father's garden. All around them a vegetable garden bloomed.

"What do you suppose we will be when we are grown up?" Tera asked Tabitha.

Tabitha plucked a cabbage and gave it to Tera. "We will always be Sisters."

A train of four donkeys was loaded with household goods. There was a fine tent to shelter them until a cottage could be constructed on the Valley floor.

Tera paid the drovers at the stone boundaries marking the point of never returning. They did not thank her. Instead they clutched their money in their fists and scurried away as fast as their legs could carry them.

Tera inhaled the last breath of freedom and stepped across the line.

She had brought kettles and clothes and medicine and gardening tools. She carried seeds for flower gardens and vegetable seeds, cabbages and apple saplings and cuttings from vines.

She stood on the high prospect of the Valley of Mak'ob, which opened up beneath her like a desolate sea. "I am not a stone," she said to the angels who went with her. "I will not sink, but will save what I can."

Tera was not afraid. The reality of living forty years suffering alone without her sister was more frightening to her than the prospect of perhaps one day suffering her sister's fate. Life was loving, after all, even though love sometimes made life hard to live. Tera knew: Existence, cold as stone and separated from love, was no life at all.

She murmured, "Even when love breaks your stony heart."

Tera had it in her power to plant hope where there was despair and loneliness.

"We will always be Sisters. . . ."

The pack animals followed Tera down the steep switchback path.

At the bottom, an old man with a stick hobbled toward her. "I am Rabbi Ahava, my dear."

She replied, "Honored sir, my name is Terebinth. I am twin sister to Tabitha, who came here two years ago this month. We are daughters of the rabbi of Jericho. Where is my sister?"

"Ah, Tera! You are the beloved. So it is true! Tabitha told us all last Sabbath . . . she said an angel revealed to her that her sister would come to Mak'ob to help us all when she was strong enough. Tabitha had a dream, you see, so she has been looking for you . . . searching the rim of the Valley for some sign of your coming every day." The old man pointed to a lean-to beneath the overhang of the cliff. "There."

The wind pushed at Tera's back. Waves drew her forward.

Tabitha, no longer stone but wounded flesh and blood, waited with arms outstretched to welcome her sister.

THE JOURNEY CONTINUES . . .

The firelight burned low. The men in the circle of the minyan were silent for a time as the Cabbage Sisters finished their tale.

"A love story." An almost-smile reflected in the eyes of one of the women.

"A love story about sisters," said the other.

Silence. Carpenter tossed a heap of dry brush onto the embers. Sparks flew up like the incantation of a magician. "How did the story end?"

The sisters shook their heads solemnly. "Don't know. Not finished. Not us," they said in unison.

Shoemaker cracked a walnut with a stone. "Delicious walnuts? Dates? Stolen fruit is always sweeter, they say."

The women exchanged furtive glances. "Not stolen."

Carpenter asked, "Every year, as long as I've been in Mak'ob, every harvest, food is sent to you from the Outside. And you share it all with us. Enough to last you two a year if you were careful. Instead, you share it all with those who suffer with you."

The sisters acknowledged this fact in their silence.

Who from the Outside delivered the harvest bounty into the depths of Mak'ob? A steward? A tenant farmer? A relative?

"Tomorrow we'll enter Jericho," the sisters declared. "He's in there, they say. We'll go to the synagogue. Surely he is there."

Carpenter wondered what would happen if these two sisters knocked on the door to their own home and demanded food or expected kindness. Surely they would be driven away.

The sisters certainly had considered this possibility. When the sun rose upon them, would they have the courage to enter Jericho and demand help from their servants in their quest to find the Rabbi of Nazareth?

"When we find Yeshua . . ."

"Find him."

"And we are healed . . ."

"Healed."

"Then you'll see."

The one leaned her bloated head against the shoulder of the other. "Yes, then we'll all see. And this . . . this night."

"This place."

"A dream."

"All a bad dream."

"Happy ending."

"Love story."

"When we find Yeshua of Nazareth."

The Cabbage Sisters set out for New Jericho at sunrise when the trumpets announced the opening of the city gates. The blind, lame, and destitute of Jericho were led or carried to their customary begging places at the city entrance. No lepers among the lowest of Jericho's society. Keen noses among the blind, who could smell leprosy at a distance and give the alarm. Keen eyes among the lame, who collected alms from travelers in their own territory for decades. They would not allow their privileged alms stations to be encroached upon by newcomers.

This could be a problem for a ragged band like the minyan.

Perhaps two lepers could sneak into the walled city undetected, but ten would be spotted at once and driven away with stones and curses.

The Sisters had a plan.

"You must stay behind."

"We're small."

"Yes. Small."

"Hide among . . ."

". . . livestock."

"Yes. Maybe camels."

"Or swine. They smell so bad."

"Gentiles of Jericho eat swine in copious numbers." This comment about the unclean diet of Gentiles also seemed ironic to Carpenter.

The Sisters continued, "Today is hog-slaughtering day in the shambles. They'll be bringing in swine. . . ."

"So maybe we can . . ."

". . . sneak in among the herds."

Carpenter and the rest of the minyan agreed. "And when you find Yeshua, and he heals you, then bring him back to us."

It was a brave and desperate plan.

The eight men of the minyan followed at a distance. If the Sisters found Yeshua, it was reasoned that they must be close enough to be found, but not so close that they would be discovered and stoned.

The Sisters—arms linked, faces covered—neared the highway, paused, and glanced back over their shoulders. Carpenter gave a signal that the minyan would advance no farther. Instead, he pointed to a heap of rubbish where they would hide and wait. The odor of garbage was a sensory disguise.

A small caravan of a half-dozen heavily laden camels approached. The Cabbage Sisters squared their shoulders and stepped onto the pavement of the highway forbidden to them by law. Heads down, eyes fixed on their feet, they marched in step with the third camel in the line.

Carpenter peered around the rubble. He saw sour looks among travelers as the whiff of something dead filled their nostrils.

The Sisters walked on, boldly.

Perhaps the travelers would think the stink was merely the decomposing corpse of a dog or rotting garbage by the road. None among the vast tide of humanity would imagine lepers so bold that they would hide among the throng. None could imagine that two lepers proceeded into the city without shouting the cry "Unclean!"

"Have they made it?" Crusher hissed.

Carpenter answered, "Almost. Brave ladies."

Moments passed in silence as all waited for the report. Carpenter whispered, "The first two camels are through."

The face of a blind man rose sharply with alarm as they passed. Chin in the air, the beggar opened his mouth as if to shout the warning that lepers were near. Then the women floated by and in. The fellow seemed to think about it a moment. He shook his head, then returned to his business. "Mercy! Alms! Alms for a blind man!"

Carpenter sighed and sat back on his heels. "They're in."

"How long do you think?" Fisherman asked. "I mean, until they find him?"

Crusher's eyes were pained.

The four Torah boys each speculated whether Yeshua was still inside the walls of Jericho or if He had already pressed on.

Shoemaker remarked, "The rumor is that he heals everyone."

His son added, "Everyone who believes."

Shoemaker stared at the beginning signs of disease on his hand. "And asks. You have to get close enough to him to ask."

A sudden look of consternation passed between Carpenter and Crusher.

Crusher moaned. "Blind men at the gates."

"The lame."

Fisherman gasped. "Still begging."

Shoemaker shook his head. "Then Yeshua isn't here. Hasn't been in Jericho."

So the Cabbage Sisters had risked their lives for nothing. Where were they now, in the quest to locate the great Healer? Would their deception be discovered in the close alleyways and streets of Jericho?

A collective depression settled on the men who huddled behind the garbage heap. The sun climbed higher in the sky, warming the open wounds of these, the human refuse of Israel.

It was midafternoon before the fearsome shrieks of citizens rose up from the city gates.

"Lepers!"
"They are lepers!"
"Chedel! Tsara!"
"Drive them out!"
"Stone them!"
"Stone them!"
"Lepers inside the walls of Jericho!"

The cries of rage and alarm caused the minyan to crouch lower and cover their heads with their filthy cloaks until they looked like mounds of garbage heaped beside one another.

Only Carpenter dared to look. The Cabbage Sisters—running, stumbling beneath a hail of garbage and stones—fled out through the gates. The guards on the parapet above them lifted a chamber pot and hurled human excrement down on them.

One Sister fell a few paces from the rug of the blind beggar. The other Sister stopped to help her up. A fist-sized stone struck her in the back. She struggled to remain on her feet, but failed.

Suddenly the blind man leapt to his feet. Long arms groped the air. Spindly legs and knobby knees shuffled forward. He towered over the two prone Sisters. One more step and he would have trod on them. Instead he turned to face the mob, which howled beneath the arch of the gate tower.

"Hey!" he shouted as something foul whistled past his ear. "Stop. Stop! Garbage all over. On the street. On my rug. Stop!" Then to the women he said, "Run away. Never come back!"

The blind man raised his arms and stood before the women like a shield. This brief respite was time enough for the Sisters to gather themselves and stagger off the highway.

The minyan heard them gasping for breath, moaning, sobbing as they came near the hiding place. Carpenter stood as the duo collapsed in a heap at his feet. Fresh wounds oozed blood. They clung to one another as if they were drowning on dry land.

It was a long time before they managed to gasp the news: "Yeshua isn't in Jericho. Never . . . been there . . ."

Carpenter did not have the heart to tell them that the

presence of the blind and lame at the city gates was evidence of what they had nearly died to discover.

The rumor that *tsara'im* were roaming free outside the city swept up the highway. From that morning on and for many days, travelers along the road to Jericho would dread meeting the two Cabbage Sisters even more than robbers.

Like injured animals, the Minyan of Mak'ob retreated to the hilltop lair above Jericho to lick their wounds. The same Cabbage Sister who received a blow to her back had also been struck on the elbow by a club. Her arm was bound close to her body. An improvised sling about her neck relieved the weight and made the pain bearable.

Tenderly, awkwardly, with the mitten-shaped stumps that remained of his hands, Crusher sponged the face of the other Sister. He plucked shards of broken pottery from her cheeks. He dabbed away the mingled blood and tears but had no answer when she moaned, "Why? Why do they hate us so?"

"We don't belong here . . . on the Outside, I mean," one of the Torah students said firmly.

"Let's go home," another agreed. "Back to the Valley."

Murmurs of agreement circled the Torah scholars.

"No one hated us there."

"No one threw stones at us."

"Or called us names."

"To die as lepers?" Fisherman observed morosely. "Yeshua's already been to Mak'ob. He won't go back there."

"Maybe we're the only lepers left in Judea," Mikki ventured.

This observation made the Cabbage Sisters sob afresh.

"How did so much change since yesterday?" Carpenter wondered aloud. "Shimona—we all saw her, healed! The hope we had yesterday! The stories about Yeshua are true."

"And Shimona now lives in a cage smaller than Mak'ob," one of the students groused. "Alone and outcast. That was never true in the Valley."

A pall of desperate silence fell over the group with the setting sun. If being healed meant living alone for the rest of life, was it worth it?

"Giving up now means giving up for good," Shoemaker warned.

"Staying out means being hunted and pelted with stones like stray dogs," a voice out of the shadows argued.

"Did you ever see anything like it?" Mikki said.

"Not me," one of his comrades replied. "I grew up in Mak'ob."

"No," Mikki corrected. "I mean up there. Look at the sky."

Suspended in the west was a trail of pinpoints of light. It was as if the departing sun had ignited a string of candles in its descent. "Does anyone know their names?"

Carpenter screwed up his face and squinted. "That bright one there, the highest? That's The Lord of the Sabbath. Below him is The Adam, beside the New Moon. And what did Cantor say?" he mused aloud, trying to recall what he had heard on starry nights back in Mak'ob. "The very brightest one is Splendor and next to it, I think, The Righteous? I'm not sure. But the little orange one, low down, that's The Messenger."

"What does it mean when all the lights of the Holy Menorah are in the sky at the same time?" Shoemaker pondered.

"It means . . . something," Carpenter asserted.

"It means we try again," Crusher stated.

"How? Where?"

"My home used to be . . . Modein. Over in the center of the country. Still have family there. Yeshua is north, or so we've heard. Perhaps he'll come to Yerushalayim for Passover. Two weeks away, yes? This time instead of traipsing around after him, we intercept him, meet him head-on."

"And if he doesn't come or returns another way?" Fisherman said bleakly. "What if that message—" he waved toward the sparkling lights in the heavens—"isn't meant for such as us?"

"Better try once more than go back to Mak'ob . . . to die,"

Crusher replied softly. "Or should we just lie down and die right here?"

"We want . . ."

". . . to try once more," urged the Cabbage Sisters through stifled groans and gritted teeth.

"I honor your wounds," Shoemaker said to the pair. Then, raising his voice to encompass the whole minyan and the starry host: "I honor them. If they are willing to try once more, and Crusher agrees, who am I to say no?"

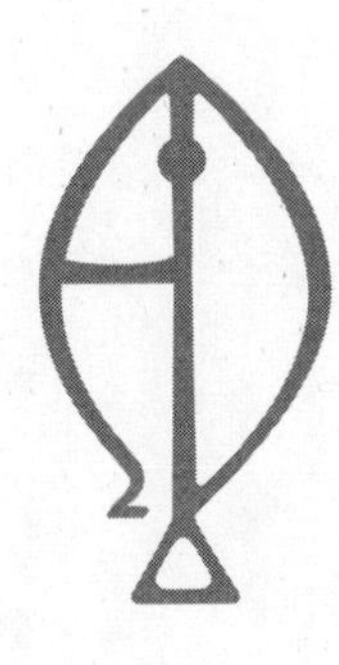

CRUSHER

And I said, "I see an almond branch." Then the LORD *said to me, "You have seen well, for I AM watching over My word to perform it."*

JEREMIAH 1:11-12

THE JOURNEY CONTINUES . . .

The minyan of lepers came to the graveyard of Modein in late afternoon. Crusher stood apart before a tomb covered with the dry stalks of creepers. The setting sun was a red ball tangled in a leafless oak. Black crows huddled together on the blasted branches.

Crusher said, "The oak trees always bloom late. It's the almonds that awaken early in these parts. Pink blossoms . . . a sea of pink, even though it's cold." He gestured toward the ridge above the desolate hollow. "Come see."

The ragged band struggled up the gentle incline after Crusher. The aroma of blooms scented the air for those who could still smell. Over his shoulder Crusher told them, "Lavender. She grows lavender in flower beds all round the cottage, dries it in the rafters, and sells it in the village."

Panting, they reached the overlook. They leaned together in a bunch like the crows.

"Ohhhhhh!" said the Cabbage Sisters in unison. They, of all the minyan, could most appreciate a well-kept garden and fields tended in geometric perfection. "So beautiful . . ."

". . . so beautiful!" One finished the awe of the other.

Lush fields stretched out beneath them. Grapevine trunks, thick as a man's leg, were just awakening after winter. New green tendrils waved from the long corridors of the vineyard. These climbed a terraced slope beneath an old deserted house on the hilltop.

Two grape arbors linked two whitewashed stone structures below in the swale. One larger cottage was surrounded by beds of lavender as Crusher had predicted. Lights gleamed from the windows, and the tantalizing aroma of cooking food made the empty bellies of the beggars complain.

"She's a good cook," Crusher said proudly. "Always . . .

always plenty." His voice caught as a woman, plump and healthy, stepped out of the front door.

The woman cupped her hands around her mouth and called, "Almost Shabbat! Hurry! Supper!"

Answering her call, a middle-aged man, tall and stooped a bit, emerged from an orchard of mature almond trees in full bloom. He was followed closely by an old dog and two young men who carried gardening tools over their shoulders. The man laughed. "Hurry, boys; your mother and sisters will not tolerate us being a minute late to Shabbat."

A young woman followed her mother out the door. "Wash up!"

"Blossom. Grown up." Crusher closed his eyes and moaned. He covered his face with his hands. "No . . . no, not a moment late," he whispered. "Wash up. Almost Shabbat."

The trees were lavender-hued in the fading light. Crusher turned away.

"Will they help us, Crusher?" Fisherman asked. "Of all of us, your family never forgot you. Cuttings from the grapevines of Mak'ob came from your people. The saplings of our almond trees. The lavender bunches that came to you in packages. They never forgot you, Crusher. Will they help us now?"

"Can they?" One Cabbage Sister clung to the other.

"We've come such a long way," sighed the Shoemaker, whose bloody right foot, bruised and travel-scarred, poked out from worn leather.

The Shoemaker's Son and the other Torah scholars studied Crusher with the suspicion of youth. "Why can't we just go down there? Knock on the door and ask?"

"Shabbat," Crusher managed to say. "I don't know the young ones." His eyes were no longer able to weep, but his throat constricted with emotion. "The man, the woman, beloved . . ." He paused. "They seem almost unchanged, and I am . . . so different. We will not, must not, come to their door in the dark. Not during Shabbat."

They followed Crusher back into the tombs. None of the graves were empty or open. They found partial shelter from the wind beneath a shallow outcropping.

The boys gathered dry brush and heaped it up as Carpenter struck the flint and sparked a fire.

"Strange, isn't it," said Fisherman as they stretched their stumps toward the warmth. "Our open wounds do not hurt. Only our empty bellies and our souls feel pain."

The last glimmer of sunlight melted away. Two stars gleamed above them, announcing that Shabbat had arrived.

Carpenter instructed the circle of downcast faces, "We have reason for thanks. We're all still alive. There's hope for us this Shabbat. Let us, this broken minyan of Israel's remnant, give thanks."

The Cabbage Sisters, with one voice, lifted their fingerless palms above the flames and made the baracha as if the burning dead branches of the graveyard were woven beeswax candles. Carpenter prayed over the last scraps of stale barley bread as though it were a golden loaf of fresh, braided challah. He broke the bread and passed it to each. Their hearts mourned as their shadows danced among the tombs.

All eyes turned to Crusher. He had led them to this place with words of hope. Perhaps the rumors were true. Yeshua at this very hour was, perhaps, somewhere near, making the blessing over the Shabbat meal, just as these outcasts had done.

Shoemaker's Son spoke for his companions: "Tell us, Crusher."

CHAPTER 14

A rowdy congregation of a half-dozen crows perched in the dead tree above the tombs, replacing the wailing of the paid mourners. Their feathers were as dark as the thoughts of the Widow and her two sons who remained behind after the small assembly of Modein villagers had gone.

Returning to the village where once the Jewish clan of Maccabee had defied the Greek oppressors, the voices of acquaintances faded away over the hill. For a moment there was sublime silence.

The crows suddenly shouted, "*Tawk! Tawk! Tawk!*" as the Khamseen wind began to keen in the east.

Obed, younger of the sons, looked past his elder brother, Jesse, for some signal from their mother. Her eyes were dry. The Widow inhaled deeply and then exhaled. She turned her back and, without a trace of sorrow, left the bones of her husband beneath the flock of crows.

Jesse, hands clasped before him, lingered a moment longer, staring at the stone sealing the mouth of the cave.

Obed followed after, grieving for what their life had been at the cruel hand of his father. What sorrow he felt was no different from what he would feel at seeing the funeral procession of a stranger. It was anguish over fleeting life—for himself, for his ultimate destiny, and for that of every living creature. His father's death proved that all men are mortal.

Obed had thought last night as his father was laid out on the bier that now he and his brother and his mother would draw close to one another.

Instead the Widow and Jesse the First Born Son had walked from the house to the vineyard and quarreled violently. It was the first time Obed had ever seen his mother displeased with the heir. Jesse had always been the light of her life and the sun around which their father's hopes had orbited.

Obed, as second son, had remained outside the circle of that light, like a hungry stray who longs to be called inside for a plate of food and a pat on the head. He did not resent his father and mother's adoration of Jesse. Obed was content to be second, to look on and love the trio of mother, father, and elder son at a distance.

Now that their father was gone, this rift between the Widow and the First Born was the one true grief Obed felt. The order of the universe had shattered. Obed had not been drawn near by the two, and now they were separated by a wide gulf of unexplained anger.

It was noon, but the sky was as dark as if the sun had never risen over the eastern hills. The low, scudding clouds seemed to catch on the buildings of the village on the ridge. Gloom surrounded their modest stone dwelling. The Widow, wordless, left her sons and forged ahead up the stone path to the house.

There would be food provided by neighbors, but this was a poor farm and there was work yet to be done. Life went on as usual, even as their nonmourning mother removed her shoes and sat shiva for a man she would not miss.

The brothers exchanged a glance. Obed understood without being told that he would take over his father's chores. A half-dozen goats had been milked by a neighbor but had not been brought in from grazing the enclosed pasture. Obed took up the staff where his father had left it against the wall moments before he collapsed and died.

Long strides gobbled the distance. His fingers untied the knot his father's fingers had tied.

Obed glanced over his shoulder at his brother, hoping they could speak about the quarrel. Jesse impatiently forked fodder for the donkey and spread grain for the pen of chickens. His face seemed to be replaying the anger of the night before. Lips moved silently, speaking again to the Widow. Perhaps Jesse was, in retrospect, adding reason to their argument. He finished his work quickly, then sat down hard on the fence to wait for Obed. Perhaps he did not want to face his mother alone.

The two brothers were as unlike as two brothers could be. The differences between them made the people of the village comment, "Jesse favors his father" and "Obed doesn't look like either side."

Jesse, at age twenty-four, was just under five feet ten inches, well muscled and hot-tempered. His black hair was curly, his beard thick. He was well educated and might have been apprenticed in the Roman countinghouse if his mother had not objected.

Obed was twenty-one, thin as his staff, fair-haired, and two inches taller than his brother. He was slow and awkward, gangly in manner and speech, and had no formal education. He was good with the animals. Got on better with the goats than with people, his father had often said. So Obed had been kept home to work the farm.

Jesse had traveled with his father on journeys as far away as Caesarea Maritima and returned full of stories about ships and the waters of the Great Sea. Obed had never been more than ten miles from home and had no desire to go farther.

The two brothers met at the head of the path and walked slowly toward the house. Obed chose his words carefully, "Jesse, you and Mother, last night . . ."

Jesse suddenly grasped Obed's arm. "Listen, Obed. I need your help with this! I'm leaving this place for good."

So this had been the source of the quarrel.

"Jesse! But you are the First Born. Half . . . between you and Mother. The land is . . ."

"I don't care. I spoke with Shem about the lower vineyard. He'll buy it. Mother can keep the rest."

The rest was rocky, inhospitable soil. "Selling the vineyard?"

"It's mine," Jesse said defensively.

"But . . . the farm."

"You stay with Mother and work her half. When she dies, you can have it. I don't care."

What could Obed say to keep Jesse from leaving? The farm would be desolate if he went away. In the rocky soil of his mother's heart, Jesse was the one budding tree. And for Obed, too, there was no one he loved so much as his brother.

He followed Jesse into the house. Food that had been prepared by friends and relatives covered the table. Too much for only three.

What would life be when there were only two?

The brothers filled their plates as the Widow glared at Jesse. He did not look at her. Obed watched them both furtively as Jesse shoveled his meal into his mouth, leaving no room for words.

The Widow sent the message of her disapproval to Jesse through Obed. "Obed, when you have eaten, I need you to sit beside me. Your older brother has something cruel to say."

Jesse barely looked up. He spoke around a slice of lamb. "I told him. Obed understands. He does not disagree with me."

The Widow seethed, glaring at Obed as though he had betrayed her. "So Obed agrees. Obed will farm this land on his own. Yesterday there were three to work the land. Now there are two. When you leave, there will be one. You will sell your father's vineyard. Those vines are like his children. And you will sell them."

Jesse tossed his empty plate onto the table. "You can hire a man to help."

"Does Obed agree to this also? There won't be enough money to hire a man. Not with the vineyard gone. There will barely be enough for us to scratch out a living."

Obed's food stuck in his throat. Both stared at him, expecting him to choose sides. He wanted to beg Jesse not to go, not to leave him alone with her coldness.

Jesse said, "Obed knows I have always hated the farm. I am no farmer. I have opportunities. I stayed because I was afraid of Father. Well, he's gone now, and I am afraid of staying here."

She hissed the words like a cornered cat: "You can't sell your share without my permission. I will not allow it. Until I die, your share is still under my control!" She drew herself up. "Well, Jesse. What do you say now?"

Jesse shouted, "You can't keep me here!"

She turned to Obed. "Obed, can you tend the vineyard? I will not permit your brother to sell it."

Obed shook his head. "It was always . . . Jesse's vineyard."

She pronounced each word distinctly. "I . . . will . . . not . . . permit . . ."

Jesse leapt to his feet and snapped up the metal box where money and receipts were kept. He emptied the contents onto the table.

Separating scraps of parchment from silver coins, he divided the money into three heaps. "My third . . . I take it in payment for the vineyard." He fumbled for the quill and ink and scribbled a note.

Received: Full payment for vineyard from Abigail, widow of Asher.
Signed: Jesse ben Asher.

He flung the paper at her. "Keep the land. Keep it, then!"

She grabbed the paper and threw it into the fire, then ran up the steps to the room on the roof.

Jesse clenched and unclenched his fists. "You see, Obed, I can't stay here."

Obed was pale. He wanted to beg Jesse to take him along. But then who would remain to take care of the Widow? Obed could not leave.

Jesse gathered his few belongings. Obed watched as his brother looked one last time around the room that had been his home . . . his prison.

Obed followed him out the door and down the path to the road.

"Will I see you again?" Obed fought back tears.

"Maybe. Maybe I'll come back someday. When I'm rich." He enfolded Obed in his strong arms. "Little brother. You were always the best. The most dependable. They just never . . . we never . . . appreciated you."

Obed wiped a tear from his cheek. "Jesse, I will . . . miss you."

Jesse pumped his hand. "You won't. You won't miss me. I made your life miserable. Marry that girl Father had his eye on for me—Livia—to keep you company. You have the vineyard. You're well enough off to marry." He looked past Obed at the house and added bitterly, "Someone new for her to order around."

Jesse refused to let Obed advance with him any farther.

Unable to speak, long arms limp at his sides, Obed stood in the center of the highway and watched his brother's broad back until he vanished from sight.

CHAPTER 15

The north winter wind howled down on the farm. Obed milked the last of the goats in the lean-to. "Three months," he said to the nanny named Jezebel, who was his favorite among the small flock. "And no letter from Jesse." He stripped the teats carefully. The goat turned as if to appraise Obed's conversation. "And I am still unmarried. But perhaps Jesse was right. With a wife I would not be so lonely."

A dusting of snow covered the land. Obed raised his gaze to the hillsides. For a moment he felt a rare flush of happiness. Jesse was done with the farm. Obed had begun to view the farm with a hopeful eye. What if he planted almond trees where the pasture was? Almond trees were early bloomers. The pink blossoms were good luck, it was said—in a spiritual sense, that is. The Rod of Aaron that budded and blossomed was almond wood. The Hebrew word for *almond* sounded like "watching." And so an almond tree announced that God was watching.

Yet Obed's father had never allowed an orchard to be planted. "Trees. They take up too much land." A man of naturally dark disposition, Obed's father had planted vegetables with curses and harvested cabbages with oaths. The vineyard had been planted generations ago, or Obed's father would never have kept it. Perhaps pink almond blossoms and shade in the searing summer would not have been to his liking. But Obed was the master now . . . almost. So now, almond trees! Or at least there would be if the Widow would allow it.

Obed could pasture the goats on the higher, rocky ground. Maybe even enlarge the flock if his mother would permit him to have a sheep-dog. Obed and Jesse had never owned a dog, though the boys had watched and admired the dogs of shepherds as they moved flocks slowly down the highway south to Jerusalem.

The Widow's express reason for refusing her sons a dog had been that she did not want a dirty animal in the house. Obed had always known the truth, however. She simply did not want to share the affection of her First Born with any other living creature. What if Jesse had loved the dog deeply? Boys often deeply loved their pets more than their mothers. In that case, something would have been stolen from her, and that she would never permit.

As a child, Obed had followed on Jesse's heels like an adoring stray. He fetched and carried and absorbed without protest his brother's flares of temper. Obed had adored Jesse unquestioningly.

Perhaps that had been enough affection for the First Born.

Obed finished the milking. He stroked Jezebel's head.

She nipped at his sleeve.

"All right," Obed said. "I will ask Mother about the almond orchard first. And later about the dog."

The wind tore at his clothes as he carried the milk bucket into the house. The Widow jabbed at the fire with a stick.

"Shalom, Mother!"

She glared at him in disappointment. He was not Jesse, after all. *Jab. Jab. Jab.* "It's almost Shabbat. I was hoping . . . well, wash up. You're late."

"Mother, I was thinking . . ."

"I was thinking," she said, not hearing him. *Jab. Jab.*

"Yes."

"Jesse will be home any day now." She held the poker aloft like a finger making a declaration of certainty.

"Mother . . ." He stopped himself from arguing with her.

"This is the first time Jesse has stayed away without sending word. Working hard, no doubt. Ambitious. Smart boy. I spoke with the rabbi and the judge today. They both said when Jesse has something to report, he will write us."

Obed nodded. "Yes. No doubt. He is busy at business."

She stared at him. "You are not listening to me. Do you care that your brother is not here?"

What could he say? He missed his brother with an ache like death. But Jesse was not returning. How could Obed convince the Widow that Jesse was not coming back? And if he did return, he would not stay. "Jesse is working hard, no doubt."

"Yes, that's what I am saying. Rabbi and Judge agree. They also agreed that you are old enough. You are the eldest son until Jesse comes home."

"I ask myself what Jesse would do every day. Mother, what shall we plant?"

"You need to take over the responsibility. For everything. I married your father, and he managed everything in the fields. I have no knowledge of farming. The vines. The fields. It all depends on you until Jesse comes home. The weight is too heavy on my shoulders. They agree. The judge drew up the papers. I have signed this. You are responsible now for everything."

Obed's long arms fell to his sides. He resisted the temptation to smile. "I was thinking . . . almond trees?"

"Do you hear me?"

He nodded dumbly.

She snapped, "I said I can't think about these things. Can't decide. You'll have to take responsibility. You're responsible. It's legal."

"Enlarge the flock . . . sheepdog . . ."

She raised her hands in frustration. "You drive me mad! I don't care."

Turning on her heels, she stormed out of his presence, retreating to her upper room.

Obed grinned at the empty steps and listened to the angry clack of her shoes on the floor above him. "Almond trees. A dog. And a wife, Mother. Yes. And I'll also be needing a wife."

Obed had first noticed the young woman the year before his father's death as she and a gaggle of cousins giggled and jostled through the open market of the village. Some called their laughter brazen, but Obed said they were young girls, and anyway, the day was beautiful enough to cause happiness.

Her father was Andrew the Wool Carder. She was small and bright. Her hair was thick and brown. Eyes were an amber-brown color, clear and deep, and always seemed amused by something. Her name was Bette, which likened her to a gentle ewe lamb. Obed smiled at her as she passed, and she blushed and smiled back. The blush was proof enough to him that she was not brazen, only happy.

Negotiations with her father and a matchmaker hired by Obed's father had begun. All had come to an abrupt end at the sudden death of Father. Obed had seen Bette from the corner of his eye at the funeral. She wiped tears from her cheeks.

He asked the Matchmaker to begin negotiations with her father again. "It is too soon," the Matchmaker scolded. "And your brother, the First Born, the heir, deserting your mother. Poor thing. People will talk."

"But I am lonely," explained Obed.

"What? With your poor mother to care for? Poor thing. Poor widow. It is too soon for her to lose a son to a wedding. Bad luck now, a wedding is, so soon, I tell you. A disgrace."

"When?" Obed pressed him.

"Six months."

Obed sighed, deeply disappointed. "Well then. This turns my plans around. I will have to get a dog first."

The Matchmaker allowed that a new dog was a more proper transfer of affection for a young man whose father had suddenly departed for Abraham's bosom.

Obed did not tell the fellow that his father had probably headed directly opposite from Abraham's bosom. And if, per chance, he had accidentally arrived in that place of heavenly rest, Father Abraham would now have a terrible case of heartburn and spit him out.

"Yes. A dog. I will need a dog when I enlarge my flock," Obed told the Matchmaker. "And I am going to plant an almond orchard as well. The judge has put me in charge to save my mother from bearing the responsibility. So tell Bette's father that, will you? Tell him I must wait out of respect—respect for my kind father who gazes down at me from . . . I hope . . . Father Avraham's bosom. But ask him not to give Bette's hand to anyone else. Tell him, please, that I am hard at work improving my position in life. And ask him, please, if with his connections with wool growers and such, does he know where I can purchase the best sheepdog? One that would be good with sheep and also with future children. For the raising of a family."

And so the word was passed on to the entire village and also to the wool carder that Obed had big plans.

Bette's father promised the Matchmaker he would not seal any other marriage bargains for his daughter. This was, in fact, like sealing the deal for Bette with Obed.

On top of all that, Bette's father, who did indeed have connections with shepherds, sent Obed the name of a shepherd who raised only the finest sheepdogs in the land.

"A dog!" the Widow cried when she heard the news.

"I told you, and you agreed that I must do what must be done."

"But a dog!"

Obed was firm. He knew well he had told her and she had agreed. He could not let her disrupt his plans now. "The money has been sent. The bargain is struck, the contract signed. I am going south to Beth-lehem to fetch him back."

"Money! A dog! Beth-lehem!" The Widow almost swooned. She groped for a chair and sat down hard. She wagged her head in misery. "One son leaves me on the day of his father's funeral. And not a word! Now this! My other son takes to the highway, where there are bandits and revolution and Romans. All to fetch back a dog."

"I will return with him, Mother."

"I won't come down from my room if such a beast is in this house. I will use the outside staircase. You will not see my face."

"We discussed it. I must have a sheepdog to help me with the flock."

She crossed her arms. "So. You are set on this. Then who will cook your meals?"

"I will do my best. You do what you must. I am sorry that you have changed your mind about the dog after it is too late."

The Widow thumped her chest. "That I have lived to see this. It may kill me. The affection of my son transferred to an animal. Perhaps you will not return. It would be justice."

"I will return. I must. Soon I intend to plant an almond orchard. As we discussed."

"An almond orchard! What! What? Your father is spinning in his grave."

Obed noted this was more emotion than she had displayed when her husband had dropped dead and turned blue before her eyes.

Perversely, he was enjoying himself. "And after I get the dog and plant the orchard, I intend to marry. A woman."

The Widow shrieked and threw herself back as if she had been struck. "Married? Married! Hear his words. Oh, angels weep. Weep. Ingrate! Do you hear my son speaking to me like this? Angels! He would bring a strange woman into my house? Replace his mother with a wife!"

"It is the way it is done. For the propagation of the race and the survival of mankind. And besides, Jesse suggested it. 'Marry,' he said to me, before he fled down the road to seek happiness. Yes! And probably he has taken his own advice and has a wife of his own."

She wailed, "Oh, my blessed Jesse! My son, my son! Where are you? Return to your brokenhearted mother. Obed will turn me out in the streets!"

A smile curled Obed's mouth. "No, Mother. You may stay. We won't come up to your room. You may live up there, like Father, looking down on us from Avraham's bosom. And we'll live down here. With the dog."

CHAPTER 16

The foundation of an ancient dwelling remained beside the vineyard. The story was that a vinedresser had lived here two hundred years ago. An earthquake had collapsed the house, and it had never been rebuilt. Part of one stone wall remained standing amid a heap of rubble.

It was a start.

Obed stepped through the broken portal, where some unnamed descendant of Abraham had once thrived. He stood before the window set in the remaining wall. It looked out on acres of the oldest vines in the territory. Why did the house remain broken while the gnarled vineyard remained alive and vibrant?

Jesse had frequently told him the only way he could stay sane was if he built himself a house apart. Obed ran his fingers through his hair. Would this be far enough? apart enough?

Sighing, Obed kicked at the heap and considered how long it would take to resurrect the little dwelling. He paced the foundation. Two rooms. A cottage. Small compared to the wool carder's house where Bette had grown up. Would she be content?

But what was it the men in the public house had whispered when

Obed's father passed by? *"No palace is wide enough for two women. No palace has enough rooms for one man and a shrew."*

Such Solomon-like wisdom seemed to especially fit his situation.

Jesse had left because of the Widow.

An odd thought rattled Obed's brain. He wondered what his father was like before marrying Obed's mother. Had he ever laughed? Did he ever speak without cursing? And was collapsing at her feet during an argument and dying before her scornful eyes the only way he could have the last word?

"Ah, Father. I am sorry," Obed whispered. "I hope you have found a quiet corner in Avraham's bosom."

Obed glanced over his shoulder at the dwelling on the hill where the Widow reigned. The room on the roof where she brooded was not far enough, not high enough. Jesse had known that. Better to give up everything and flee to a far country than become an actor in the Widow's version of a Greek tragedy. Oedipus had rightly run away.

Obed missed Jesse, but he could forgive him for going.

Now Obed had inherited the question: How to protect a wife from a mother?

"I will build a fortress for Bette. Stone by stone," Obed said aloud.

He stooped to pat a block covered by weeds. This house must be rebuilt before he could bring Bette to share his life.

Obed's route took him south to Emmaus, where the track from Modein met up with the main road to Jerusalem. As he tramped through that village without stopping, Obed reflected how he had recently passed some important milestones. He chuckled at his own joke. He had never before in his life been farther from home than Emmaus.

A solid Roman highway now lay underfoot: paved, maintained, channeling runoff like a polished tabletop. If Obed had turned west instead of east, he would reach the seaport of Joppa in a few hours. From Joppa another road ran both up to Caesarea Maritima and down to Azotus and beyond. From Joppa one could also take to the highways of the Great Sea—and then who knew what exotic destinations lay within reach?

Obed shook his head. Only in imagination would he be going to Joppa, let alone over the sea. Jesse might launch his life on such a voyage, but not his younger brother.

Obed sighed, but not with discontent. This trip to Beth-lehem would end with a dog of his own. An almond orchard would follow, and soon, a wife.

It was enough.

On the trail from Modein, Obed had passed a solitary trader plying a willow switch on the backs of a trio of heavily laden donkeys. When Obed bid him good day, the merchant barely interrupted his cursing of the mud, the weather, the greedy priests, and his recalcitrant beasts to nod in reply.

In marked contrast the highway was crowded with travelers. Pilgrims headed for the Feast of Dedication sailed uphill in a laughing, chatting flotilla of billowing robes. The wind from the sea at their backs and the sun in their faces, they were a cheerful lot, despite the chill. Though those returning from Jerusalem faced the bite of the breeze, they recognized journey's end by the smell of the ocean.

A jovial, red-bearded, red-faced wine merchant from Apollonia on the Plain accosted Obed. "Alone?" he boomed. "Not on your life. Join us! Daughters never been to Yerushalayim. Made enough money on last year's vintage to take them all. Promised I would, and here we go."

Three auburn-haired girls, from twelve down to six, ranged beside their boisterous father and resigned-looking mother. The ruddy flock surrounded Obed and pestered him with questions: Why was he alone? Where would he stay in Jerusalem? Wasn't it exciting to be going to the Holy City?

"Not going to Yerushalayim," Obed replied when the chatter momentarily paused. "Business in Beth-lehem."

"Yerushalayim and Beth-lehem! So near!" the protests erupted. "Miss the festival? the lights? Go right by it almost anyway."

The wine trader studied Obed as if sizing him up. "You don't look old enough to be so world-weary," he ventured.

"Maybe he's a bandit," the twelve-year-old ventured. "Or a dangerous rebel with a price on his head." Her eyes gleamed with excitement.

"Hush, child," the mother said sharply. "A man's reasons are his own business."

"Quite right," the father agreed. "And none of ours."

"Nothing so interesting," Obed corrected quickly but with a smile. "I have business waiting for me back in Modein, so this is just a quick trip and then I must hurry back home."

The mother looked relieved, the daughters disappointed.

"Modein," remarked the father to his daughters. "The very place where the first Maccabee hacked the false priest to pieces and achieved the miracle we celebrate this season."

From that point on in the journey it was not necessary for Obed to contribute anything. The merchant kept up a running stream of anecdotes about the Maccabees, mixed with reminiscences and jokes at which his family laughed, groaned, or exclaimed as required. None of it was consequential, nor was the account of the Maccabee rebellion correct in the details recounted, but the wide-eyed devotion of the daughters toward their ebullient sire was memorable.

In Obed's mind all that mattered was that it was pleasant. They were a family, and they were enjoying life together. The merchant was the master of his own house and surrounded by gullible and adoring children.

It was a novel thought. For many miles Obed's smile remained fixed.

All too soon the highway intersected the trail that bypassed Jerusalem and offered a shorter route to Beth-lehem. In a series of switchbacks the byroad climbed out of the canyon. At each eastward turn of the ascent Obed watched as the red heads bobbed and dwindled in the distance.

Jerusalem was just ahead there. The family from Apollonia would reach it before nightfall.

Perhaps Obed's brother, Jesse, was in the great City of David, making his fortune, making a name for himself. Perhaps Obed could find him there and join him in a great adventure. He shook off the thought and trudged upward.

Emerging onto a ridge where the wind howled in earnest, Obed stopped at the sight that confronted him there: Flanking a Roman mile marker half buried in mud was a pair of crosses. The features and bodies of their occupants were frozen in agony. They were young men, not much older than Obed . . . or Jesse.

The dead man on the right bore some resemblance to his brother. Obed's eyes widened. Could it be? Was it?

He mentally measured the length of the tortured body that hung on the cross like a tree blasted by lightning.

Tall, but not so tall as Jesse . . . hardly human at all. No, he decided. The vision was a trick his mind played on him from months of worry and wondering about his brother.

Obed, as awkward in prayer as he was in conversation, breathed a request to heaven for the safety of the trader and his family . . . and for Jesse, wherever he was.

He turned away. "I have come too far—too far from Modein," he muttered, pressing on.

The streets of Beth-lehem were crowded with pilgrims who had come for the holiday. White houses clung to the hills like boulders embedded in the rocky soil. The stink of livestock wafted on the cold air.

Obed's eager gaze was drawn to the handsome dogs that followed close at the heels of their masters.

At the well Obed plucked the parchment fragment from his leather bag and presented it to a young man flanked by two canines.

The fellow read the letters, then exclaimed, "Aye. It's Zadok you're lookin' for, is it?" He jerked his thumb toward a tidy house on the lower slope. "Chief Shepherd. Business with 'im?"

"I've bought a pup." Obed stretched his hand out to pet one of the lad's canines and was met with a snarl.

"Don't want to do that," the young man warned, signaling his beast to back off. "She don't know you. Protective. See? Not a pet."

"Is this . . . one of his?"

"Zadok's? Nay. But they're fine. Fine. Naught'll get past 'em."

Obed thanked him, backed up a bit before he turned, and set out down the narrow path to Zadok's house. Beyond the village a field full of grazing sheep stretched out. Vast. Here and there tendrils of smoke rose from fires where shepherds gathered. Canine sentinels kept watch at intervals around the perimeter of the pasture.

Obed was met with the clamor of angry barks as he approached the house of the Chief Shepherd.

A woman gathering wash from the line studied him a moment, and with a sharp whistle, the clamor fell silent.

Obed stayed outside the stone fence. He called, "I am Obed of Modein. Come for a pup."

The woman, her arms full of linens, disappeared into the house. Moments later, an imposing figure emerged.

The man who introduced himself as Zadok, the Chief Shepherd, was the single most intimidating form Obed had ever confronted. White-haired and bearded, he had a patch over one eye. From beneath the patch ran a scar like a ravine. It seemed to have been inflicted by someone or something determined to cleave the shepherd's head in two.

Zadok growled, "You've come early. Didn't expect you 'til next week."

"Planting next week. Almond trees."

The shepherd was unimpressed. "Plantin'." He snorted. "What'll y' be needin' a fine sheepdog for?"

"Goats."

Zadok's lip curled in a scowl. He did not give Obed opportunity to reply. Stepping aside, he signaled his animals that Obed was a friend. "Come on, then. The wife's brewin' tea."

Obed was conscious of the eyes of a half-dozen grown dogs upon him as he followed the master inside. The crook of Zadok's finger would have set them upon him.

Bundles of dried lavender hung from the beams above their heads and covered the strong odor of the flocks.

Obed stared at the stone floor of the cottage and swallowed hard for the third time. He felt the shepherd's stare boring into him.

"Modein, y' say?" Zadok grilled him. "Goats, y' say?"

Obed's head bobbed like a nervous schoolboy confronted with being a miserable failure at his lessons.

"Oh, Zadok, leave the poor lad alone," the plump, pleasant-faced housewife urged. "You haven't even asked him to sit down. He paid in advance, and he's come all this way. Be polite."

Harrumphing, Zadok indicated a wooden bench and gestured for Obed to sit. "Payment's not so important as character, woman. Payment can be returned." Then to Obed he explained, "My wife, Rachel. Tender-hearted, eh? But character. Hard t' judge on short notice. A good dog can tell the worth of a man—" he snapped his fingers—"like that."

Obed thought about replying that he had come to buy a puppy, not to make a marriage proposal, but instead noted, "I am betrothed to the daughter of a wool carder, Andrew of Modein. He said you . . . he gave me your name." Obed offered the slip of paper from Andrew as proof.

"There, you see, Zadok?" Rachel offered. "Don't let him scare you, young man. He's like this every litter."

"And how else should I be?" Zadok growled. Then, almost grudgingly, he softened. "Andrew of Modein. Good man. Daughter likely make a good match for you. Pretty country around Modein, too. But jackals, caracals too, sneak out of the canyons at night, eh? Wild, demony-lookin' creatures, those caracals. I knew a fellow who raised an orphan caracal from a kitten. Fine pet—'til it ate the chickens. Need a good dog about, in Modein."

While Zadok pondered, rubbing his beard, Rachel prepared the brew.

She must have been a pretty thing as a young woman, but life had engraved some unnamed sorrow into her face. Warm brown eyes were pools of resignation.

Zadok slapped his thigh as if he'd reached a decision. "All right. Got just the one for you."

"When can I see them? Are they far?"

Zadok frowned as if the question was preposterous. "Right now, of course," and he whistled a sharp note.

The depths of an alcove beside the fireplace stirred into motion and a pile of puppies untangled themselves and emerged into the lamplight. Wooly, squarely built, colored as though mingling smoke and ashes and charcoal, five sheepdog pups with stumps for tails and eyes focused only on Zadok trotted out to sit obediently in a row.

Zadok pointed to the male second from the end. He was not the biggest but had a way of holding his head on one side as if listening attentively.

"Go on, call him," Zadok urged.

"I . . . what? I don't even know his name."

"Doesn't have one yet," Zadok returned. "Do this: Make sure he sees you."

Obed focused his gaze on the speckled face of the puppy. He smiled as the ears pricked up and the head tilted in attention.

Zadok coached, "There, that's got it. Now point t' the floor by your feet. The crook of your finger. 'Tis enough."

Obed complied, then was amazed to find that the pup not only immediately came forward but turned about and sat beside Obed's left foot, just where he directed.

Zadok nodded. "You'll do. Just so y' remember," he added, raising an emphatic hand, "he's your partner, eh? Not your slave. He works 'cause he respects you. No man'll get by him t' harm your wife . . . your children. With his last breath he'll protect what's dear t' you. See y' treat him well and respect him in return."

"He'll have a fine home. Children to watch over, I hope, one day."

Zadok plucked the puppy up by the scruff and dropped him in Obed's arms. "Well. He's a good'un. He's yours now." One final kneading of the puppy's ears. "Be good, son. Make me proud."

Obed smiled at Rachel and said cheerfully, "Like children, eh?"

Rachel nodded in reply, but not without giving Obed a glimpse of even deeper sadness glistening at the corners of her eyes.

CHAPTER 17

The pup waited patiently just at the edge of the firelight while Obed toasted a scrap of unleavened bread on a stick. Supper would be a frugal affair tonight, camped out here in the wilds. Unwilling to sleep near the crosses still laden with their horrifying burdens, Obed had pressed on 'til hunger and aching muscles forced him to camp in a canyon off the road.

The sheepdog watched him with bright, inquisitive eyes. When the time had come to leave brothers and sisters behind in Beth-lehem, the animal had accepted Zadok's final command and followed his new master with only a single backward look.

Obed placed a bit of dried fish and a scrap of bread on a flat rock but did not yet invite the beast to eat. In this, Obed thought, he was proving himself to be as obedient to Zadok's instructions as the dog.

At last he said, "Now" and pointed at the food.

The puppy walked into the light with great dignity, sniffed, and began to eat. He showed much more decorum than Obed, who tore off a chunk of bread and stuffed it in his mouth.

It was hard to chew around the grin on his face. "You make me happy," he said to the dog. "Just watching you makes me feel . . .

happiness." Obed had never owned a pet. If he had dared to express interest in a particular kid or lamb, Father and Mother had been quick to point out the ultimate fate of all livestock, calling him weak and womanly.

"You are truly an amazing pup," Obed continued. "A Solomon. Or a Daniel. And I can't go on calling you 'pup.' So what is your name? Remember!" He held a slim finger aloft in conscious imitation of Zadok's pronouncements. "It's not enough for you to be wise. You must also be brave—fearless even. A great warrior."

The puppy cocked his head to the side and listened.

"Samson, then? Goliath?"

A skirl of wind released a smatter of ice crystals from the overhanging brush, scattering them down the back of Obed's neck. Hastily he threw more branches on the fire, but the wood was damp and the blaze sputtered. Pulling the hood of his robe up over his head, Obed snuggled down into the coils of a blanket.

"Barak? Nimrod?"

The puppy curled himself beside the flickering embers but kept his gaze fixed on Obed. With the next gust of wind a shiver started at the puppy's tail and worked its way out his shoulders.

Obed bit his lip, trying to maintain his resolve. Quickly abandoning the pretense, he lifted a corner of the blanket and offered, "Come on, then."

As the puppy snuggled close to his chest Obed said with contentment, "I won't tell Zadok if you won't. There's no reason to steal his *samek*, his joyfulness. Is there . . . Samek?"

And both fell asleep.

Years of goats inhabiting the pasture had left a rich layer of manure in the soil. Perfect for nourishing an orchard of almond saplings, Obed thought, as he labored to prepare the land.

The new goats and their kids fared well on the grass and weeds of the rocky slope above the pasture. The pup proved to be better at his work than any human hireling. Though he walked far around the Widow's snarl and stony looks when she appeared, the pup had no fear of goat horns or hooves. Work was a game. He lay on a boulder, keeping the flock in their place as Obed dug the holes for the orchard in the rich soil of the pasture.

The saplings arrived on an oxcart from the Galil. They had been many days on their journey, and it was important to set them quickly, lest the dream of an orchard be stillborn.

The servant sent to deliver and help plant thirty-six trees was an old man, a Jew from the Decapolis. His name was Charuz. He knew well the birthing of almond orchards. It was said his hand was upon every almond tree that bloomed in Eretz-Israel.

"Almond trees. See? Their little buds already know spring is coming, eh?" Charuz flicked a branch with his cracked, dirt-caked nail. "Lovely trees, they are. They'll give you pink blossoms within a fortnight if you love them. If they do not bloom, then all is lost. Alas!"

"What does that mean?" Obed caressed a branch that looked perfectly barren and dead to him. The thirty-six saplings had cost him one-third of a year's income. He could not afford dead sticks planted in neat rows.

"Listen!" Charuz cocked his head and leaned down close to the cloth-wrapped root balls. He clacked his toothless gums rapidly in a sound like kisses. "Roots are stirring even now as we speak. Awake. They smell the soil of home, and if they do not soon find earth, they will die of longing. Love them, boy, and in seven years they'll support you and your wife and children." He gazed around Obed's arm to where the Widow perched like a black-winged crow observing the delivery. "Is that your wife?"

"My mother."

"Ah. Old, eh? My eyes. Not so good anymore. So. Where is your wife?"

"I am going to be married soon."

"Good. It will take two to love the almond grove. Two with vision to see the future. You plant trees for your children, boy. Always. An orchard is for a man with vision and a future and a hope." He swung the first tree onto his shoulder and marched toward the first hole. "Goats, I see. On the hill. Good. Manure."

Obed was instructed to dig the holes bigger, wider, deeper. Then Charuz expertly set the trees, filled in the soil, and tamped it down with his broad, spadelike foot.

All the while the Widow observed their work without offering a drink of water or a bite to eat. At the third row of saplings Charuz lifted his gaze. "She does not approve, your mother?"

"She prefers goats in the pasture. Keeping down the weeds. Or vegetables."

"A field of vegetables is planted by frightened women—women worried about what they will eat tomorrow. Maybe she is jealous that she will not live as long as the trees. And she will not. They will live long after we are gone. But a good cabbage is in the kettle for today, eh? This is perhaps how she thinks." He tramped the loose earth around the base of the sapling.

"Yes. Cabbages." Obed did not look at her.

"She will enjoy the pink blossoms when they open two weeks hence." Charuz placed the next tree in its new home.

Obed did not reply. The Widow had no appreciation of blossoms, pink or otherwise. He blurted, "My betrothed—now there is a girl who loves blossoms."

"That's all you need. It takes two to raise these little ones up. You'll have to mind the cold. Protect them. Build a smoke fire in the freezes. Water them in the dry season. A few generations of goat dung will feed them well enough."

The two men worked in silence, punctuated by the pronouncement of blessing as each sapling was in place.

What a contrast this cheerful, shared labor seemed to the curses of Obed's toiling father.

Obed felt a rush of pride when all the straight rows were complete. "So. It's done." He visualized tall, strong nut trees spreading their limbs and cooling the sun-baked pasture.

Charuz raised his arms. "*Shaqed* and *shaqad.* These almond trees—*shaqed*—say to you now, the Almighty never sleeps or slumbers. He is watching over your life. *Shaqad.*"

Obed felt a glow of warmth at the pronouncement of the old man. "I will take care of them."

The Widow remained on her parapet, frozen and glowering down like a statue.

Obed counted out the coins into the open palm of Charuz, who recited yet another blessing. Only when the old man led the empty oxcart off, down the road, did the Widow turn on her heel and vanish into her room.

That night the Widow called down from the top of the steps, "Well, now you've done it. The waste. The waste!"

Obed ladled stew into a bowl and placed it under the pup's grateful nose. The dog lapped up his reward. "I've made some supper. Would you like some, Mother?"

She did not reply to his offer. "A laughingstock! Obed's great almond orchard. Rows of thirty-six dead sticks in the ground. Fit to pull out and play fetch with that mongrel dog of yours. You've wasted our money. Wasted. If your father was here . . ."

Obed sat down with his supper and tried to recapture the joy and pride he had felt this afternoon. "They're only saplings. It will take time."

"If he was only here . . . your father would pull one of those dead things out of the ground and beat you with it. Beat you until you could not stand."

The pup whined at the sound of her unhappy words and slunk off under the table. Obed knew she was right. He thought, *Father never could see past the profit of weeds digesting in the belly of a goat.* But he did not answer her.

She shrilled, "Do you hear me? Are you listening? If your brother was only here."

Obed snapped, "Jesse's not coming back . . . not ever."

"Jesse will come home to me," she cried. "And then we'll see. . . . We'll see." Then he heard her mumble, "I should set a torch to your folly tonight!"

That night Obed and the pup slept in the lean-to beside the gate to protect the orchard. The madness of the Widow would pass, he thought, when the pink blossoms of the almond trees bloomed.

18 CHAPTER

The blooms of the almond orchard broke open just at the right moment: two weeks to the day after they were planted. Just as old Charuz had predicted, it was proof that new life existed in the old earth.

The Widow came to the gate and scorned the beauty of the pink flowers. "Weeds bloom beneath the feet of pigs, do they not?" Casting her glance to the one-room stone shelter Obed had constructed beside the vineyard, she said, "So. Your dog. Your orchard. But do not think you will ever bring that woman into my house."

That very morning Obed knocked on the door of the Matchmaker and said he would wait no longer.

The next day the marriage *ketubah* between Obed and Bette, daughter of the wool carder, was signed at the synagogue in the presence of the rabbi and two witnesses.

"A shame your father could not be here," the rabbi said to Obed.

Obed only tucked his chin and did not reply. This gesture was taken as emotion by those gathered in the room.

"And your mother?" asked Andrew, father of the bride. "She is well, your mother? She will welcome a daughter-in-law?"

There were rumors that the Widow was still mourning the death of her husband and the desertion of her First Born. Obed replied truthfully, "These last few months I have been building a small house beside the vineyard where Bette and I will live apart for a time. It is almost ready."

The rabbi clapped his hands together. "And the Lord said, *It is not good for man to live alone.*[23] So. When shall the wedding take place?"

Obed did not mention that the Widow had vowed she would not attend a wedding and would never welcome Obed's new bride into her home. "Worse than the dog," the Widow had declared.

Obed replied, "The sooner the better. Our home will be finished in two weeks."

Bette's father nodded and extended his hand to his new son. "Two weeks, then."

Morning light poured through the open windows.

It was cold, but Obed would not close the shutters just yet. The twisted trunks of the ancient vines waited for spring. Obed pictured them sending out green tendrils as Bette walked through their ranks. He imagined her everywhere, but this morning she was really coming to visit.

It had been arranged. His beloved was arriving with her family to tour the house. He wanted Bette and her clan to see the new home in full daylight.

The stone cottage was finished except for the last detail. Remembering the house of the shepherd's wife in Beth-lehem, Obed purchased bunches of dried lavender from the spice merchant in the village souk. As Samek observed, Obed braided the stalks and hung the bouquets upside down from the rafters. The aroma filled every corner.

There was very little furniture. The Widow would not permit him to take anything out of the big house. So be it. He purchased a bed from the rotund butcher who had outgrown it.

A rug made of four large fleeces was on the floor beside the fire pit. As for the rest, perhaps Bette would want her own things anyway.

He crossed his arms over his chest and said to the pup who stared at the rafters and whined with pleasure, "Samek, what do you think? Are you happy? Familiar, eh? Smell that? Lavender. I thought you would like it. She'll like it too."

A shadow fell across the room as someone stood in the doorway.

"She would like anything," the Widow said grimly. "She is desperate to be wed. Desperate. That's the gossip."

Obed whirled around to face his mother. "What are you doing here?"

"I came to tell you what I heard." She did not cross the threshold. "The gossip. About the Wool Carder's daughter. Your beloved Bette. She's been had by someone. Pregnant, they say."

Rage boiled up in Obed. "Go back to your lair! Everyone knows you're mad! You are not welcome in my home!"

Samek leapt to his feet and growled at the apparition.

She stepped back, continuing her attack from the step. "Yours? Every stone on this property still belongs to me."

"Get out! Mother, please! This . . . you . . . you are what drove Jesse away. Madness!"

"You'd still marry her? Pregnant with another man's child?"

He shouted, "It's a lie."

"We'll know in a few months, won't we?"

"Even if she was, I'd still want her."

"You're ten kinds of a fool." She laughed bitterly. "This place. You rebuilt this house for her. Then I'll tell you the secret of your pretty cottage. It was the house of a leper. Your father's sister. He kept her here until they couldn't hide it any longer. The stones . . . contaminated! Torn down after you were born!"

"You are a liar. A thief of joy. Get out. Get away from here. This is my house. And Bette's. Built for her!"

The Widow shrugged. She was enjoying his pain. "This is your inheritance, then. You will raise another man's child in a house where lepers lived. A fool, Obed. You are a fool. Not like anyone in my family. Certainly not like me. Or Jesse. Or the man you called 'Father.' He was not your father. Didn't you ever wonder?"

Obed took a step toward her as if to strike.

She smiled cruelly and turned on her heel. "Every rock and tree on this place is mine . . . and Jesse's. Second born? You were first born to a woman with leprosy. We kept you, out of the kindness of our hearts, when she left for Mak'ob, so you would not die of the disease. So I give you this house—these leper's stones where you were born. This house, the truth . . . your wedding present. You might as well not have been born at all."

The pup licked Obed's tears as he crouched on the sheep fleece by the fire. "Oh, Samek. Where is my rejoicing now?"

The dog nudged him hard with his muzzle.

Obed heard the laughter of Bette and her family as they turned off the highway and onto the narrow track that led to the vineyard and the cottage.

He stroked the head of Samek, who mourned with him. "What will I tell her? What? Oh, they are coming! If what the Widow says is true, Bette cannot enter this house! Must not . . . I cannot marry her!"

The pup buried his head against Obed and trembled at his master's grief.

Bette called cheerfully, "Obed! Friend! Husband! Are you inside?"

The company of bride's maids with her exclaimed over the beauty of the house. The whitewashed irregular stones, the high windows that would let the morning sun stream in.

He struggled to his feet and groped for the door. Samek pressed tight against his legs.

Bette's mother and father were in the midst of a flock of relatives all bearing gifts of furniture and dishes and food. Bracing himself against the frame, he blocked their entry and tried to smile as they roared at him to let them pass.

No stopping them. Like a wave, they knocked him aside and streamed in. Table and chairs were arranged beside the fire. Cups and platters and cooking utensils were placed on the empty shelves. Exclamations of approval welled up. Every detail of the house was praised. From the smooth plastered walls to the lavender in the rafters.

"I'll have to plant a garden. Flowers."

"And vegetables. Important to always have fresh vegetables on hand."

"Something bright along the walkway. Roses."

"Sage is heartier. And blooms purple."

"But roses . . ."

Bette noticed Obed's face was as pale as the walls.

"Obed? Husband? The wedding is tomorrow. Are you unwell?"

His smile flickered, but his heart had died within him. He could not speak. His thoughts reeled: *First born child of a leper . . . kept by my uncle out of charity . . . hated by the woman I thought was my mother. Oh, Lord! I can't marry this girl. Can't . . . oh, God in heaven! The angels mock my joy.*

He leaned heavily against the wall as the troop continued to examine and praise the house. Samek wagged and accepted friendly pats and praise.

Bette gazed up at Obed. "Husband? Are you unwell?"

He nodded bleakly. "Not feeling . . . well."

Bette's father strode up and clapped Obed on the back. "The stress of it. Prospect of the wedding. I remember. I was sick for a week before I married. Got over it soon enough the first night!"

Bette blushed at her father's words and turned away quickly.

Obed thought, *See the color on her cheek . . . the blush of innocence. She's never been with any man. I will be the first.*

So that much of the Widow's tale was a lie. Bette was pure. Untouched. She was not pregnant.

Obed reasoned that if the Widow was lying about that, then no doubt she was lying about his birth. He was not the child of a leper. The Widow was lying about everything, except, perhaps, that Obed was not her son. That much seemed entirely possible. Such a fact would be good news to his ears.

Obed inhaled deeply. He roused himself. "I-I'm all right. Just nervous. Hoping you liked it," he said to Bette.

Her mother roared, "Like it! Oh, she is a woman in love! With the house and also with the fellow who built it, I think."

The resounding approval of the wedding committee comforted Obed. As they charged off to prepare for the wedding, he felt certain the Widow had been lying about everything. He would speak to the rabbi next week when the celebration was over. Surely the rabbi would be able to help him as the Widow grew more mad every day.

CHAPTER 19

As Samek looked on, Obed knotted the sash of his wedding garment with trembling hands. He glanced around the furnished cottage to which he would bring Bette tonight. He had always been uncertain about prayer, but this evening he raised his eyes to the rafters, his prayers like the fragrance of the lavender. "Lord, I am awkward and foolish. I am worth nothing. But you have given me everything. I am the happiest man." Obed closed his eyes, resisting the image of the Widow's accusations. "As I was saying, Lord, the happiest man in the world. My bride—may she be blessed all the days of her life." Tears of joy brimmed. "You have given me a fine, loyal dog. An almond orchard. And now this . . . a wife. What can be better?"

Men and boys from the village sang when they came to accompany Obed to the wedding feast. Torches held high lit the landscape.

Obed emerged from the stone cottage as they gathered with the rabbi at their head, outside in the yard.

A cheer arose when Obed raised his hands and stammered his awkward thanks for their company.

"Well, Obed," said the rabbi, "this is your hour." His eyes flitted nervously toward the Widow's house.

Obed shook his head in the negative. He whispered, "Not coming."

The rabbi coughed into his hand. "As I was saying, your finest moment! Marriage. The culmination of life's purpose for every son of Avraham. And we have come—" he gestured broadly toward the congregation—"we, your friends, to share in your joy."

Obed wished Jesse were here to be his best man. He wondered if his brother had found the happiness he sought by leaving the village.

Obed had found every joy in spite of staying behind.

The pup stuck to Obed's heels as they marched forward to the sound of the drum and flute. Obed was grateful for the little dog's presence.

Little Samek, my family, eh?

There was no leaving him behind, Obed explained to the rabbi. Samek would not be denied. His name meant "rejoicing," and he must, therefore, rejoice with his master.

Bette and her mother, aunts, and bride's maids, waited at the well in the center of the village. Obed remembered how Rachel of old had met Jacob at the well. Jacob, a shepherd, no doubt also had a sheepdog at his heels. But that first Rachel, who won the heart of Jacob so long ago, could not have been so beautiful as Obed's bride.

Her dress was embroidered by her own hand with pink almond blossoms in honor of Obed's new orchard. The scent of her perfume filled the evening air, intoxicating him. A veil concealed her face, but Obed knew Bette's amber-brown eyes shone with love, only for him. Obed had survived his childhood, and now everything but the future melted away.

Let it come!

Obed tried to focus, tried to listen to the rabbi.

"If any man has cause . . ."

The garlands woven with almond blossoms and lavender were placed on their brows.

Bette: the dream who came only when I awakened!

Obed's brain seemed incapable of understanding simple words as the rabbi pronounced the blessings of Israel upon them and their children.

Children!

Obed's hands trembled as he drank and passed the cup of blessing for Bette to share.

You are the wine which quenches my thirst!

So it would be with their life together. One measure of blessing, pressed down, shaken together and overflowing.[24]

At your breathing the endless stars rise and set!

Obed's life was before him. He vowed he would leave the sorrow of his past behind.

". . . *For this cause a man shall leave his mother and father and cling only to his wife, and the two shall become one flesh.*"[25]

From now on everything was Bette.

Because you have loved me, the almond tree blooms.

Bette, the sum of Obed's every wish and dream.

So Obed brought his bride home, home to their stone cottage by the vineyard. It had all been prepared in advance by the bride's maids for their arrival: the fire lit, the bed strewn with rose petals, two cups of wine beside the bed.

He opened the door. Lifting her easily, he carried her across the threshold into the room. He felt her heart beat fast against his chest. Was she afraid? He wanted to tell her he would not hurt her, but words stuck in his throat.

Her breath was sweet against his neck. She raised her face and kissed him.

Tender. Tender. She seemed so small and fragile in his arms, like he could break her if he was not careful.

"I never want to let you go," he moaned.

She laughed. "Put me down." She whispered, "I'll only be a minute."

He obeyed, in agony, and she disappeared into the bedchamber.

Turning toward the fire, he grinned and stretched his hands to warm them. His eye fell on a scroll sealed with red wax that lay on the table. He picked it up, examining the cramped writing on the exterior. The hand of the Widow. Not to be ignored. She meant for it to be found and opened.

A gift for Bette, new wife of Obed, son of a leper.

So the Widow had decided she would have the last word on his wedding night after all.

He broke the seal and examined the document.

It was cruelly titled *Deed to Leper's Cottage granted Obed and Bette and their heirs.*

The flush of anger swept over him, blocking out his anticipation. Even on this night, the Widow had found a way to impose herself as the center of attention.

But only for a moment. The rustle of Bette's movements in the next room drew him back from anger.

"Obed?" Bette called to him.

"A minute," he croaked.

Rolling up the Widow's curse, he placed it in the wooden box where he kept his receipts.

"Obed?" Bette called again.

He sighed and shook himself free from the creature who surely looked down on their lighted windows from the dark house on the hill.

He slid the bolt, locking the cottage door. He secured the shutters and pulled the curtains.

He saw his shadow on the whitewashed walls of the room. Obed vowed he would not be a shadow any longer. How long had he been waiting for one thing to change his life? Stupendous. The awakening of a mighty man! With Bette he could be all these things.

This was it. All at once he knew she was what he had been waiting to discover. He had been something broken until now—a cracked cup, incapable of holding wine. With Bette all things would be mended. All.

He drew himself up and glanced at the pup, who gazed at him with mournful eyes. "What are you looking at?" Obed challenged.

Bette called again, softly. "Obed?"

"Yes," he answered.

Undressing, shy, he wound a blanket around himself.

Carrying a small clay lamp, he entered the room where Bette lay covered by the clean, crisp linens. Her round shoulder shone in the light like the first white milestone on a long journey.

This way to your future, traveler. You are not lost.

She smiled up at him, inviting him to join her. Her eyes gleamed as brightly as the lamp. She pulled back the covers.

His breath caught at the vision.

Smiling at his admiration, she whispered, "Obed, Husband, as far as your eye can see, this land I give you forever. . . ."

She reached for him and pulled him to her.

It was August. The ancient vines outside their door were heavy with fruit from their doubled labor. It was, Obed told the rabbi, Bette's love that called forth prosperity from heaven. The wheat stood taller than the almond saplings, but the blossoms, against all expectations, had produced some nuts. Obed had never seen such a thing.

"A portent of great things to come," Bette said to Obed as they shelled the entire crop into one bowl. "And by the way—" she smiled across at him—"next spring you'll be a father."

His mouth fell open. No words formed.

Samek's ears perked up at Obed's sudden start and shiver.

Bette laughed at Obed's expression and patted the worried canine, who came round to whine at her foot. "Yes, Samek. A new puppy. Tell your master it is true."

"A child?" Obed stammered.

"If we had worked at it morning, noon, and night, instead of just morning and night, we might have accomplished this sooner. I would prefer a winter baby. Remember that. Next time I'd rather have a baby in winter when there's not so much to do. And have the hard part over by planting."

She told him she had suspected it for a month, but now she was certain. She laughed and then asked him if she could give the news to the Widow. "Maybe such happy news, news that your mother will have a grandchild in seven months, will bring her round."

Images burst from his mind like a covey of quail startled in the field. *The accusation the Widow had made against Bette the day before the wedding. Her mocking gift of the leper's cottage. Her refusal in over half a year since their marriage to acknowledge Bette. Her denial of Obed as her son . . .*

He balanced these things with the glory of a living child—his child—blooming in Bette's womb.

"It won't change her. Don't hope to be friends with her."

"Not even this?"

"She doesn't care. As long as I work the fields and bring her income and see to it she is cared for, there is no affection in our arrangement. I am a hired hand to her."

Bette frowned at his pronouncement. "I'm sorry."

"That's the way it is."

"I mean, I am sorry for her. So bitter. So alone."

"She has always been alone. Even when we were all around her. That's why my . . . father . . . died. And why Jesse left. But me? I meant the least to her obsession, yet I stayed. She hates me even more, I think, for not leaving."

Bette shrugged and popped a raw almond into her mouth. "But this . . . this is our life, Obed. My dearest. These four walls. The vines, the orchard. Our little flock. What she thinks means nothing to our happiness. You believe that, don't you?"

Involuntarily, Obed glanced up toward the Widow's house. "I wish it were different. I miss my brother. But he was right to leave."

"And you are right to stay, to honor her with your labor. It is written: Long life and honor to you, Obed. Blessings and prosperity."

"Long life . . . with you." He moved to sit beside her. She took his hand and guided his fingers to her belly. It was flat, no sign yet. Like the saplings waiting to bud. "And this little one of ours. May he grow strong and know that we love him. I ask for nothing else."

CHAPTER 20

The tapestry of trees and vines turned red and gold, then fell to fallow earth as harvest ended. Autumn melted beneath the winter rain. Everything beyond the walls of their cottage turned gray with waiting. It grew colder each day.

Only Bette bloomed like a rose.

The sky was bucketing, water filling the cistern for the year to come. Bette lay in Obed's arms and he felt the baby *tap, tap, tapping* beneath her skin.

"'Shalom, Papa,' he is saying to you, Obed."

He laid his lips upon her stomach and mouthed, "Shalom! My son . . ."

Tap. Tap. Tap.

"He heard you," Bette said, pleased they were already a family of three.

"Well then," Obed said, "if I could sing, I would sing for him."

"Why not?" She hummed a dancing tune.

"Not me. I'd throw him off of music for life." Obed rolled over and gazed at the ceiling like he was looking at the sky.

Bette curled herself around the baby and lay close to Obed.

He said, "I see what you mean about having the next baby in winter.

It would fill the hours. Eh? Is it time to milk the goats yet?" Obed spoke to the dog.

Samek, now a gangly adolescent, wagged his tail-less behind but made no move to stand or go to the door.

"See?" Bette said. "He knows it's raining. Only fools go out in such a rain." She pecked Obed's cheek and lay back down.

"Fools and fellows with goats to milk." Obed groaned and sat up slowly. He searched for his cloak and scanned the floor for his shoes.

A loud rapping startled them both. Samek leapt to his feet and bellowed. His hackles raised, he stared at the door as if an army or a gang of bandits were there.

Obed and Bette exchanged curious glances. "Who on such a day?"

Obed wrapped his cloak around him and tossed a blanket over Bette. "Stay here. Wait," he instructed.

With a signal of one finger he drew Samek to his side. Cheek against the rough wood, he called through the door, "Who's there?"

Thunder rolled outside, shaking everything.

The timorous voice of an old man replied, "Obed, it's Charuz. Of the almond trees!"

The old tree man's cloak hung over a chair to dry. He greedily gulped down the warm stew Bette put before him. Between mouthfuls he explained. "I was a few miles hence. The air has the portent of death upon it. A freeze is coming. Soon as the rain has passed, it'll be here."

Obed and Bette exchanged a worried glance. "How can you tell?"

He spoke around a morsel of bread. "I've seen it well enough after so many years. Your trees have a good start, aye. Twice the size as last year when I brung them. But you'll lose 'em unless you set to work."

The old man had warned him the day of the planting that this country was hostile for an orchard in winter.

"What shall we do?"

In spite of his urgent warning the old man was in no hurry to leave the table. "A fine, hospitable shore this is to fetch up on." He slurped his stew. "Nectar of heaven this food be for an old man who plants saplings from morn 'til night and has no family to come home to, nor no home but the highway."

Bette ladled more into his bowl. "How can we save Obed's trees?"

"Freeze tonight'll kill the saplings." Charuz was matter-of-fact about his statement. "Not like these Canaanite vines. Stand the test of four hundred years and shed the cold like water off a duck. But these . . . the saplings. Like young children they are. They've only got the strength you give them these first years."

"What can we do?" Obed felt helpless. "How can a man fight such weather?"

"Tarps. We'll tent the saplings. Then embers in firepots beneath the shelter to keep them warm."

"Who has such things—firepots and shelters?" Obed asked.

"I carry such weapons. I have got them. Lucky for you I came. It ain't a big orchard." He cupped the bowl in both hands and drank the steamy liquid. "Lucky, too, for me." He laid a glassy glare on Bette. "Feed us well. We'll be at this war all night. Stoke the fire and bank the embers. Not a consuming blaze, mind you. Just hot enough to give us embers. Understand me? We'll tent the trees first. Then set the firepots."

Obed and Charuz had not completed spreading the oiled-cloth shelter over the rows of thirty-six saplings when the temperature dropped dramatically. It was as if the Judean hills had been plunged into an icy sea. The tips of Obed's ears and nose reddened instantly. His fingers ached and his fingernails tore as he tugged at the obstinate tarps. The rain pelting the windward heights changed to a curtain of sleet slicing downhill, slashing into the back of Obed's neck and rattling the improvised shelter.

If the struggling almond grove was a city under siege, Obed thought, the hammering frozen raindrops were the attacker's arrows.

How had Charuz known such a storm was coming? Obed had lived here all his life and he had seen such a savage onslaught only twice before in his life. On one of those occasions he had found a goat frozen to death on the morning after the tempest relented.

The memory made Obed redouble his efforts to secure the remaining tenting over his orchard. Poles driven into the sodden soil at the end of the rows provided anchor points for a line stretched above the saplings. Over this went the waterproof material.

The trick was to throw a loop of cord over the tarp and secure the end of the line to a peg driven into the ground. This maneuver had to happen before the wind whipped the whole construction out of Obed's frozen grip. The flapping fabric was like a billowing sail, threatening to carry the whole of the orchard away to Moab.

"Tie down the upwind seam first," Charuz shouted over the blast. "T'other edge can flap but we'll make all fast after."

A shawl pulled up over her head, her feet slipping in the mud, Bette struggled up the slope. A trio of clay pots slung from cords billowed a trail of smoke behind her, mimicking her icy breath. Obed met her just as her feet went out from under her. "Save the embers," she cried.

Grasping under the arms, Obed preserved both the firepots and his wife.

Charuz did not stop to praise Bette's efforts. "Need a lot more," he shouted. "After this tempest passes, temperature's going to drop like a rock. Got to warm up the whole space beneath the cover or they'll die."

Obed pictured the struggling almond saplings as fragile, defenseless babies. "Empty out our supply crocks if you have to," he called, his mouth close to Bette's ear. "Save the olive oil and wine for last, but we'll dump it and use them too, if we must!"

Bette indicated understanding without replying and struggled back down the hill toward the cottage.

By the time the cloth shelters were all secure and a dozen firepots placed, the air trapped beneath was sensibly warmer than outside—well above freezing.

But already the first of the embers had faded to cold, gray ash. "Can't stop," Charuz ordered. "From now on we take turn about. Bring back three dead ones at a time, scrape in a load of fresh embers, and back you come."

"Not Bette," Obed corrected. "She keeps the fire going and a pot of stew on for us. How long do we keep this up? All night?"

"Bless the Almighty! All night and all day tomorrow if need be!"

The sleeting rain stopped. Clouds parted. The sun rose. Bette prepared Obed and the old man a victory meal. Providence, it was, that old Charuz had been passing by when the hint of frost pricked his ears and bit his nose.

The table was crowded with heaps of food before the two exhausted men. Charuz prayed a mighty prayer of thanks to the Almighty that he had come in time for the saving of the little trees.

Obed and Bette sat unmoving, eyes closed, during the prayer, which continued for several minutes.

Charuz reminded the Almighty at length that years on the roads had taken a toll on him. He asked plaintively, as steam rose from a baked apple and eggs, "Might there be someplace where an old man could live and labor in a small orchard until the end of his days?"

Silence. The eggs grew tepid. Outside the sun warmed the little orchard saved by the oiled tarps and still-warm firepots and the labor of the old man.

No one said "Amen."

Bette opened one eye and lifted her head. "Obed, we could use a good hand on the place. I won't be much help to you when the baby comes, and then there may follow other children."

Charuz scooped up a morsel with his bread and crammed it into his mouth. He said as he chewed, "A fine idea, Bette. Good time for you to implement such a plan. There is little work to do in the fields with winter full upon us. We could concentrate on other matters." He directed his full attention to Obed. "Obed, I myself will help you build myself a small house—a room no bigger than the height of someone my size will do. But big enough for a man to sleep and to store braziers and gardening tools. Perhaps a fireplace. Yes. A table and one chair."

Obed stammered to Bette, "But perhaps Charuz does not mean this place."

Charuz squinted at the lavender in the rafters. "It will do. Yes, I like it here. Children coming. I am told by some customers I would have made a good grandfather if my own children had lived. Alas. I have always liked children, but none of my own have survived. Alas. Obed? You are a good worker. Prosperity is not far from you. You only need a man of wisdom and experience to teach you." He pointed to his own chest with his thumb. He paused in his chewing as some new idea simmered behind his eyes. "Almond oil. A good start. Almonds are not just for eating if you are wise. Press them. Spread the word that this is the oil of great beauty. The women of Yerushalayim love the oil of almonds for their skin. Smells nice. So?"

Obed explained, "The almond orchard belongs to the Widow. I tend it, but only this house and the land it stands on are my own. The boundary is the stone fence. Bette has planted flowers and—"

Charuz pursed his face like a dried apple. "You say the old vines of this vineyard are not your own. Belong to the Widow who resides in the house yonder? But you own this house and this patch of land within the fence where your house stands?"

"That's the size of it."

"Well then. By my reckoning, about two acres of ground belong to you. Flower gardens are fine for dreamers. But I know the steward of the priestly family who inspects and purchases the wines for sacred use at the Temple in Yerushalayim. I have planted five fine orchards for his family in my youth. He says there is a fortune in sacred wine. But few know the secret of the best grapes." He snapped his fingers. "Promise to feed me, and I will tell you."

Bette laughed. "I will feed you."

He raised his eyes and mouthed thanks to heaven. "And here is the secret. Old vine cuttings and grapes grown on arbors. High above the ground." He spread his hands to Bette. "Forsake your flowers for great wealth. Or maybe just a little wealth—I should not exaggerate—*a good living*. But a woman may also love to sit beneath the shade of her own grape arbor, I am told. Am I right? What do you say?"

What could Obed say? Bette agreed. It was settled.

Before the almond trees bloomed, the one-room cottage for old Charuz was built behind Obed and Bette's house. A fireplace. Bed. Table and chair. Room for tools and such. The old man had a yellow cat, and she moved in as well. Samek accepted her presence.

The first arbor for growing sacred wine was constructed, linking a walkway between the two buildings.

"Prosperity," Charuz prayed as he showed Obed how to plant and nurture the cuttings from the old vines and train them to climb the arbor. "This year I teach you how to make the finest oil from almonds and kosher wine from the Widow's first crush. Three years and you will sit beneath your own vines as a man of means."

21 CHAPTER

Charuz told Bette that Obed would just get in the way, so they sent him to the village to fetch the midwives. Pale and breathless, trying to hide his anxiety, Obed returned with a team of two steady, brown-faced farmer's wives who knew everything about birthing calves and lambs and kids.

They sent a boy on to fetch Bette's mother and sisters.

On the highway Obed walked too fast, scurrying far ahead of the midwives, then turning and coming back like Samek did when going to the field.

The midwives plodded and discussed other things. Babies arrived frequently, after all, so they talked about the weather and rheumatism.

Obed beckoned from the gate. "Here. In here! She's in labor, you see. . . ."

The midwives, who already knew where Bette lived and why they had been summoned, exchanged a look by which they expressed wordlessly to one another that Obed was one of those difficult husbands—more trouble in labor and delivery than either his wife or child.

They pushed past him at the door and told him it was best if he found a place outside to wait. "These things generally take some time. Especially the first."

The door shut in his face. Samek, likewise banished, sidled up to him and leaned against his knee. Obed pressed his ear against the door, attempting to hear what was happening inside.

Pleasant conversation. He recognized his name. A bit of laughter.

He blushed and turned to see Charuz inspecting the almond grove. Pink blossoms had just begun to emerge.

The old man waved and smiled, calling Obed to his side.

Reluctantly, Obed left the house, feeling desolate, deserted, and strangely afraid for Bette.

"Well," Charuz said, rubbing soil from his hands, "she's fine."

Obed said, "They won't let me in the house."

"You'd just be in the way. Find some work to do. I've left the goats for you to milk."

Obed did not feel like milking goats.

Charuz patted his shoulder. "It's all right. Children are born every day. You've seen goats give birth. Bear down and out pops a kid. An hour later, everything's clean and well and they're grazing again. No different for humankind."

"Even so." Obed's head ached as it had never ached before.

Bette's relatives came like a gaggle of geese along the road. He went to greet them, hoping they might gain admittance for him.

Bette's mother, a bright-eyed, laughing, elder version of the daughter, promised she would keep him informed. She pinched his cheek. "Don't be so mournful." She shivered and laughed. "You've done your part. I'm going to be a grandmother."

He milked the goats and did the chores. Charuz whittled outside his little house. Obed joined him and drank a cup of wine.

Hours passed before Bette's twelve-year-old sister came out and hurried toward him. Her eyes were wide and she was pale.

Terror gripped him. Obed stood, unable to make his feet move.

The sister whispered, "Mama said I should tell you. The pains are coming faster now. Mama says the baby'll come soon. Come in and have a word with her."

Obed's throat was dry. He had no spit. He could not swallow as he entered the crowded space. The faces of nine women turned to consider him as if he was the enemy; after all, his pleasure was Bette's pain.

Bette lay pale and small on their bed. Her hair was damp on the pillow. The mound of her belly was still as it had been that morning. She turned and almost smiled as he entered. Kneeling beside her, he kissed her hand.

"Oh," he said. "Oh."

She looked terrible, exhausted by the agony.

She panted, "They told me it's good for the husband to see his wife toil the last hour . . . so he knows." Her pretty face twisted. She made no noise but squeezed his hand so hard her knuckles turned white. He knew this must be some slight reflection of the force that gripped her, crushed her, and moved their child toward the light.

The midwife laid her hand on Bette's midsection as the contraction intensified, tightened and hardened like a stone. She counted the seconds slowly until it began to ease.

"You're doing fine," she whispered to Bette. Then to Obed the midwife said, "Not long. You can go now."

"But . . ." Obed stared at Bette's face, which was red from the effort to remain silent.

The veins in her neck and temples stood out. She did not care that he was terrified of losing her. Did not care if he stayed or went.

The contraction ended, and her breath exploded from her lungs.

"Breathe slowly when the next one comes. Breathe with it," the midwife instructed. And then more harshly to Obed, "Get out. We'll fetch you."

"Bette." He kissed her on the forehead. Bette did not look at him. He was only one among the crowd of faces. Her only focus was the vise crushing her middle.

Her relatives patted him kindly, propelling him forward from one to another, then out the door.

Miserably, Obed slunk away to sit with head in hands outside the old man's lodgings. Samek rested his muzzle upon his knee.

"All will be well," Charuz consoled, peering through the carved bore of a whistle. "I will give this to the baby. Oh. Did I tell you? The almond trees blossomed this morning. The vine cuttings for the sacred wine have today put out the first new leaf."

The call of Bette's mother was a trumpet blast—triumphant. A shout of victory from the walls of Jerusalem. The foe was vanquished. Life had prevailed!

"Obed, you have a daughter!"

Charuz tapped the finished whistle on his open palm. "A female on the day the first buds open. A good omen. May she be fruitful in joy and blessing to the house of Obed."

Bette's mother, who had borne all females to her husband, said, "I knew it. She carried it high."

Obed walked like a prince through the congratulations of the women to Bette's bed and child. The midwife shooed the audience away and closed the door, leaving the three alone.

Bette was washed and anointed with soft perfume. She wore a clean shift. Her hair was brushed and braided. Could it be that less than an hour before he imagined her laid out on a bier?

She smiled and pulled back the swaddling to reveal his daughter. He gazed at the child in amazement. She was not a calf or a lamb. He had never seen a newborn human before, and this chalky pink, perfect, wrinkled creature was in part his making. He felt very proud. He knew now why roosters crowed and bulls bellowed.

The crown of the baby's head was thick with wet dark hair that had been curled around a finger and made to stand up on her head like the comb of a chicken. She was quiet, staring at the light with cloudy blue eyes. Perfect little hands and feet were connected to spindly arms and bowed legs drawn up to a tummy like a frog. The stump of the umbilical cord reminded Obed of Bette's battle.

"Are you all right?" he asked.

Bette nodded. "How did we do?"

"She is beautiful." His voice trembled. Tears brimmed. He meant it. *Beautiful.*

Bette gazed at her. "We shared the same heart for nine months. Strange. You'd think I'd recognize her face. But I don't. Me? Or you? Or both of us?"

"I can't tell. You know everyone . . . your mother . . . they'll all have an idea which side—your side, I hope. A girl after all."

"Disappointed?"

"Never. I love her mother more than my life. And she . . . born on the day the almond trees blossomed. A sign. God is watching."

"I've been thinking. Look at her. A name. You didn't know I was preparing for the possibility of a girl, did you?"

"It never mattered. You . . . well and happy. It doesn't matter to me."

"Blossom. That is her name. Yes."

Obed sent the message to his mother's house on the hill, asking her to come see her granddaughter. The Widow did not reply.

After the harvest she sent her servant to fetch the accounting and her share of the income. But there was no semblance of a mother's love for son or grandchild.

In the open market of Modein, she spotted Obed and Bette as they strolled through the booths. She approached them with an arrogance that startled the onlookers.

"The child." She snapped her fingers at Bette. "Let me see it."

Bette held Blossom tight against her shoulder and blinked at the Widow as though she was some strange creature that might hurt the baby.

The Widow scowled at Obed, and for a moment, there was some flash of regret or loneliness in the woman's expression. Bette, compassion overcoming fear, lowered the baby to let the Widow see her face.

The Widow took the baby's tiny hand and held it in her bony fingers. She stooped to examine the petal-soft flesh of the infant, and for a moment those around her believed the Widow might smile.

"Her name is Blossom, Mother," Obed said, hopeful.

"Hmmm." The Widow stiffened and raised her chin. "Sure, it is Jesse's child. She is not a leper. Yet."

Smiles of the observers faded instantly, replaced by horror at the Widow's words. Jesse had been gone over two years. How could the Widow believe such a thing? How could she speak it out loud? The ripple of shock swept through the souk like concentric circles on a pond after a stone has been dropped.

This time the whisper of certainty came back, "She's mad."

The echo of truth multiplied. "Looking for Jesse, she is. Servant says she wanders through the house calling for Jesse. Doesn't even recognize Obed. Thinks he's a hireling."

"Who's heard from Jesse?"

"No one."

"Not once since he went away?"

"Never."

"And what she said about little Blossom being a leper?"

"The Widow's mad, and there's an end to it."

CHAPTER 22

Bette rocked Blossom by the fire. She stroked the infant's hair and smiled down at her. "Beautiful girl. Beautiful . . ."

Obed was disconsolate. He stood with his arms crossed. Anger furrowed his brow. "She's insane. Mean to the core. But to make such an accusation in public. In the souk!"

Bette glanced up at him. Her doting expression did not change as it shifted from baby to husband. "Insane, yes. By definition she can't help herself. Poor thing."

"You have pity on her if you want. As for me, I'd be just as willing to sell what little I own and move away forever. Like Jesse. And not a word from him, the center of her obsession. Well, he had the right idea. Vanish. Disappear forever and never, never even bother, never remember he has a brother." Obed suddenly sank to the chair and sobbed. "My brother—why hasn't he written? Why?"

Obed covered his face with his hands lest Bette see his womanish tears.

She put Blossom on the bed and stood behind him, encircling his aching head with her arms. She let him weep awhile before she spoke. "You need to know. And so does she."

He wiped his eyes on his sleeve. "It's made her crazy, I think. I hoped, you know, that she would find some joy in our life. A baby, our little Blossom, to bring her some happiness. But she's wild—really, beyond anything—and she doesn't know me. Not at all." He groaned. He had not spoken about his mother or his brother in a long time. His longing for Jesse was a physical pain.

Bette pressed her palm on his brow and kissed the crown of his head. "Obed, here's the plan. You must find Jesse. Somehow. We must find him."

Charuz stroked the head of the young dog as he and Obed shared a midday meal beneath the arbor. Sun shone through the grape leaves, weaving a dappled pattern of light on the two men.

Obed said, "Thanks for your help, Charuz. I've got so many ideas. So much hope for this place. The land blooming, like it never did when my father was alive."

Charuz tore his bread and blessed it. Then he looked up with a flash of anger in his eye. "The Widow, your mother, is talking about it to anyone who listens to her. She says that you're working for Jesse—holding his place, as it were. And when Jesse comes back? Well then, the land, she says, is still his. I don't want your heart broken, lad."

Obed winced at the Widow's campaign to keep Jesse first in her heart. Needing a moment to think before he answered, Obed pulled a grape leaf and rolled a mixture of hummus in it. Dipping it in olive oil and vinegar he tasted it, chewed, and swallowed. What if Jesse came home, rich and powerful? Or defeated and crushed by life and needing a place to stay?

At last Obed answered. "I don't think Jesse is coming home." In this admission, Obed's heart was filled with longing to see his brother again. "I don't know why. Don't know why he's never written, to tell me where he's at or how he's doing. But even if he came home? If she gave him everything but what is truly mine—" he raised his eyes to the grape arbor—"Charuz, I'd gladly give up all my dreams to see Jesse again."

Charuz inhaled deeply. "Well then. I needed to hear that." The old man fished in the leather sack at his side and pulled out a sealed scroll: a message addressed to Obed in Jesse's broad handwriting.

"When?"

"Two days ago it came to me. A tree grower. Friend of mine. Eastern territory. The border of the wilderness."

Obed's hands were trembling as he broke the seal and began to read.

My dearest brother, Obed,

I pray for you daily and think of you and Mother often. Though you have not heard from me since I left after Father's death, my thoughts and prayers are with you every day as I labor. I have a vineyard of my own now. The work is my life.

I cannot come home again and will not see Mother again. But I long to see you, my dear brother, and hear all the news.

When the grapes are harvested and the vines are pruned, I will come. On the first night of the full moon's rising in the month of Kislev I will meet you at the tomb of our father. I beg you, do not share the content of my letter with anyone, especially not our mother.

My heart looks forward to the moment when I may see you again, my dear and faithful brother and friend.

Your loving brother,

Jesse

Obed scanned the missive again and again before he raised his face to Charuz. "He says I can't share this with anyone! There is no address, no city where I can write him back. Charuz? How did your friend come by this?"

Charuz stroked his beard. "It came to me . . . without explanation of how or where . . . or when. I have no message for you but the one you hold in your hands."

Obed rolled up the scroll and tucked it into his pocket. "Jesse is alive. At least that's something. But no real news. Nothing. Nothing I can share. My mother must not know . . . even this. These are Jesse's instructions."

"The letter is written to you. As far as I am concerned, I am an old man. I forget things." He tapped his temple. "What letter? Eh? From whom? I'll never remember long enough to speak of it."

Obed reflected. "So, back to your original question. Bette and Blossom are everything I care for in this world. This little house. It's mine. I built it. You and I have built and planted this arbor together. It's enough. In spite of all my dreams, it's enough. If my brother came home? If Jesse . . ." He paused, fighting back the emotion of yearning. He imagined the reunion, the joy! "If Jesse asked me to turn over everything beyond this little plot. The orchard? The vineyard? I would give it gladly to welcome him home and share his friendship again."

"Would that I had ever had a brother like you," Charuz lamented. "But alas!" He spread his cracked and calloused hands. "Brothers are often the most unfaithful friends. Most ready to betray." He sighed. "Ah, well."

The parchment was tucked away in a safe place. Throughout the coming weeks, Obed secretly reread it as Bette and Blossom slept.

Full moon rising. The month of Kislev . . .

CHAPTER 23

The tithe had been paid on income of the vineyard. It was double what it had been last year. Obed credited the expertise of Charuz for the bounty.

Pruning hooks in hand, Obed and Charuz worked the long rows of ancient vines, cutting and casting off dead branches. The old man worked twice as fast as the younger and soon reached the end of his row.

He straightened his back and grinned at Obed, then spit though his gapped teeth.

Strange how one season in the care of the gardener had doubled the harvest. And the clusters were heavier; each individual grape seemed twice the size of last year.

Obed was sweating when he came to the end of his row. Charuz handed him a cup of water; then, as Obed drank, Charuz whispered, "Blessed are you, O Lord, master of the vineyard, who causes this vine to grow strong for the harvest which will come forth next year."

Obed wiped his mouth with the back of his hand and said, "Omaine."

Charuz gazed at him with amusement. "It is written, '*Honor the Lord with your wealth, with the firstfruits of your crops; then your barns will be filled to overflowing, and your vats will brim with new wine.*"[26] Obed, my son, if you could entreat the Almighty, and ask of him anything, what would you most like to see in the next year? A greater harvest? Wealth? Standing in this spot next year, what would you most like to see?"

Obed replied, "I would most like to see my brother. Jesse."

Charuz raised his sparse eyebrows as if the answer surprised him. "This was his vineyard?"

"He's the heir. It was his when my father died. If he returns, then it will be his."

"He had little regard for what was meant to be his."

Obed had to agree, yet he defended Jesse. "My brother. You just have to know him. Always first. Always the strongest and the smartest. The best. I say that from the bottom of my heart. Not bitter. Jesse is all that. He had greater things to do with his life than stay at home and tend a little vineyard, I suppose. My brother was always destined to be a great man. And I? I am a small thing in the eyes of the Lord."

Charuz cleared his throat and rubbed his knobby fingers over the knotted branches of the vine. "You know the story of this vineyard?"

"Only that it is very old."

"It was cultivated from the rootstock of the vines of Canaan, which were here before Joshua brought Israel into the land. Ah yes. Holy. Proof of a promise. Few of these ancient vines remain."

Obed studied the old man's hands for a moment. Intertwined with a vine, his fingers seemed one with the branches.

"You know, I won't mind returning it to Jesse. It was always to be his. And then I heard he was leaving and I said, you know, when he comes home I'll have it here for him."

"*Let love and faithfulness never leave you; bind them around your neck; write them on the tablet of your heart.*"[27]

"Well spoken. Yes. I haven't stopped looking for him."

Charuz commended him, then inquired, "And your brother? Is he faithful to have left when he did?"

Obed brushed the thick mulch of fallen grape leaves with the toe of his boot. "He's always been the smart one. Better than I ever could hope to be. Why, if it was Jesse working beside you, you'd both have it finished by now."

Charuz snapped his fingers. "Like that, eh?"

"That's about it."

"But he is not here. You are here. And the work will be accomplished." Charuz inhaled deeply and looked to the road. "My work's almost done here. I'll be moving on soon."

The announcement stung Obed. "But I thought you'd stay on . . . stay with us. Blossom loves you."

The old man sharpened his pruning knife on a whetstone, then continued his work. "You'll be needing my cottage."

After the harvest, Charuz left suddenly one night without a word of explanation.

Bette stood with hands on hips and frowned into the empty cottage. The dog whined at her heels. "He took everything. His gardening tools. Gone. Not even a note of farewell."

Obed cradled Blossom and stared at Bette's back. He did not want to look in at the empty place where the old man had lived. He would pretend that Charuz was still inside.

"I don't think he's coming back." Bette turned away. Obed followed her gaze to the grape arbors he and Charuz had labored so hard to complete.

Obed shook his head and turned away. Some nameless emotion weighed him down. "Oh well. He's used to moving from place to place," he said lightly.

"He could have at least said good-bye to Blossom."

"Maybe, but maybe he means to come back," Obed ventured. But even as he spoke the words aloud, he knew Charuz was gone for good.

Bette took the baby from Obed's arms and strode into the house.

Obed stared bleakly at Charuz's cottage.

Abandoned.

That was the word and that was what Obed felt. The little house was abandoned, and Obed was abandoned too.

Like when Jesse had left him alone to care for the Widow.

Obed followed Bette into the house and watched her in silence as she nursed Blossom, then placed the baby in her bed for a nap.

Bette held a finger to her lips, warning Obed to be quiet; then she led him back out into the autumn afternoon sun.

"Another fall. Another year. High Holy Days coming," she said.

"Your mother gets more restless this time of year. And still no word from your brother."

"Maybe he'll come back." Obed searched the road in the distance and thought of the letter from Jesse, which he had secreted away. "Maybe."

"You'll miss him, won't you? Charuz, I mean."

"He was . . . a good worker."

"More than that, I think." She raised her hand to brush the brittle grape leaves on the arbor.

"Yes," Obed admitted, "I will miss him."

Obed perched on the stone fence beside the empty highway. The red autumn sun hung low in the sky. The Day of Atonement was close at hand. Without Charuz for Obed to confess his faults to, he had no man he trusted to serve as his *bet din*.

He laid his hand lightly on the head of his dog. "I'm glad for your company," he said. "And you and Bette and Blossom seem content with me, though I know I'm just an insignificant fellow."

The dog licked his hand and lay down at his feet.

This was the time for inner reflection, for *teshuvah*, turning like the seasons.

The smell of Bette's bread baking in the oven made his stomach rumble, but he would not eat. He could not eat.

He covered his head with his plain woolen cloak as if it were a prayer shawl. Obed could talk easily to his dog, who adored him. Why could he not speak to the God of his fathers with the ease with which old Charuz had always prayed?

"Lord, it is because I am nothing. So small in your eyes, O Lord. I am ashamed to open my mouth. Afraid to open my heart, though you know me better than I know myself."

Obed fixed his eyes on the tall date palm, the landmark at the gateway of the caravansary of Modein. His mind wandered to Charuz, who had traveled the length and breadth of Eretz-Israel planting orchards and vineyards everywhere. The old man never stopped praying.

And then Obed thought about his brother. Jesse had traveled the world, no doubt, and made his fortune a thousand times by now. Jesse had never prayed for as long as Obed had known him.

The bare branches of the almond orchard reached skyward, scraping the underbelly of the heavy clouds. "Charuz said that an almond orchard is a reminder that God is watching. But does God watch over little men like me?"

Did the God of Abraham, Isaac, and Jacob see and hear an ordinary fellow like Obed, who had never really accomplished anything of importance?

Obed closed his eyes and exhaled. "What difference do I make? If only I could see myself as you see me, Lord. Then I could fix the broken places in my life and . . ." His prayer faltered. He was suddenly exhausted by the effort. He fell silent and lay back, stretching out on the ground beside the dog.

And Obed dreamt, unaware of how much time passed. The sun melted into the mountains in the west. A voice whispered on the wind, *Discretion will protect you, and understanding will guard you. . . .*[28]

Obed looked around to see who had spoken. A man stood nearby. It was Charuz, only it was not Charuz. He was tall and straight and strong. Ancient, but not old in human years. His clothes were white linen, like the clothes of a priest. His beard was white as snow and his eyes were older than old. He looked into Obed's heart and spoke without moving his lips.

"Who are you, really?" Obed asked Charuz. "And what about your name? You think I never noticed?"

You asked to see yourself. So pay attention, Charuz instructed, raising his glowing arm and pointing at the distant highway.

The sky was ablaze with a hundred shades of rust and orange. Beneath Obed the ground trembled as the even cadence of a footstep approached.

"Who is it? Who's coming?" Obed asked Charuz, but Charuz had vanished. Obed asked the dog, "Who is that giant coming?"

Because it was a dream, the dog answered. "That is you. Yourself. My master. Don't you recognize yourself? To those you love, and those who love you back, you are Obed the Giant."

Obed the Dreamer sat up. In the distance he saw someone who certainly resembled himself. Only the Obed he saw in his dream was enormous. The giant Obed was grinning, whistling, swinging his arms like a soldier whose long legs devoured the miles in his march toward home.

Towering on the horizon Obed the Giant approached the date palm by the caravansary. At the base of the tree slept Obed's brother, Jesse. Jesse awakened with a shout and raised his fist as if to strike Obed the Giant on his ankle.

Wrapping his hand around the tree as if it were a walking stick, Obed the Giant pulled the palm out by its roots, raised it high, and then used it to scratch his back. Jesse, terrified, ran into the caravansary and slammed the door.

Obed the Giant laughed and the almond trees shook, sending pink showers of blossoms floating in the air.

Obed the Dreamer whispered in his sleep, "Ah, I know this is a dream. I don't know who Charuz is supposed to be, but he cleaned up nicely and does well as an angel. And my brother, Jesse? He was afraid of me . . . afraid. So he ran inside and shut the gate. But why was he afraid? The blossoms are my little Blossom. And this giant Obed, myself, is who I am in the eyes of my child. And also in your eyes, my dog. You believe I am a giant and you would love me even if I beat you."

The dog replied, "True."

"But I wouldn't beat you, dog. Not ever. Not even in a dream. However, I would be happy to scratch my back with the date palm. I don't know what that part of the dream means. Maybe Bette can tell me, since dogs can't really talk."

Obed was still laughing when he awakened. His back itched from sleeping on the dry grass.

It was too dark to see if the date palm still stood at the gate of the inn.

Bette called to him from the house. Supper was ready.

24 CHAPTER

Winter came in fierce one night. The moon was halfway to full in the month of Kislev. A gust of wind shook the little house as Obed lay beside Bette.

He opened his eyes as a shutter banged open and a blast of cold filled the house.

Leaping from bed, he struggled to close it and lock it in place.

"Check the baby," Bette instructed dreamily from beneath the fleece.

Obed held the clay lamp over the baby's crib and made certain she was tucked in. He stoked the fire to a roaring blaze; then, as Bette dozed off again, he took out Jesse's letter and scanned the content.

First rising of the Kislev moon . . . Father's tomb.

Would Jesse really come back? Obed read the strange message again and again. Had Jesse chosen the tomb as their meeting place so no one would see him? none could report his return to the Widow? The parchment rustled as he read by the firelight.

"Obed?" Bette called.

He turned to see her eyes shining as she studied him. "What are you doing? It's freezing."

"Just be a minute." He rolled up the letter and laid it aside. Climbing back in bed, he tried not to put his cold feet against her. She moved close to him, her warmth warming him as the wind howled around the corner of the cottage.

"What were you reading?"

"Nothing. A list."

She did not ask what sort of list. She laid her head on his chest. "Do you think he'll come back?" she asked.

He held his breath for a long moment as if she had punched him. "What?"

"Do you think he'll—?"

"Who?"

"Your brother."

Outside, a blast of lightning lit the sky. Seconds later thunder rolled across the land. "You read it."

"An accident."

"How long ago?"

"The night after the old man left. It was on the table in the morning."

"Ah," Obed replied, remembering his scramble to hide it away that morning.

"You could've told me."

"Yes."

"Well?"

"I-I'm afraid he won't come."

"But you could've told me." She kissed his cheek and then found his lips. "Are we enough? Me and Blossom?"

He kissed her back, urgently, searching for something to fill the ache of his loneliness. "You . . . are . . . everything. . . ."

Obed sat in the overgrown garden overlooking his father's tomb. He seldom visited, except once a year out of obligation, to mark the anniversary of the cruel man's demise. The Widow had not returned to her husband's grave since the day he was buried.

A tangle of dead vines covered the stone like a deserted spiderweb. The pall of something rotten hung in the cold winter air. It was, Obed thought, the last place anyone would imagine for a family reunion. Jesse must have known this would be the case. A meeting of the living would never be suspected in such a place. Jesse's presence in Modein would be undetected by their mother. The brothers could talk without fear of hindrance or interruption.

Obed's hands were clammy with excitement. He fingered the parchment of his brother's message, reading it over again several times in the waning light.

Would Jesse come? Was this some sort of elaborate joke? *Meet me in the deadest place on earth—the tomb of a man who loved no one while he lived and who lies in his grave unloved. . . .*

The strange thing about it was that Obed had always loved his father. Always. He had loved him even when the curses had rained on him like physical blows. Obed had pitied his father too. The desolation of this place seemed the most appropriate memorial to his life.

Obed would rather have met with Jesse among the new stand of almond saplings. Or beneath the arbors in the newly built cottage.

But the Widow's windows looked down on Obed's property. She would see a stranger walk across the yard and recognize the long, loping gait of Jesse. She would know at once and howl and swoop down on Jesse from her perch. The joyful reunion Obed imagined would become all about her instead of the meeting of two brothers.

Obed searched the darkening sky and asked the God of Abraham, *What if Jesse decides not to come? What if he has pieced together a vision of the Widow following after me, seizing him, holding his life captive with guilt?* Perhaps that possibility was what Jesse feared most, what he had run from in Obed's dream.

Obed muttered, "Don't be afraid, Jesse. It's just me and you. The old bones of the past can't harm us."

The round red sun descended in the western horizon. At the same moment, the full moon ascended slowly in the east. Obed glared at it, willing it to hurry.

"Jesse?" he called when it was nearly risen. No reply. Dead leaves rattled across the path. Starshine winked on above him.

Where was Jesse?

Obed clutched the edge of the stone bench. The full moon of Kislev rose higher. Now a finger's breadth above the mountain. Now a fist.

Obed's heart sank as minutes passed and Jesse did not come.

"Jesse?" he cried, certain no one would hear his voice.

So. It was some sort of joke. Or Jesse had been delayed on the way. Or he was sick. Or dead.

"Jesse?" His call was tentative, like a mourner speaking the name of the dead, wishing for an answer but not expecting a voice to reply.

"I have . . . missed you . . . my brother. My brother. So much to tell you."

The crunch of gravel behind him interrupted his reverie. He gasped, leapt to his feet, and turned.

Searching the darkness behind him, he shuddered, certain someone . . . something . . . had entered the graveyard. The stink of rotting flesh made him cover nose and mouth.

"Who's there?" Obed stammered. "Jesse? Jesse? Is that you?"

From the darkest shadows a voice replied, "Unclean . . . do not come near."

"Jesse!" Obed cried with joy at the familiar sound of his brother's voice.

"Stop, Obed. Come no closer!" came the terrified reply as Obed charged into the darkness. "I am . . . a leper."

Obed followed the voice, tracing the sound to an outcropping of stone. "Jesse," he cried, reaching out. "Brother! Where are you?"

"No nearer, I beg you!"

Obed touched a ragged cloak, closing his fingers around it and pulling Jesse to him in an embrace.

"Let me go," Jesse begged. "I am unclean. Don't you understand? Unclean! Defiled! Obed, no!"

Obed held his brother tighter. The foul stench of Jesse's illness told him everything. He understood it all now. Love had driven Jesse away. His suffering hidden, to spare Obed from suffering, had instead caused a wound too deep for words.

"I will not let you go unless you promise you won't run away!"

Jesse's brittle weight sagged in Obed's strong arms. He began to sob.

Obed led him to the stone bench beside their father's tomb. The full moon rose, casting cold, colorless light on the scene. Jesse's wounds in monochrome were not so fierce as they must appear by harsh daylight.

"I told Mother. She would not accept it."

"Nor will she," Obed answered. "She calls my cottage the leper's house."

"Better if she believes I am dead already."

"You are thin." Obed wiped away Jesse's tears.

"Tried living on my own to hide the sickness. I was on the move until money ran out, and people began to notice. So I came back. Came to Mother's door and asked her for help. She said . . . I was not her son. So I lived here in the tombs." Jesse laid his head on Obed's shoulder and gasped out his words. "I watched your life from a distance. Your wife, you . . . made me happy, see? The baby . . . you . . . working in the vineyard. Every day I watched . . . prayed for you. Little stone house. The almond orchard. I stole food from the rubbish heap at the caravansary. I had planned to take my own life this very night and end it all, if you had not come."

Obed stroked Jesse's hair as if he were a child. "I'm here now. And you must live."

"How did you know? How did you find me?"

Obed did not answer that question directly or show his brother the letter that had told him where to meet and when. He said simply, "An angel. The message said I was to come to you."

"Now you know the truth, I can let go. I can say farewell to you."

"No. No, Jesse. You must stay awhile. Like the old vines, meant to grow strong here again in your own soil. Stay with us and you will find a new life."

And so that night, arm in arm, trembling matched with trembling, Obed took his brother home to meet his wife and child.

Obed bathed his wounds, anointed him with oil, and clothed him. Bette fed him and made a bed for him in the little cottage behind the house. Blossom smiled at him and gave him a will to live.

So it was that Jesse the leper did indeed grow strong again. He had a will to live, in spite of his sickness.

He lived happily in Charuz's cottage. His presence remained a secret for two years, unknown to the villagers of Modein or to the Widow.

THE JOURNEY CONTINUES . . .

Stars began to fade. A rooster crowed from the farmyard. Dawn lit the eastern sky as Crusher's tale came to an end.

He closed his eyes and inhaled deeply. "She's up already. Can you smell the lavender warming in her garden?"

Fisherman blinked at him. "But . . . but . . . you are Jesse?"

He said, "You know my name. I lived for two years in the cottage Obed built for Charuz. My sickness did not progress in all that time. Obed told anyone who was curious that I was a bondservant. My mother never recognized me, or if she did, she never acknowledged me. She died by and by and is buried here. No one knew me because I did not go into the village. I was never seen by anyone who knew me. I was home. Bette and Obed and little Blossom. Here with my family. Loved and cared for. They would not have sent me away."

"What happened?" asked Shoemaker.

"The rabbi came one day. Unexpected. A simple thing. I came in from the field and he saw me. Recognized the wound on my hand as leprosy. I had forgotten . . . and . . ."

Suddenly behind the minyan a dog barked. Gravel crunched beneath the heavy step of a man.

Crusher stood to face the encroacher. He called, "Come no closer. We are unclean! Lepers!"

The footfall paused. A voice rang out joyfully, "Jesse?"

Crusher answered. "Obed! Come no closer. There are ten of us here."

A woman with Obed cried, "Ten! Jesse! There are ten of you! We've brought breakfast, but not enough for everyone. Come to the house. There's plenty for you and your friends."

Obed—just as Crusher had described, but fifteen years

older—appeared at the head of the path. Bette was beside him and an old, half-blind dog with a gray muzzle followed at their heels.

The minyan covered faces and open wounds with ragged cloaks and drew back.

Carpenter warned, "Sir, we know you are a good man. Your brother has told us. But we are a minyan of lepers sent out from the Valley of Mak'ob. Sent to bring back the Nazarene to help us. Lepers, you see. Please come no closer!"

Obed was not intimidated. He placed a basket of food on a stone and rushed ahead with arms outstretched to embrace Crusher. "Jesse! Jesse!"

The brothers wept.

Bette explained, "We smelled the smoke of your campfire last night. Obed guessed it might be Jesse. So much happening these days. We were praying Jesse would return."

Shoemaker addressed Bette. "We've come in search of Yeshua of Nazareth. There are rumors. Miracles, they say."

Bette declared to all, "Not rumors! True. Messiah. He heals the sick. Obed was afflicted with a cancer last year. Dying, the physician said. A month ago Yeshua touched Obed's hand and he is healed. The blind see. The lame walk. Lepers are cleansed, and the dead are raised."

Now all the minyan stood up at this news.

The Cabbage Sisters let their veils drop, revealing the inhuman blooming of cauliflower faces. "How do you know this?"

Obed answered, "Yeshua was here in Modein at our own synagogue. We saw Yeshua. Heard him teach. I am alive. I am witness of the miracles." He turned to his brother. "Then Bette and I sent word to you at Mak'ob. That you must return. We've been expecting you. Looking for you every day."

"I never got your letter," Jesse told his brother. "We ten left Mak'ob months ago. Looking for Yeshua. Hoping to bring him back to the Valley. There are so many in need there. We have never found Yeshua."

Breathless, Fisherman asked Obed, "Where is he now? Where has he gone? Where can we find him?"

Obed replied, "We heard the Herodians wish him dead. So he's headed east . . . out of Herod Antipas' reach. Toward Jericho, last I heard. And then I don't know."

The Cabbage Sisters clung to each other. "Jericho!"

"Jericho!"

"Back there!"

Bette took the arms of the women and gently led them up the path. "Come on. There's plenty for you to eat at the house. Clean clothes. A bath. A day of rest. It will do wonders for you."

Jesse protested. "Bette, our presence will put you in danger."

Bette replied, "No. No more fear, Jesse. Only hope. Hope for us all. We've all been afflicted in one way or the other. But no more. If they kill us, Yeshua can raise the dead. What harm can come to us now if we are his? Jesse, I wrote you in the letter. Though your eyes never read the words, your heart drew you home. Now you are here. The one we were waiting for has come at last."

For three days the Minyan of Mak'ob rested in the cottage that once had belonged to Charuz and later to Jesse. Fed and bathed and dressed in new clothing, the ten felt almost human again.

Almost.

Bette packed food for their journey. A money pouch filled with silver was slipped into Jesse's pocket.

The brothers embraced a final time.

"I wish you would let me come with you."

"You can't. This journey is meant for the last lepers of Mak'ob. I'll be back, a new man." Jesse filled his eyes with the forest of pink blossoms. "Pray for us."

Obed replied, "God is watching over you."

The minyan set out early, and they almost made it out of Modein without incident.

Almost.

It was barely dawn. Pink, swirling clouds raced each other through the sky toward the Holy City, like almond blossoms blown from the orchards of heaven.

Skirting the edges of the town en route to the Joppa/Jerusalem highway, the lepers passed the rear of a bakery. What appeared to be an apprentice baker emerged from the shop, but he didn't spot the pilgrims of hope. He glanced around furtively before upending a basket into a ditch, then skulked back inside.

"Burned . . ."

". . . them," the Cabbage Sisters observed.

"Barley bread," Shoemaker commented, sniffing the air. He didn't notice the envious looks of those who could no longer appreciate aromas. "Too bad."

"Burned or not: traveling rations," Carpenter said. "Burned bread keeps. We should glean it."

Shoemaker accompanied two of the Torah school students. The trio, selected because each possessed all his limbs, was delegated to retrieve the windfall.

The rest waited in back of a row of acacia trees.

Barley bread was dark brown at all times, but these loaves were nearly black and hard as rocks. Shoemaker loaded four into one student's waiting arms, then heaped the other scholar's grasp as well.

He then stacked three more, one atop the next, before stuffing the last beneath his chin.

That was when the bakery door banged open again, accompanied by scuffling feet and protesting noises from the apprentice. The baker, clearly in a foul mood, dragged his protégé out by the earlobe. "You liar! Scoundrel! Where'd you dump them? Where?"

Then he spotted the lepers. The two students redoubled

their efforts to scramble out of the ditch, spilling loaves in the process.

Shoemaker froze in place, like a pack rat caught raiding a campsite freezes in a torchlight's revealing gleam. Law-abiding by nature, Shoemaker gave the required warning: "Unclean! Lepers."

Seeing the opportunity to divert attention from himself, the apprentice squealed, "Lepers! Lepers stealing the bread. That's what happened. They broke in and stole the bread."

The loud noises brought other shop owners out to locate the source of the early morning outcry.

Eager to prove his loyalty and worth, the apprentice seized a rock about the size of one of the loaves and heaved it. Shoemaker ducked, slipped in the mud of the ditch, and was struck in the back.

Carpenter could not restrain Mikki from rushing to the aid of his father. Both Carpenter and Crusher—Jesse—lunged forward after the boy.

Fisherman slid down the bank to help Shoemaker to his feet.

At the sight of more lepers emerging from the thorn trees and apparently attacking, the bakery knave set up a loud howling. In rapid-fire succession he pitched three more rocks. One landed harmlessly. One sailed into the culvert, striking Fisherman in the collarbone, breaking it.

The third hit Crusher squarely in the face, knocking him to his knees, senseless.

By now rocks were raining all around the lepers. A hailstorm of limestone lumps pelted all the minyan, except the Cabbage Sisters, who stayed huddled in the trees.

"Lepers! Go away!" the townspeople chanted.

"Good people, we're trying." That was as much as Carpenter managed before another rock hit him in the eye.

Mikki and one of his Torah school colleagues dragged Shoemaker out of the streambed.

His arm dangling at his side, Fisherman shouted instructions for two more students to assist in carrying Crusher.

Carpenter stood atop the far bank, his arms spread wide.

He did not try to plead for mercy; he merely made himself a target so the others could escape. The deadly hail of stones increased. Carpenter cut the bag of silver coins from Crusher's belt, emptied the contents into his hand, and flung the coins into the howling mob.

The attack ended as men, women, and children dove to the ground, scrambling to retrieve the money.

"Hurry!" Fisherman shouted to Carpenter.

Limping, shuffling, and toting the unconscious Crusher, the other nine wheezed their way up a canyon. They didn't stop even after putting a tangle of brush and the city dump between themselves and the aroused citizens of Modein.

Crusher came around. He sat on a stump and cradled his blood-soaked head. "What do we have left?"

Carpenter said with grim finality, "We've lost everything . . . everything. The money's gone. A few loaves of bread left for the journey . . . and we are finished."

A trio of crows mocked them from a dead tree.

The men were silent and grim as they set out again.

One Cabbage Sister leaned against the other when they moved, in a kind of three-legged gait. "Whatever will we . . ."

". . . do now?" they moaned.

There was no discussion and no need for a vote.

Carpenter said what they all were thinking. "Back to Mak'ob. There's nothing for us Outside. Let's go home, where we can die among friends."

They had failed. They stood on the rim of the precipice overlooking the Valley of Mak'ob. Dusk settled on the Valley floor, though the sunset flamed in the west. No familiar campfires gleamed up from the desolate refuge where the hopeless had once lived.

The Cabbage Sisters gazed at the overgrown vegetable patch. The fence was broken. Stones tumbled down onto once neat furrows. "It wasn't so bad here," said one.

"It was home," agreed the other.

The Torah boys chorused: "Empty."

"Empty."

"Empty."

"All gone," Carpenter said flatly.

"All healed but us." Shoemaker shook his head slowly in disbelief. "He came here while we were out looking for him."

Mikki said, "Poor Mother. She'll be waiting for us to come home. And we never will."

Carpenter scanned the switchback trail they had ascended with such hope so many months ago. He imagined what the night must have been like when Yeshua came and healed them all.

Fisherman completed his thought. "All of them."

"But not us." Shoemaker put his arm around Mikki.

Crusher rummaged through the bag Bette had prepared. Two loaves of flat bread remained. "It's too dark to travel down the path. We should eat."

Carpenter agreed. "We should build a fire. To keep warm tonight. It's cold on the rim." He set the Torah boys to work gathering fuel. The instinct to live remained strong, though death was now a certainty.

The fire was built from the dead branches of scrub oak and acacia wood. The ten sank down in misery. The cold spring wind whistled past, but they hardly noticed.

Crusher gave the bread to Carpenter, who blessed it with a mumbled blessing. He broke it.

"Our homecoming feast," Crusher said, yielding to bitterness as the torn bread was passed hand to hand. "The end of our journey."

Ten distorted faces gazed into the flames. Ten who did not look into the eyes of those friends who had made the journey together.

Why had it ended thus? Always beyond reach. Always in the next village. Yeshua the Healer, Messiah of Israel, would not be found beyond the boundaries of Mak'ob. He had come into the Valley of Suffering and had taken upon Himself the disease of the most vulnerable.

Mikki broke a crumb off from his meager portion and held it up in the firelight. "I saw Yeshua. Was this close to him . . . before I was sick. When I didn't need him. I could have asked him anything, but I didn't need his help. When Yeshua was in the Temple, driving out the money changers, I saw him. He opened the cages of the doves. Set them free."

The minyan understood what Mikki meant. They too were caged, like birds destined for slaughter. If Yeshua was so kind that He set caged doves free, why, why had He remained hidden from the Minyan of Mak'ob who had sought His help for so long?

The ten ate in silence after that.

One morsel of bread remained. From the darkness came the quavering voice of an old man. "The Valley will fill with suffering when Yeshua is gone."

All turned to see who had spoken. Carpenter stood. "Who's there?"

"My name is Charuz." A wizened old fellow stepped into the ring of firelight.

"Be warned. We're lepers here. Ten of us. Waiting for morning when we can go down into the Valley floor."

"Ah," the rail-thin figure in the broad straw hat replied.

"But I know you," commented Fisherman. "You're the man with the citron trees."

"Grapevines," Mikki and Shoemaker corrected.

"And I know all of you," Charuz said, bowing. "I know vines and etrogs. I also know pomegranates and almonds."

The Cabbage Sisters and Crusher started upright.

"Are you determined to die in Mak'ob? Because if you are not, I can take you to him . . . to Yeshua."

"You know where he is?" Carpenter demanded.

"It's too . . ."

". . . late," the Cabbage Sisters said mournfully. "Too tired to travel."

"Ah, but there's my cart," Charuz offered. "Come aboard, First Fruits of Israel. Come see where he who cares for the tender shoots waits for you."

The ten lepers, First Fruits of Israel, leaned against one another and slept as Charuz drove the oxcart through the long, dark night.

Too weary to hope, they no longer cared where they were being taken. The groaning of ungreased wheels masked the soft moans of ancient, intractable anguish.

Only twice along the uncharted route did Charuz stop and awaken his passengers, urging them to drink and to eat a morsel of bread. Offering water and grain to the oxen, the old man pressed on as if these were ten rare, precious trees that must be delivered to a field and planted by morning.

Planets danced above their heads. Starry skies and constellations shone overhead, just as they had upon the shepherds Abraham, Isaac, and Jacob in Israel's beginnings. The wagon jolted along the same river road where Joshua led the children of Israel into the Promised Land after 440 years of slavery and exile.

At the top of a rise, facing east, Charuz stopped the oxen.

Shoemaker was the first to awaken. Stars paled in the predawn sky. "Where are we?"

The old gardener swept his hand over rolling orchards and vineyards toward the pale pink walls of a city a half mile distant. "Jericho."

"Where is . . . he?" Shoemaker asked.

"Within."

The Cabbage Sisters raised their heads with difficulty and whispered to each other, "Look, Sister. Home again."

"They'll kill us if we come closer," said Fisherman.

"As good a place to die as any," noted Crusher.

"So we have come to this." Shoemaker caressed the head of his sleeping son. "How will we get through the gates? past the guards?"

Charuz fixed a curious smile on his wizened face. "He has been waiting for you."

"Waiting?" asked one of the Cabbage Sisters.

"He? For us?" echoed the other.

"You are the last from the Valley. All must be fulfilled. He would not leave before that work is finished." The old man was matter-of-fact as he placed feedbags on the noses of his oxen. "It is almost Passover."

Charuz fetched a skin of water mixed with wine that was passed from hand to hand. Bread was blessed, broken, and distributed. It was fresh and soft and easy to chew, even though the lepers did not have more than ten teeth among them.

The last morning stars gleamed as the gates of the city swung open. A caravan passed through, on its way out from Jericho. Drovers turned their heads and covered noses and mouths against the stench of rotten flesh.

Crusher called after them, "We are searching for Yeshua the Nazarene! The one they call Messiah!"

A boy leading the last camel shouted back, "Yeshua is in the city! At the house of the tax collector!"

"How will we reach him?" Fisherman asked softly, not expecting an answer.

Charuz gazed at the gate in silence for a long time but did not move the cart. The first light of dawn danced like molten gold on the blue mountains of Moab.

The solitary figure of a man emerged from the shadowed eastern portal. Ordinary. Just a man. He carried a staff, but nothing else. He walked with a purpose, his long stride gobbling up the distance between the walled city and the rise in the road.

"It's no one," said Carpenter with disappointment.

Charuz did not speak or move. He only stroked the noses of his oxen as he watched the approach of the one.

Then the traveler raised his staff high above his head in greeting. "Shalom! My friend!" the lone pilgrim shouted joyfully to Charuz.

Only then did the old man stir. "It is he. Yeshua," Charuz said calmly.

Heads snapped to attention. All eyes turned toward the approaching stranger. Some stood. Still, no one spoke. The ten remained rooted in the wagon as Charuz ran forward to meet the Master.

Yeshua embraced the old man with a laugh, paused for a moment. Voices carried on the crisp morning air.

"The last," Charuz said. "Those who were lost."

Yeshua smiled and gazed across the distance at the ten who had suffered so much. He saw them. "And now they are found. Well done, my friend." Yeshua clapped an arm around the gardener's shoulders.

Side by side, the old man and the Messiah started up the slope toward the wagon.

Yeshua looked so ordinary: brown hair with a touch of bronze. Warm, gold-flecked brown eyes.

Could this be the Messiah of Israel?

One by one they slipped from the bed of the cart and staggered toward Yeshua. Each saw the anointing in His eyes: Yeshua Himself shared their sorrows. He was the eleventh guest at the banquet of suffering.

He spoke their names—naming the nameless, calling them to His side. Souls trapped in broken bodies were healed first.

First Light broke full upon them as they came to Him. All the time in the world. . . .

He wrapped His arms around them, smiled down, and commanded unspeakable wounds to be healed. And . . . the wounds obeyed. He healed them all.

All, you ask?

Yes. It is written. All.

Our friend, John the Apostle, has recorded that all the books in the world cannot hold the stories of what Yeshua did while He lived among us as a man.[29] But this is the truth, the testimony of what we witnessed with our own eyes. We ten, the last minyan of suffering, went on our way joyfully home, with skin . . . and hearts . . . as of little children.

The leaves of the tree were for the
healing of the nations.
No longer will there be anything
accursed. . . .

REVELATION 22:2-3

Digging Deeper into ELEVENTH GUEST

Dear Reader,

Have you struggled to hang on to hope, when everything seems hopeless? Do you wonder if God sees your suffering, the worries that keep you up at night? Have you experienced a rift in a relationship that needs mending, but you don't know how to go about it?

The journey of the lepers of Mak'ob is all about these questions, and so many more that might be your questions or situations too.

Did Mikki deserve such a dread disease, just when his life was beginning? Was it right that the Shoemaker—a very honest, upright man—had to struggle to keep his business afloat in a tough economy. Isn't God supposed to watch over the righteous?

Judah the Fisherman was a businessman who kept both profits and people in perspective. Yet his biggest battle of all was at home, with a shrewish wife.

The Cabbage Sisters, in their immaturity, fought over a what-if situation (the shared love of a young man) . . . until the reality of Tabitha's illness pulled them together and helped them realize what was truly important.

The brothers Obed and Jesse took very different paths in life. Jesse chose to flee home and his mother's domination. Obed chose to stay home and endure his mother's abuse. Yet it was their shared love and Obed's forgiveness that brought Jesse, the wanderer, home again.

Do any of these situations hit home for you? Do you long for answers? acceptance? love? hope?

Following are six studies. You may wish to delve into them on your own or share them with a friend or a discussion group. They are designed to take you deeper into the answers to questions such as:

- Are some people just "destined" to suffer?
- Why doesn't God answer my prayers? And how can I deal with the what-ifs that haunt me?
- How can I make the best of an unhappy home situation?
- How can I know what's really important in life?
- Is God really watching? Does He care about what's broken in my life?
- How can I hang on to hope, even in the midst of difficult circumstances?

Can lives, bodies, and hearts truly be transformed? With Yeshua, *anything* is possible! Through *Eleventh Guest*, may the promised Messiah come alive to you . . . in more brilliance than ever before.

1 THAT'S ANOTHER STORY?!

They were meant to be a minyan of ten, chosen by lot to go out in search of Yeshua the Miracle Worker. The Galilean Rabbi was said to be able to heal every disease.

—P. 3

If you heard that a "miracle worker" was walking this earth, would you believe the stories? Why or why not?

____

____

____

What proof would make you believe in the claims of that miracle worker?

____

____

____

The Valley of Mak'ob was also known as the Valley of Suffering—and with good reason. Once a person with leprosy entered the Valley, the only way to leave was through death. It was dangerous to go Outside, for those with leprosy were greatly feared. No one else wanted to risk coming in contact with the "walking dead" for fear of contracting the disease themselves.

Staying Inside the Valley was so much safer . . . but there was only one end result.

How do you respond when you see those who are considered "untouchables" today (whether through social, mental, or physical conditions)?

____

____

____

Have *you* ever felt "untouchable"? If so, when? How did people respond to you during that time of your life? How has that experience influenced the way you treat others who are suffering now?

____

____

____

READ

Carpenter explained to the rabbi, "With Cantor flown away? It's like this, Rabbi. Those of us with a few years on us—mind you, not these four youths, but the rest of the party—we're thinking maybe it's a sign. Maybe we're meant to stay Inside."

Other voices broke in while the four teenaged lads scowled.

"Aye," agreed Crusher.

"That's it," concurred the two Cabbage Sisters in unison. "Thinking it's a sign we shouldn't . . ."

Fisherman, who had grown content with a life without the uncertain sea, added, "Never was too keen on the idea of leaving the Valley."

Carpenter added, "So, if Your Honor agrees with what we're saying? Well, Rabbi, we'd rather just . . . you know." . . .

Carpenter squirmed. "I'm not as young as I used to be."

The four young Torah scholars sat forward eagerly. Their leader, son of the Shoemaker who lay close to death, proclaimed, "But we're still young.

Still strong! Ah, Rabbi! We've never been Outside since we were small. Since we entered. Let us go! We'll go." He included the other scholars with his sweeping gesture. "Let us go Outside on our own. If there's a Messiah, we'll find him."

Rabbi raised his hand for silence. "Fine lads, all of you. Cantor would be proud of your eagerness. You're sons of his brave heart, that's certain. But without a leader. Without Cantor or Carpenter . . ."

—PP. 3–4

ASK

If you were one of the minyan chosen to leave the Valley, what concerns would you have (whether you dared to voice them or not)?

____

____

____

Which one of these people or groups would closest express your feelings? Explain.

- Shoemaker's Son (Mikki) and the other young Torah scholars
- Fisherman
- Crusher
- Carpenter
- the Cabbage Sisters
- Rabbi Ahava

____

____

____

READ

"I didn't want Cantor to leave the Valley. But it seems to me he wouldn't have wanted the rest of you to give up the quest just because he's not here to lead you. . . . And what if Messiah was just over the next hill? if hope was within reach? Just a mile away? Would you have turned back?"

Crusher studied the patch of sky as if he saw the future there. "Well now, that's altogether another story."

Lily held up her clawlike left hand. "And if you knew a touch or a word could restore this? And the One we've all been waiting for was close enough for you to shout to him? to grasp his knees and not let him go until . . . until . . . ?"

Carpenter, ashamed of his willingness to stay in a familiar place and die, relented. "If you put it that way, Lily, of course we'd go on."

"Yes. Yes, Carpenter," the young widow encouraged. "Cantor would expect it of you. Expect you all to be brave."

—PP. 4–5

ASK

How did Lily's words change the course of the journey for the entire group?

____

____

____

What individual has encouraged you—with a word or touch—when you weren't sure if you could go on? How?

____

____

____

In what way(s) have you seen a single individual change the course of a family, an organization, or a nation—for the better? Tell the story.

READ

"I've lived too long in Mak'ob to tell a good true story with a happy ending. No. I've forgotten all such stories."

—Carpenter, p. 10

Carpenter scanned the switchback trail they had ascended with such hope so many months ago. He imagined what the night must have been like when Yeshua came and healed them all.

Fisherman completed his thought. "All of them."

"But not us." Shoemaker put his arm around Mikki.

—p. 217

ASK

Do you agree with Carpenter's assessment that there's no such thing as a true story with a happy ending? Why or why not?

When have you felt hopeless—or wondered if suffering is simply the lot dealt to you in life?

What has happened (if anything) to change your perspective?

READ

Even though I walk through the valley of the shadow of death,
I will fear no evil,
for You are with me. . . .
You prepare a table before me
in the presence of my enemies. . . .
Surely goodness and mercy shall follow me
all the days of my life,
and I shall dwell in the house of the Lord forever.
—PSALM 23:4-6

ASK

In what way(s) does the ending of the minyan's story in *Eleventh Guest* give you hope and encouragement for your own story?

How can you share with others about your time in "the Valley" to encourage them in their suffering?

____

____

____

WONDER . . .

"The end is within reach. The goal is in sight. We will take hold of the Truth. It is finally attained. . . . The future is written in the Book, is it not? What was. What is. What will be."

—Eben Golah, pp. xvi–xvii

If you believe that everything written in the Book—God's Word—is the truth, and that the end is in sight, how will that influence the way you live today?

2 LIVING WITH WHAT-IFS . . .

Her eyes brimmed with what-ifs.
—CALLISTO, P. 20

What one circumstance in your life would you change if you could? What event would you turn the clock back on? Why?

___

___

___

What what-ifs and worries keep you awake at night?

___

___

___

All of us live with what-ifs. *What if he hadn't boarded the plane that day? What if I had gone to college, instead of deciding to work for a year? What if I lose my job? What if my child gets hurt? What if my coworker lies and blames me? What if we can't make our house payment this month? What if I had just let that little thing go and not stood my ground? How would my life be different?*

Tycho, Callisto, Linus, and Mikki knew all about the worry of what-ifs. They were living in a dangerous time—both politically and economically.

READ

"Mikki!" someone above and behind called to him. "Mikki!"

"Here!" He raised his hand.

Suddenly Linus appeared, fighting to reach him, to rescue him, to pull him up from drowning in a sea of sweaty tunics and frantic bodies. . . . Linus' grim and determined face appeared. The older brother managed to look both angry and relieved at the same moment. "Stay close to me," Linus urged, setting him on his feet and breaking a path to safety beside a pillar. . . .

With a growl Linus rounded on Mikki, seizing him by the scruff of his neck and pulling him down from the pillar. "Are you trying to get killed?" Linus worried aloud. "Keep to business and leave politics alone! Isn't that what Father always says? You can be so much trouble, Mikki!" Then he walked Mikki back to their stall with his arm around Mikki's shoulders.

—PP. 19–20

Tycho . . . grabbed his younger son and embraced him, but was unable to speak. . . . Tycho closed his eyes, as if trying to erase the nightmare image of what could have happened to Mikki.

—P. 20

Her eyes brimmed with what-ifs. "Mikki could have been killed!"

Tycho rubbed her hand in a calming gesture. "But he wasn't. We're all safe. No one got hurt."

—P. 20

ASK

In what different ways did these three family members express their concern for Mikki? How did they handle their what-ifs? Explain.

- Linus
- Tycho
- Callisto

When you've been concerned about a loved one who might be in danger, how have you responded? More like Linus, Tycho, or Callisto? Why?

____

____

____

READ

Callisto fretted, "But we ordered all that extra leather, expecting to sell a lot more sandals this year. The way pilgrims are staying away from Yerushalayim, we'll be lucky to sell enough to pay for the hides, let alone make any profit."

"Everyone's in the same boat," Tycho replied. "Lamp makers. Tinsmiths. Weavers. Since Passover, shoppers are staying home. Guilds are putting workers on half pay. . . . Don't worry. . . . We'll manage. The tannery will give me more time to pay. They don't want the hides back. Who else is there to sell to? We're all in the same fix."

"How bad is it? Can we hang on?"

—PP. 28–29

ASK

What what-ifs are Callisto and Tycho discussing? What impact could these events have on their family?

____

____

____

Have you ever found yourself in a similar situation, when money was tight and business prospects weren't good? How did you handle those worries? How do you handle them now, in today's tight economy?

____

____

____

READ

If only he'd never shown his father the wounds! If only he'd used the thimbles. If only he'd been more careful with the needle. Mikki couldn't breathe. It had nothing to do with his hands. He felt like he was drowning. *Leave home? Go somewhere unknown? Live with strangers? Never come back?*

—P. 49

"I can't! I can't do this!" Mikki heard his father assert. "I can't let him go alone. I'm going with him. . . .This is my fault. I must go! You understand, don't you, Callisto? Linus, you run the shop. Take care of your mother, yes?"

"If you go into the Valley," the priest observed sternly, "you may never come out to live again, except as a leper, outcast from city and society, unclean as death. Do you understand?"

"Yes," Mikki heard his father shout.

His father ran to embrace him, snatched Mikki up in his arms. A deep breath, and then his father cried, "Unclean! Leper! Unclean!"

—P. 52

"I-I wish my father was here. He could tell you the rest. How the Shoemaker went with his son. Gave up everything. Left Yerushalayim behind and . . ."

—P. 53

ASK

Step into Mikki's shoes. If you realized you were going to have to leave everything and everyone you knew, how would you respond?

____

____

____

What did Shoemaker give up to accompany his son to the Valley of Mak'ob? Why do you think he made this choice?

____

____

____

Knowing you'd be leaving some of your family behind, would you have made the same decision? Why or why not? What what-ifs would you continue to live with, depending on the choice you made?

____

____

____

READ

The heaviness of despair settled in Mikki's bones as he hurried away from Eli's house. Sure, they had learned the prayers of praise and healing and thanksgiving together. . . . He had prayed, really prayed.

Where was the God who answered? Why was Eli sick? Why were shops of the tradesmen's lanes being shuttered and abandoned as business dried up?

Don't you care? We are drowning in Yerushalayim. Drowning in the sea of hopelessness.

Mikki raised his eyes, imagining Messiah, Son of David, breaking through the clouds to vanquish their oppressors and heal their land.

"Oh, that You would rend the heavens and come down," he whispered.

But the clouds did not part.

—PP. 34–35

"The stories are true!" Linus asserted. "You remember the blind beggar at Nicanor Gate? The Nazarean healed him."

"Peniel?"

Callisto nodded eagerly. "And a cripple by the Pool of Bethesda," she added, her words spilling all over each other. "And—"

"And Eli!" Linus said triumphantly.

A mighty wind roared in Mikki's ears, and his mother's face swam in front of his eyes. *Eli, healed?*

Then the stories were true! The journey was not pointless! There was hope for the lepers of Mak'ob!

—P. 57

ASK

When you pray, do you feel like God answers? Why or why not?

____

____

____

Compare Mikki's thoughts in the first passage above to his thoughts in the second. What makes the difference in his perspective?

____

____

____

Have you experienced a long period of waiting before you received an answer to prayer? If so, how did you change during that waiting period?

___

___

___

WONDER . . .

"They say he heals everyone who asks . . . who believes."

—P. 53

In your distress you called and I rescued you.

—Psalm 81:7

Do you really believe that Yeshua can heal you? Then why not pray like you believe it to be true?

3 PLANTING A DREAM

> Was he staring into the fulfillment of someone else's life, someone else's dreams?
> —P. 61

Do you ever wish you could live someone else's life? If so, whose—and why?

____

____

____

Look back five or ten years. What dreams did you have then that haven't yet been fulfilled?

____

____

____

If one of those dreams could be instantly fulfilled, which would you choose? How would receiving that dream change you? How would it affect the other people in your life?

____

____

____

Judah the Fisherman has lost so much. Although he's surrounded by friends from the Valley of Mak'ob, he grieves when he sees his old home in Joppa. He wonders about his sons: *Where are they? What are they doing?* He wonders if the property has been sold. If the trees that he planted for each of his children—symbolizing his dreams for them—are still there . . . or if someone else is living the life he wishes he still had.

READ

Before Judah could complete his shouted warning, wave and wind and plunging cable sucked Breen over the side and into the depths.

Ripping his knife from the sheath at his belt, Judah bit down on the blade and threw himself headfirst into the sea after the boy. . . . There had been no time to shed his tunic. Now the clothing threatened to drag him to the bottom.

God of my fathers, Judah prayed, *help me now!*

—P. 65

It had been a near thing, this rescue. Judah had jumped in without thinking of his own safety, and it was a good thing too. In another moment Breen would have been impossible to locate until they hauled in his drowned body still knotted in the net. . . .

Among the houses of the fisherfolk of Joppa town there were many empty places at tables where the sea had not been so forbearing. Judah was grateful to God he did not have to report such a fate to Breen's father and mother.

—P. 66

ASK

What do these passages say about Judah the Fisherman's character? Why does being "under fire" usually bring out the truth of a person's character?

Look back at a stressful life event. How did you respond? Would you respond the same way if the event happened again? Why or why not?

____

____

____

READ

After the weary row back to Joppa Harbor, Judah wanted only to sleep. Instead he dispatched Lech to help Breen get home. . . . Judah himself did not go home. He waited on the docks for the other two boats to return.

—PP. 66–67

He reviewed what the night had cost him. The catch of fish had escaped, the net would have to be mended, the purse line was so chopped up it would need to be replaced, and a whole night's fishing had been wasted, but praise the Eternal, a life had been spared.

—P. 66

"I'm sorry . . . my fault . . . stupid," Breen kept repeating.

"Go home." Judah pushed the young man away good-naturedly. "To be a fisherman you learn many lessons . . . . Just thank the Almighty that tonight's lesson didn't cost you your life and . . . don't ever step in a coil of rope again! . . . Now get home! But out of your next pay packet, save enough to buy a thank-offering for HaShem your next trip to Yerushalayim."

"You mean I still have a job?"

"After I saved your life? You'll be years working that off."

Breen looked worried.

Judah offered his crooked smile to relieve the tension. "'Course you have a job. Be back here midday. Nets to mend. Now go!"

—PP. 66–67

Shomer protested. "You already saved me from a beating . . . or worse. Can't take your charity, too."

"Can you weave nets? Fishing nets?" Judah inquired.

"S'pose so. I can weave anything if I have a frame and a pattern to follow. Why?"

"Then it's not charity. Call it an advance on your pay. I'm hiring you to work on my nets for me. Now take this, get a room and a meal, and come to harbor tomorrow at midday. Ask for Judah the Fisherman. Anyone can tell you where to find me."

—P. 81

ASK

What kind of businessman was Judah the Fisherman? Is he a person you'd want to work for? Explain.

____

____

____

In your work (whether at home, school, or in the workplace), how easy is it to keep what's important in perspective? Do you tend to err on the side of getting things done or looking out for people? Give an example.

____

____

____

READ

"And you could have been killed," Emma protested. "Then where would I be? . . . Answer me that: where?"

Judah tried to step forward to embrace her, but she backed away. "You're soaked and you stink, and you could have been killed. You never think of me at all, do you?"

"Emma, what if it had been one of the boys? You'd want someone to—"

"Never! Our boys will never risk their lives out on the ocean in those foolish, dangerous, little boats. They will own a fishing business, not be smelly fishermen. . . . And why are you out on the water anyway? Don't you own the business? Don't you have three boats and all those men who work for you? Why can't you be home at night and go to an office like the Carpet Importer or the Dried Fruit Merchant?"

The wives of those two shopkeepers were two of Emma's best friends. They often came up when comparisons were required. . . .

When did she change? Judah pondered wearily, recalling the loving, laughing beauty of his bride.

—PP. 69–70

ASK

What does Emma complain about? What do those complaints reveal about her dreams? about her perspective of the present and the future?

Are there ways in which you can identify with Emma? If so, did you always feel that way, or did your thoughts and feelings change? What triggered the change?

READ

"The one you're standing in front of right now is your tree. It'll be yours forever. Next year, five years, ten years, when each of you comes here with your own babies, you'll say, 'I remember when my papa and me planted this . . . 'course he was a lot stronger then.'"

There was a chorus of "Really?" and "Mine, Papa?"

Judah nodded and pointed to the last tree on the left. "And that one'll be for your baby sister when she gets here."

Judah felt Emma's eyes boring into the back of his head. He had invited her to come to the "ceremony," but she had refused. "Dirt and smelly trees?" she griped. "Are you trying to make me sick? You know how dirt and smelly things make me sick."

Even now she came no farther than the doorway of the house. She leaned her back against the doorframe, the bulge of her pregnancy prominently displayed.

"Thank you, Papa," Tamuz said, hugging Judah around the neck. Not to be outdone, Rin hugged even harder from the other side. Two-year-old Tor stared and said, "My tree," as he patted a branch.

Judah wiped his cheek. "Got dirt in my eye," he said. Then, "Wash up good, boys. Hands, faces, and necks. And don't track anything into the house."

Emma was no longer watching.

—PP. 74–75

Her face was drawn up in an unhappy frown.

Judah wished her good dreams.

—PP. 84–85

ASK

How does Emma respond to Judah's idea of planting the trees?

____

____

____

Does Judah allow her attitude to influence him in doing what he wants for his children? Why or why not?

____

____

____

What could you do, even in the midst of a difficult home situation, to "plant dreams" and not give up? How can you wish an unhappy person "good dreams"?

WONDER . . .

Hope deferred makes the heart sick,
But a desire fulfilled is a tree of life.
—PROVERBS 13:12

What dream do you need to plant in the soil of your heart today?

4 FIXING THE BREACH

She had severed her welded heart from Tabitha's. . . . The breach, though unrevealed to Mama and Papa, was open between the sisters.

—P. 117

"What do you suppose we will be when we are grown up?" Tera asked Tabitha.

Tabitha plucked a cabbage and gave it to Tera. "We will always be Sisters."

—P. 128

If you had siblings (or cousins who were close in age), what did you fight about when you were young?

____

____

____

Looking back, were those fights about issues worth fighting over? Why? What, if anything, has changed in your perspective?

____

____

____

Tera and Tabitha, as twin daughters of the rabbi of Jericho, share everything—until it comes time for the first born daughter to be wed. Then their relationship explodes into what's best known as a "catfight," escalating into furious, resentful, hateful words and a startling act of violence that invokes guilt.

READ

Tabitha said, "I see it clearly. Marry off the first born daughter to . . . to a relic! . . . Then when I am out of the way, you . . . marry this Yeshiva Adonis!"

Tera could not deny that this had crossed her mind. "But you! You would have me, your own sister, marry with you . . . to this old fellow . . . and share your misery. You would marry us both to this decrepit inhabitant of an ossuary just so you would not be lonely!"

Poised like cats with claws unsheathed, the sisters glared at their own reflections in their faces.

Fury! Betrayal! Jealousy! Resentment roiled the depths of their evenly matched souls. So, Tera would have love and youth and the challenges of poverty, which knit one's soul to its mate, while Tabitha would have wealth and impotence and a life without passion or joy!

—P. 112

ASK

What do the sisters accuse each other of? What is the fight *really* about?

Have you ever found yourself in a fight like this that you can't win? What happened as a result?

If you had to choose love, youth, and poverty *or* wealth, impotence, and a life without passion or joy, which would you pick? Why?

____

____

____

READ

Tera denied that this horror could be possible. Why? In the family of such a righteous rabbi? Tera prayed to wake up from the nightmare. To no avail.

"You still have one . . . one beautiful daughter," Tabitha said in farewell to her parents. "Tera, now you will have to live for both of us."

—P. 119

Tera would stand in her place at the wedding to Nachman the Elder. A bargain: Even if she was forced to be a wife to him for the sake of Tabitha, she would do so.

"But only, please HaShem, will you not give her back to us? For Mama. For Papa. She may have my life and I'll take hers. She may marry my young man . . . have children. And I will hold steady for everything. But only just . . . I want my sister's life back."

But it was not to be.

—P. 119

Vain and vapid, self-absorbed and selfish, Tera grew up in an instant.

—P. 121

ASK

What breaks the tension of the twins' fight? What circumstances result, for both of the girls?

____

____

____

How does Tera's prayer reveal her change of heart toward her sister?

Have you ever felt like you have to live for yourself *and* for someone else? Why?

READ

The doctor said, "Tabitha is resigned. Accepting that this is God's judgment for her sin."

"What?" the rabbi exclaimed. . . . He grasped Tera by the hands. "Dear daughter, do you know what it is your sister is talking about?"

Tera knew. Tabitha thought their anger at each other had brought on the punishment. Tabitha felt the pain of their disagreement as well, but surely the Almighty was not so cruel in judging the vanity of girls. God had not joined in and taken sides in the argument between two siblings. The Almighty would not cause one to die of sickness and the other of a broken heart because of a silly argument.

Tera would not tell her father the details of what had passed between them. "It was nothing. She was afraid to marry Nachman the Elder; that's all."

"Afraid?" Papa sat down slowly. "Afraid is not a sin. I am afraid now." He spread his hands out on his lap and said slowly over the low weeping of Mama, "No . . . no judgment. This sickness, our beautiful daughter—just the way things are in this world."

—P. 120

ASK

Do you believe sickness is God's judgment for sin, as Tabitha thinks? Or is sickness "just the way things are in this world," as her papa says? Explain your answer.

How can "silly arguments" cause tremendous damage? Have they influenced your life in any way? If so, how?

READ

Both sisters would suffer, each in a different way. Their great love for each other could not save them from life. Love demanded that no matter who suffered first, both would suffer.

—P. 122

Tera called to her, but Tabitha could not hear her. Instead, Tera heard Tabitha say to the sea, "I'm going under. My own weight dragging me beneath the waves. I know it. Who loves me enough that he will give his life for me? Who will die in my place so I will no longer be stone, but live, redeemed?"

Tera shouted, "I will!"

Tabitha answered her, gasping out each word. "Oh, Tera! It can't be. You dying for me. Or me dying for you. Our Love. It isn't enough. Our Love can't fix this. No matter who dies for who, we each still suffer for the other. Sorrow will drag us under in the end."

Tera cried out, "Then who? Who can save us?"

Tabitha did not reply. The wind pushed and the waves pulled until she vanished beneath the water.

Tera stood rooted on the shore. She could not save her. "Someone! Lord of heaven, help us. Save us!" she cried.

The waves thundered. The wind howled.

Lightning cracked, rending the heavens and striking the sea. And then? Then the gentle voice of a man sighed from somewhere far away, "I will go. I will die for her. And you."

—PP. 121–122

"I am not a stone," [Tera] said to the angels who went with her. "I will not sink, but will save what I can."

Tera was not afraid. The reality of living forty years suffering alone without her sister was more frightening to her than the prospect of perhaps one day suffering her sister's fate.

—P. 128

ASK

How did each of the sisters suffer? Which one do you think bore a greater burden—Tera or Tabitha? Why?

____

____

____

Do you think love is enough to fix any situation? Explain.

____

____

____

What's the difference between human love (for example, the compelling sacrifice Tera made in going to the Valley to be with her sister) and the Lord of Heaven's sacrificial love?

WONDER . . .

Life was loving, after all, even though love sometimes made life hard to live. Tera knew: Existence, cold as stone and separated from love, was no life at all. . . . "Even when love breaks your stony heart."

Tera had it in her power to plant hope where there was despair and loneliness.

—P. 128

Is there a breach in your relationship with a friend or loved one? If so, what step(s) can you take to end the argument? (Remember: you are only responsible for *your* actions, not the other person's response.) How can you plant hope where there is despair and loneliness?

5 IS GOD WATCHING?

"Does God watch over little men like me?"
—Obed, p. 203

Do you ever wonder if God is watching? Does He really notice what's happening in the world—and in *your* world? What makes you think He does . . . or doesn't?

___

___

What's the most prominent memory you have of growing up? Is it a happy one or a traumatic one? How has this childhood memory become a part of who you are now and how you live?

___

___

___

Obed and Jesse grew up in a very unhappy home, with both an abusive mother and an abusive father. When his father dies, Obed doesn't really grieve the loss. He only grieves what their life has been like at the cruel hand of his father. And now he's left with his shrewish mother, who only has interest in her other son, her first born. There's nothing like being on the outside, looking in. . . .

READ

Obed had thought last night as his father was laid out on the bier that now he and his brother and his mother would draw close to one another.

Instead the Widow and Jesse the First Born Son had walked from the house to the vineyard and quarreled violently. It was the first time Obed had ever seen his mother displeased with the heir. Jesse had always been the light of her life and the sun around which their father's hopes had orbited.

Obed, as second son, had remained outside the circle of that light, like a hungry stray who longs to be called inside for a plate of food and a pat on the head. He did not resent his father and mother's adoration of Jesse. Obed was content to be second, to look on and love the trio of mother, father, and elder son, at a distance.

Now that their father was gone, this rift between the Widow and the First Born was the one true grief Obed felt. The order of the universe had shattered.

—P. 146

Obed watched as his brother looked one last time around the room that had been his home . . . his prison.

Obed followed him out the door and down the path to the road.

"Will I see you again?" Obed fought back tears.

"Maybe. Maybe I'll come back someday. When I'm rich." He enfolded Obed in his strong arms. "Little brother. You were always the best. The most dependable. They just never . . . we never . . . appreciated you."

Obed wiped a tear from his cheek. "Jesse, I will . . . miss you."

Jesse pumped his hand. "You won't. You won't miss me. I made your life miserable." . . .

[Obed] missed his brother with an ache like death.

—PP. 149, 153

ASK

How do these passages reveal Obed's character—who he really is? And how he handled his circumstances?

____

____

____

If you were the second son, unloved and unappreciated, how would you respond? Would you have been glad or sorry to see Jesse go? Why?

____

____

____

READ

"You're ten kinds of a fool." She laughed bitterly. "This place. You rebuilt this house for her. Then I'll tell you the secret of your pretty cottage. It was the house of a leper. Your father's sister. He kept her here until they couldn't hide it any longer. The stones . . . contaminated! Torn down after you were born!"

"You are a liar. A thief of joy. Get out. Get away from here. This is my house. And Bette's. Built for her!"

The Widow shrugged. She was enjoying his pain. "This is your inheritance, then. You will raise another man's child in a house where lepers lived. A fool, Obed. You are a fool. Not like anyone in my family. Certainly not like me. Or Jesse. Or the man you called 'Father.' He was not your father. Didn't you ever wonder?"

Obed took a step toward her as if to strike.

She smiled cruelly and turned on her heel."Every rock and tree on this place is mine . . . and Jesse's. Second born? You were first born to a woman with leprosy. We kept you, out of the kindness of our hearts, when she left for Mak'ob, so you would not die of the disease. So I give you this house—these leper's stones where you were born. This house, the truth . . . your wedding present. You might as well not have been born at all."

—PP. 173–174

Obed's life was before him. He vowed he would leave the sorrow of his past behind.

". . . *For this cause a man shall leave his mother and father and cling only to his wife, and the two shall become one flesh.*"

From now on everything was Bette.

Because you have loved me, the almond tree blooms.

Bette, the sum of Obed's every wish and dream.

—P. 179

ASK

If you were Obed, facing this barrage from a bitter woman, how would you respond? What would you say? want to say?

______

______

______

How does Obed respond?

______

______

______

Have you been able to leave any sorrow of your past behind and cling to what is "now"? If so, how have you accomplished that? If not, what holds you in the past?

______

______

______

READ

Images burst from his mind like a covey of quail startled in the field. *The accusation the Widow had made against Bette the day before the wedding. Her mocking gift of the leper's cottage. Her refusal in over half a year since their marriage to acknowledge Bette. Her denial of Obed as her son . . .*

He balanced these things with the glory of a living child—his child—blooming in Bette's womb.

"It won't change her. Don't hope to be friends with her."

"Not even this?"

"She doesn't care. As long as I work the fields and bring her income and see to it she is cared for, there is no affection in our arrangement. I am a hired hand to her."

Bette frowned at his pronouncement. "I'm sorry."

"That's the way it is."

"I mean, I am sorry for her. So bitter. So alone."

"She has always been alone. Even when we were all around her. That's why my . . . father . . . died. And why Jesse left. But me? I meant the least to her obsession, yet I stayed. She hates me even more, I think, for not leaving."

Bette shrugged and popped a raw almond into her mouth. "But this . . . this is our life, Obed. My dearest. These four walls. The vines, the orchard. Our little flock. What she thinks means nothing to our happiness. You believe that, don't you?"

Involuntarily, Obed glanced up toward the Widow's house. "I wish it were different. I miss my brother. But he was right to leave."

"And you are right to stay, to honor her with your labor. It is written: Long life and honor to you, Obed. Blessings and prosperity."

"Long life . . . with you." He moved to sit beside her. She took his hand and guided his fingers to her belly. It was flat, no sign yet. Like the saplings waiting to bud. "And this little one of ours. May he grow strong and know that we love him. I ask for nothing else."

—PP. 181–182

ASK

How does Bette help Obed balance his perspective of his mother? Who helps you keep a balanced perspective amidst life's difficulties? How?

What things do you do just because it's right to do them?

____

____

____

What person or people are you letting infringe on your happiness? What do you need to focus on instead?

____

____

____

READ

Obed reflected. "So, back to your original question. Bette and Blossom are everything I care for in this world. This little house. It's mine. I built it. You and I have built and planted this arbor together. It's enough. In spite of all my dreams, it's enough. If my brother came home? If Jesse . . ." He paused, fighting back the emotion of yearning. He imagined the reunion, the joy! "If Jesse asked me to turn over everything beyond this little plot. The orchard? The vineyard? I would give it gladly to welcome him home and share his friendship again."

—P. 198

ASK

What does this passage say about Obed's priorities? about the state of his heart?

____

____

____

If others were to judge your priorities by watching how you spend your time, what would they say? Would this be an accurate reflection of your true priorities? Why or why not?

____

____

____

READ

Obed replied, "I would most like to see my brother. Jesse."

Charuz raised his sparse eyebrows as if the answer surprised him. "This was his vineyard?"

"He's the heir. It was his when my father died. If he returns, then it will be his."

"He had little regard for what was meant to be his."

Obed had to agree, yet he defended Jesse. "My brother. You just have to know him. Always first. Always the strongest and the smartest. The best. I say that from the bottom of my heart. Not bitter. Jesse is all that. He had greater things to do with his life than stay at home and tend a little vineyard, I suppose. My brother was always destined to be a great man. And I? I am a small thing in the eyes of the Lord."

—P. 200

ASK

If you had a sibling destined for great things, and you were simply ordinary, how might you feel? How might you respond?

____

____

____

Which sibling are you most like in your thoughts and actions—Obed or Jesse? Why?

READ

The bare branches of the almond orchard reached skyward, scraping the underbelly of the heavy clouds. "Charuz said that an almond orchard is a reminder that God is watching. But does God watch over little men like me?"

Did the God of Abraham, Isaac, and Jacob see and hear an ordinary fellow like Obed, who had never really accomplished anything of importance?

Obed closed his eyes and exhaled. "What difference do I make? If only I could see myself as you see me, Lord. Then I could fix the broken places in my life and . . ." His prayer faltered. He was suddenly exhausted by the effort.

—P. 203

ASK

What two big questions is Obed asking? Have you ever asked these questions? If so, when?

Have you ever wished that you could fix the broken places in your life—or in a loved one's life? What prayers have you sent heavenward as a result? What actions have you taken?

____

____

____

WONDER . . .

"The Almighty never sleeps or slumbers. He is watching over your life. *Shaqad.*"

—CHARUZ, P. 168

An "ordinary person" can truly accomplish great things. Obed's love for his brother brought Jesse home not once, but *three times*; he continued to honor and care for his mother, who only viciously harmed him; he built a home for Bette and Blossom and later his boys, in spite of the fact that he had grown up in an abusive home; he showed kindness to the lepers and provided for them, without fear of touching them. In the perspective of eternity, the influence that Obed had over people was enormous! If you truly believed that the Lord was watching over your life, and that even an ordinary person like you could accomplish great things, what might you accomplish with the Lord's help?

6 HANGING ON TO HOPE

Carpenter instructed the circle of downcast faces, "We have reason for thanks. We're all still alive. There's hope for us this Shabbat. Let us . . . give thanks."

—P. 143

Do you know someone who is in the midst of difficult circumstances yet seems to hold on to hope and peace? Why does this particular person come to mind? Tell the story.

____

____

____

Is it easy for you to give thanks, no matter the circumstance? Why or why not?

____

____

____

The lepers of Mak'ob, outcasts of society, experienced disheartening and horrific circumstances on their journey to find Yeshua. They were hungry, exhausted from traveling, bleeding from wounds, fearful, discouraged, shunned by society, and even stoned. They wavered between hope and discouragement.

READ

"We don't belong here . . . on the Outside, I mean," one of the Torah students said firmly.

"Let's go home," another agreed. "Back to the Valley."

Murmurs of agreement circled the Torah scholars.

"No one hated us there."

"No one threw stones at us."

"Or called us names."

"To die as lepers?" Fisherman observed morosely. "Yeshua's already been to Mak'ob. He won't go back there."

"Maybe we're the only lepers left in Judea," Mikki ventured.

This observation made the Cabbage Sisters sob afresh.

"How did so much change since yesterday?" Carpenter wondered aloud. "Shimona—we all saw her, healed! The hope we had yesterday! The stories about Yeshua are true."

"And Shimona now lives in a cage smaller than Mak'ob," one of the students groused. "Alone and outcast. That was never true in the Valley."

A pall of desperate silence fell over the group with the setting sun. If being healed meant living alone for the rest of life, was it worth it?

—PP. 136–137

ASK

If you were one of the minyan, what would you be saying after nearly getting stoned in Jericho? What's the general consensus of the group?

____

____

____

How is it possible to swing from great hope to depression or discouragement in just twenty-four hours? Has this ever happened to you? If so, tell the story.

____

____

____

If you could be healed from a physical, emotional, or mental ailment, yet it meant living alone for the rest of your life, would you choose to be healed? Why or why not? What benefit can you see on both sides? How could seeing the benefit(s) of suffering alter your perspective?

____

____

____

READ

"Better try once more than go back to Mak'ob . . . to die," Crusher replied softly. "Or should we just lie down and die right here?"

"We want . . ."

". . . to try once more," urged the Cabbage Sisters through stifled groans and gritted teeth.

"I honor your wounds," Shoemaker said to the pair. Then, raising his voice to encompass the whole minyan and the starry host: "I honor them. If they are willing to try once more, and Crusher agrees, who am I to say no?"

—PP. 137–138

Obed held his brother tighter. The foul stench of Jesse's illness told him everything. He understood it all now. Love had driven Jesse away. His suffering hidden, to spare Obed from suffering, had instead caused a wound too deep for words.

—P. 208

ASK

What makes the Minyan of Mak'ob decide to try again? Would these reasons be enough for you, if you were part of the group?

What does it mean to honor someone else's wounds? If someone has been in the trenches of suffering, do you look at them any differently? Explain.

Which is more difficult for you to handle—a physical injury or an emotional wound? Why?

READ

"No. No, Jesse. You must stay awhile. Like the old vines, meant to grow strong here again in your own soil. Stay with us and you will find a new life."

And so that night, arm in arm, trembling matched with trembling, Obed took his brother home to meet his wife and child.

Obed bathed his wounds, anointed him with oil, and clothed him. Bette fed him and made a bed for him in the little cottage behind the house. Blossom smiled at him and gave him a will to live.

So it was that Jesse the leper did indeed grow strong again. He had a will to live, in spite of his sickness.

—P. 209

Bette took the arms of the women and gently led them up the path. "Come on. There's plenty for you to eat at the house. Clean clothes. A bath. A day of rest. It will do wonders for you."

Jesse protested. "Bette, our presence will put you in danger."

Bette replied, "No. No more fear, Jesse. Only hope. Hope for us all. We've all been afflicted in one way or the other. But no more. If they kill us, Yeshua can raise the dead. . . . Jesse, I wrote you in the letter. Though your eyes never read the words, your heart drew you home. Now you are here. The one we were waiting for has come at last."

—P. 213

ASK

What actions of Obed give Jesse a will to live again, in spite of being sick?

____

____

____

How does Bette's response to the Cabbage Sisters and to Jesse help them hang on to hope, even though they have once again missed the Healer's touch?

____

____

____

Do you agree that "we've all been afflicted in one way or the other"? Explain.

____

____

____

READ

"The last," Charuz said. "Those who were lost."

Yeshua smiled and gazed across the distance at the ten who had suffered so much. He saw them. "And now they are found." . . .

One by one they slipped from the bed of the cart and staggered toward Yeshua. Each saw the anointing in His eyes: Yeshua Himself shared their sorrows. He was the eleventh guest at the banquet of suffering.

He spoke their names—naming the nameless, calling them to His side. Souls trapped in broken bodies were healed first.

First Light broke full upon them as they came to Him. All the time in the world. . . .

He wrapped his arms around them, smiled down, and commanded unspeakable wounds to be healed. And . . . the wounds obeyed. He healed them all.

All, you ask?

Yes. It is written. All.

—P. 221

ASK

Why would it be important for Yeshua to speak the names of these lost ones? to share their sorrows?

____

____

____

What "wounds" of your own do you long for Yeshua to heal?

____

____

____

WONDER . . .

He who dwells in the shelter of the Most High
will abide in the shadow of the Almighty. . . .
You will not fear the terror of the night,
nor the arrow that flies by day. . . .
A thousand may fall at your side,
ten thousand at your right hand,
but it will not come near you.
—PSALM 91:1, 5, 7

"What harm can come to us now if we are his?"
—BETTE, P. 213

If you truly believed Bette's words, how might that bring hope and peace to your present circumstances? How might you help others hang on to hope?

Dear Reader,

You are so important to us. We have prayed for you as we wrote this book and also as we receive your letters and hear your soul cries. We hope that *Eleventh Guest* has encouraged you to go deeper. To get to know Yeshua better. To fill your soul hunger by examining Scripture's truths for yourself.

We are convinced that if you do so, you will find this promise true: *"If you seek Him, He will be found by you."* —1 CHRONICLES 28:9

Bodie & Brock Thoene

Authors' Note

The following sources have been helpful in our research for this book:

- **The Complete Jewish Bible*. Translated by David H. Stern. Baltimore, MD: Jewish New Testament Publications, Inc., 1998.
- **iLumina*, a digitally animated Bible and encyclopedia suite. Carol Stream, IL: Tyndale House Publishers, 2002.
- **The International Standard Bible Encyclopaedia*. George Bromiley, ed. 5 vols. Grand Rapids, MI: Eerdmans, 1979.
- **The Life and Times of Jesus the Messiah*. Alfred Edersheim. Peabody, MA: Hendrickson Publishers, Inc., 1995.
- *Starry Night™ Enthusiast Version 5.0, published by Imaginova™ Corp.

Scripture References

[1] Rev. 2:13
[2] Isa. 59:17
[3] John 15:5
[4] Dan. 7:13-14
[5] Rev. 1:10-13
[6] Rev. 22:13
[7] Rev. 1:8, 11
[8] John 2:16
[9] Ps. 81:1-2
[10] Ps. 81:3
[11] Ps. 81:7
[12] Ps. 81:8-9
[13] Ps. 81:13-14, 16
[14] Isa. 64:1
[15] Zech. 3:10
[16] Ps. 107:9
[17] Deut. 5:9
[18] Lev. 23:40
[19] Ps. 127:4-5
[20] See Josh. 6:26
[21] Isa. 64:1
[22] Job 1:21
[23] Gen. 2:18
[24] See Luke 6:38
[25] Gen. 2:24
[26] Prov. 3:9-10
[27] Prov. 3:3
[28] Prov. 2:11
[29] John 21:25

About the Authors

BODIE AND BROCK THOENE (pronounced *Tay-nee)* have written over 50 works of historical fiction. That these best sellers have sold more than 10 million copies and won eight ECPA Gold Medallion Awards affirms what millions of readers have already discovered—the Thoenes are not only master stylists but experts at capturing readers' minds and hearts.

In their timeless classic series about Israel (The Zion Chronicles, The Zion Covenant, and The Zion Legacy), the Thoenes' love for both story and research shines.

With The Shiloh Legacy and *Shiloh Autumn* (poignant portrayals of the American Depression), The Galway Chronicles (dramatic stories of the 1840s famine in Ireland), and the Legends of the West (gripping tales of adventure and danger in a land without law), the Thoenes have made their mark in modern history.

In the A.D. Chronicles they step seamlessly into the world of Jerusalem and Rome, in the days when Yeshua walked the earth and transformed lives with His touch.

Bodie began her writing career as a teen journalist for her local newspaper. Eventually her byline appeared in prestigious periodicals such as *U.S. News and World Report*, *The American West*, and *The Saturday Evening Post.* She also worked for John Wayne's Batjac Productions (she's best known as author of *The Fall Guy)* and ABC Circle Films as a writer and researcher. John Wayne described her as "a writer with talent that captures the people and the times!" She has degrees in journalism and communications.

Brock has often been described by Bodie as "an essential half of this writing team." With degrees in both history and education, Brock has, in his role as researcher and story-line consultant, added the vital dimension of historical accuracy. Due to such careful research, the Zion Covenant and Zion Chronicles series are recognized by the American Library Association, as well as Zionist libraries around the world, as classic historical novels and are used to teach history in college classrooms.

Bodie and Brock have four grown children—Rachel, Jake, Luke, and Ellie—and seven grandchildren. Their children are carrying on the Thoene family talent as the next generation of writers, and Luke produces the Thoene audiobooks. Bodie and Brock divide their time between London and Nevada.

For more information visit:

www.thoenebooks.com
www.familyaudiolibrary.com

THOENE FAMILY CLASSICS™

✪ ✪ ✪

THOENE FAMILY CLASSIC HISTORICALS

by Bodie and Brock Thoene

*Gold Medallion Winners**

THE ZION COVENANT

*Vienna Prelude**
Prague Counterpoint
Munich Signature
Jerusalem Interlude
Danzig Passage
*Warsaw Requiem**
London Refrain
Paris Encore
Dunkirk Crescendo

THE ZION CHRONICLES

*The Gates of Zion**
A Daughter of Zion
The Return to Zion
A Light in Zion
*The Key to Zion**

THE SHILOH LEGACY

*In My Father's House**
A Thousand Shall Fall
Say to This Mountain

SHILOH AUTUMN

THE GALWAY CHRONICLES

*Only the River Runs Free**
Of Men and of Angels
*Ashes of Remembrance**
All Rivers to the Sea

THE ZION LEGACY

Jerusalem Vigil
Thunder from Jerusalem
Jerusalem's Heart
Jerusalem Scrolls
Stones of Jerusalem
Jerusalem's Hope

A.D. CHRONICLES

First Light
Second Touch
Third Watch
Fourth Dawn
Fifth Seal
Sixth Covenant
Seventh Day
Eighth Shepherd
Ninth Witness
Tenth Stone
Eleventh Guest
and more to come!

CP0064

THOENE FAMILY CLASSICS™

✪ ✪ ✪

THOENE FAMILY CLASSIC AMERICAN LEGENDS

LEGENDS OF THE WEST
by Bodie and Brock Thoene

Legends of the West, Volume One
- *Sequoia Scout*
- *The Year of the Grizzly*
- *Shooting Star*

Legends of the West, Volume Two
- *Gold Rush Prodigal*
- *Delta Passage*
- *Hangtown Lawman*

Legends of the West, Volume Three
- *Hope Valley War*
- *The Legend of Storey County*
- *Cumberland Crossing*

Legends of the West, Volume Four
- *The Man from Shadow Ridge*
- *Cannons of the Comstock*
- *Riders of the Silver Rim*

LEGENDS OF VALOR
by Luke Thoene

Sons of Valor
Brothers of Valor
Fathers of Valor

✪ ✪ ✪

THOENE CLASSIC NONFICTION
by Bodie and Brock Thoene

Writer-to-Writer

THOENE FAMILY CLASSIC SUSPENSE
by Jake Thoene

CHAPTER 16 SERIES
Shaiton's Fire
Firefly Blue
Fuel the Fire

✪ ✪ ✪

THOENE FAMILY CLASSICS FOR KIDS

BAKER STREET DETECTIVES
by Jake and Luke Thoene

The Mystery of the Yellow Hands
The Giant Rat of Sumatra
The Jeweled Peacock of Persia
The Thundering Underground

LAST CHANCE DETECTIVES
by Jake and Luke Thoene

Mystery Lights of Navajo Mesa
Legend of the Desert Bigfoot

THE VASE OF MANY COLORS
by Rachel Thoene (Illustrations by Christian Cinder)

✪ ✪ ✪

THOENE FAMILY CLASSIC AUDIOBOOKS

Available from
www.thoenebooks.com or
www.familyaudiolibrary.com

CP0064

Jerusalem

FIRST CENTURY A.D.

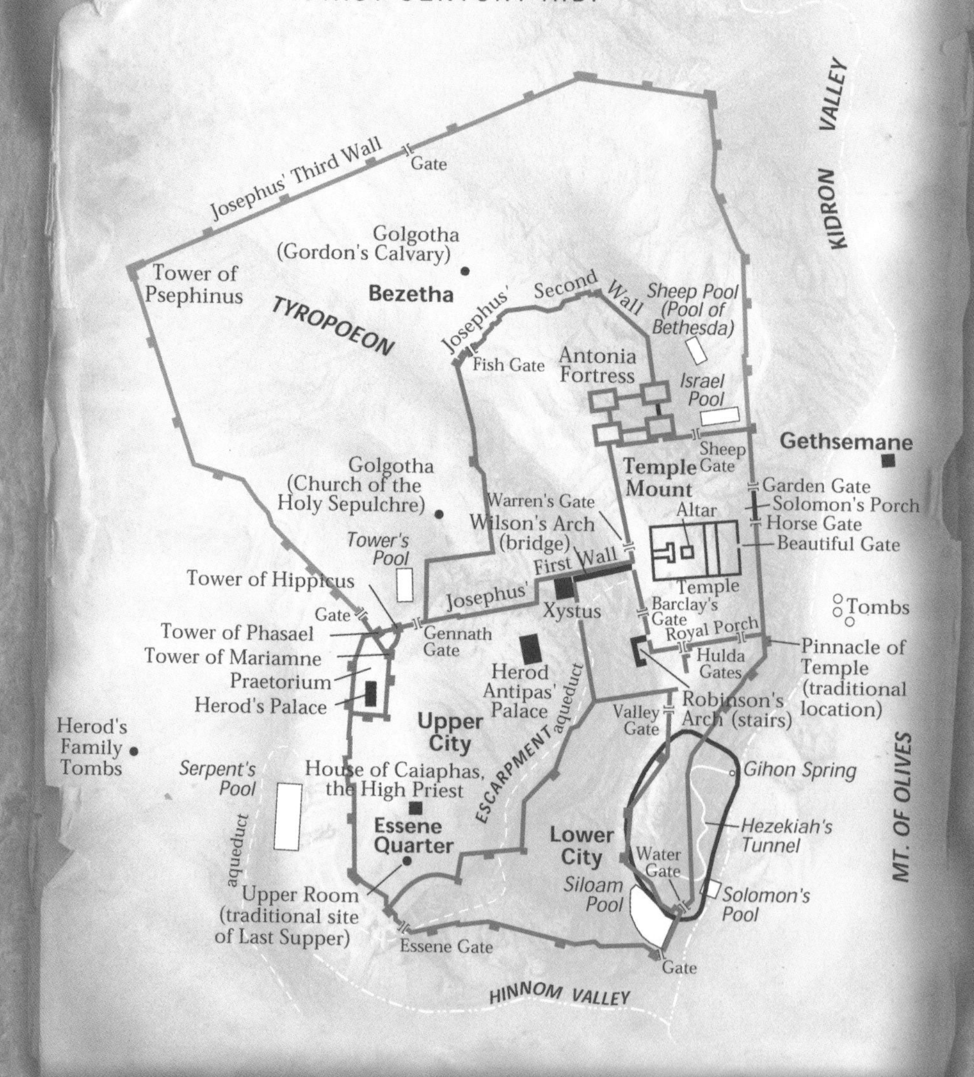